LA Deadly

A Detective Howard Drew Novel, 4

Larry Darter

Fedora Press

eBook ISBN 979-8-9876944-0-4

Paperback ISBN 979-8-9876944-1-1

Hardcover ISBN 979-8-9876944-2-8

For my sister, Debbie. Thank you for your unfailing support. I appreciate it so much.

LOS ANGELES, Calif. (February 5, 2023) — Two women killed in separate homicides in Downtown Los Angeles.

Los Angeles Police Department officers are investigating a pair of homicides that occurred in Downtown Los Angeles early Sunday morning in separate locations. The victims were both women in their early thirties. Police are still searching for suspects.

"It's worse than a war zone around here lately." — unnamed police official

Contents

One

It was the third day of the battle. As Sergeant Howard Drew and his squad moved cautiously down a narrow side street toward the courtyard of a two-story building, they came under heavy small arms fire. A brutal gun battle erupted, leaving two of Drew's soldiers shot and trapped in the open. Drew dove behind the blackened hulk of a burnt out vehicle as one of his team leaders, Specialist Conner Atkinson, crouched behind the trunk of a date palm in the center of the courtyard. As the gunfire slackened, Drew and Atkinson heard the cries and screams of the wounded. Atkinson sprang into action and darted across the kill zone as enemy fire raked past him. Drew, laying down suppressing fire, watched as Atkinson sprinted forward, leaned down, and in one fluid motion, grabbed up a wounded soldier, threw him over his shoulder, and ran across the courtyard toward a door at the front of a building. Before Atkinson reached it, the door swung open. A figure clad in a black abaya stepped out. Drew's brain registered the tan suicide vest strapped over the abaya as Atkinson continued running toward the open door with the wounded soldier. In horror, Drew swung his M4 carbine toward the female insurgent as an urgent shout of warning erupted from his throat. The shrill ring of his cell phone yanked Drew out of the nightmare. He sat bolt upright in bed and reached for the phone with a shaky hand, the all too familiar panicky feeling in his chest. The trembling, quavering voice sounded unfamiliar to his ears, as though it belonged to someone else. When he had whispered into the phone, the word hello had sounded feeble, almost whimpering.

"Detective Drew?"

For a moment, Drew felt too embarrassed to speak further. He wondered if the caller had recognized the fear in his voice.

"This is Captain Kenneth Mann. Is this Detective Drew?"

Sweat trickled from Drew's forehead and armpits. His breathing was rapid and ragged, and he seemed unable to think clearly or focus. The name meant nothing to him at first. Then he remembered who Mann was—Robbery-Homicide Division's commanding officer. Drew looked at the glowing blue numerals on the LED display on the clock beside the bed: 11:21. After a moment, he worked out it must be 11:21 P.M. since there was no sunlight coming through the bedroom windows. He'd slept for less than two hours. With one hand, Drew gripped the phone he held to his ear while he absently rubbed his chest to relieve the feelings of tightness.

"Detective Drew?"

Another long moment of silence passed; Drew's eyes closed.

"Detective Drew, are you there?"

"Yes, I'm here," Drew croaked after gaining control of his breathing.

"Detective, I'm calling because I need you and your partner for a special assignment, a homicide, in Studio City. Are you able to respond to a call out?"

"I can respond. Sorry, I just woke up."

"Well, I'm sorry if I woke you. But I'm sure you're accustomed to it."

Drew suppressed a snort. *Accustomed to it—why would I be?* Drew hadn't received a middle of the night call out since leaving West Bureau. Assigned to the Open-Unsolved Unit, Drew investigated murders that had happened years, often decades ago. There were no call outs, no homicide scenes to report to, or dead bodies to examine in the middle of the night.

"No, problem. What happened?"

"Lieutenant Lou Moreno will brief you on the scene. Call your partner and get going without delay."

Now wide awake, Drew recognized Moreno's name. He commanded the RHD Homicide Special Section. Drew wondered why Mann was summoning him and Li to a scene belonging to Homicide Special.

"What scene?"

"Spirito's, an Italian restaurant in Studio City. Do you know it?"

"Yeah, on Tujunga Avenue. Why—"

"Moreno will explain everything. Find him first when you get there. He will brief you."

"What about Lieutenant Howard? He should—"

"We will inform him we've temporarily reassigned you and your partner to Homicide Special, Detective. We're wasting time. Get your partner and get down there. Am I making myself clear?"

"Yes, Captain, you're clear."

"Then Moreno will expect you."

Mann hung up without waiting for a reply. Drew stood up and headed to the kitchen to make coffee, wondering what was going on. The restaurant Mann had named was within the North Hollywood Division's boundaries in the San Fernando Valley. If Mann had a body there and RHD was handling it, not the Valley Bureau detectives, that probably meant media sensitive or celebrity involvement. The question was, why did command want him and Li there?

Drew glanced out the patio doors at the twinkling lights of L.A. after dropping the pod into the machine and pushing the button. While waiting for the single-serve brewer to do its thing, Drew leaned with his back against the kitchen counter, feeling a sense of relief. He had no clue what awaited him at Studio City, but it would certainly save him from revisiting the nightmares this night. Drew wanted a smoke. He looked for the pack of cigarettes he habitually left on the counter before remembering there was no pack. Drew had quit smoking again recently. He picked up the phone instead, found Amy Li on his contact list, and pushed the call button.

Li's sleepy voice answered after three rings.

"Amy, it's Howie," he said. "We've got a call out."

"A call out?" Li sounded confused.

"Captain Mann just called. We've caught a special assignment. There's a murder in Studio City and Mann wants us to take it."

"Okay, we meeting at the PAB to pick up the car?"

"No, let's meet at the scene to save time."

"Where in Studio City?"

"Spirito's. It's an Italian restaurant on Tujunga Avenue."

"Yeah, okay, I know where it is. See you there." Li disconnected.

Drew dumped the coffee into a travel mug, put another pod in the machine, and pressed the brew button again. Then he went back to the bedroom to dress.

Two

On the way to Studio City, Drew tuned his car radio to KRLA. He picked up a breaking news report on a shooting investigation underway at Spirito's Italian restaurant on Tujunga Avenue. The reporter on the scene said a large LAPD presence at the location was investigating the circumstances of a body found in a car outside the popular restaurant. She concluded her report by saying a wide cordon of yellow crime scene tape kept her and other members of the media from getting a close look, and LAPD media relations hadn't yet given a statement to the press. Drew tuned out the broadcast once it returned to the usual late night news-talk programming.

He took Wilcox Avenue to the 101 and then cruised north on the freeway in minimal traffic, given the hour. He exited at Tujunga Avenue and arrived at the restaurant about fifteen minutes after leaving his apartment. As he looked for a parking spot, Drew saw an unusually large number of police vehicles present throughout the area, patrol cars and unmarked detective sedans. He also noted SID and coroner's vans were present along with a red LAFD EMS ambulance. After parking, Drew sat in his car sipping his coffee, waiting for Li to arrive. He had been to Spirito's a few times, a restaurant that had served contemporary Italian fare in Studio City for over fifty years. The restaurant was not only a favorite of everyday locals and tourists, but a popular hangout for L.A.'s celebrity crowd. The restaurant hosted a popular jazz nightclub upstairs for those in the mood for live music.

Five minutes after Drew arrived, Amy Li walked up to his door and tapped on the window. Drew got out. Li wore a muted navy business suit with a cream-colored shirt and shiny black shoes, making Drew feel uncomfortably under dressed. He had only taken time to put on a pair of jeans and a polo shirt. He grabbed his blue LAPD raid jacket from the front seat and shrugged it on to look more official. Then the detectives walked toward the scene. Drew held up the yellow crime scene tape. After ducking beneath it, the detectives gave their names and badge numbers to the uniformed officer with the crime scene log. They then walked down the street past the restaurant's parking lot to where the preponderance of cops and other official personnel stood around a silver Dodge Challenger.

Amy Li, a short, trim, and attractive Asian-American woman, was born in Los Angeles a few years after her parents immigrated to the United States from Mainland China. Like Drew, she had been a bureau detective before transferring to Open-Unsolved a couple of weeks ahead of him. They had been partners since Drew had joined the unit.

Drew spotted Moreno. Leading the way, he headed toward the lieutenant.

"Lieutenant? Drew and Li. Captain Mann told us to report to you."

"Right," Moreno said. "Thanks for coming out. Here's the deal. COVID-19, vacations, and the budget cuts have my guys spread pretty thin. Staffing is down. Murders are up. As long as the defund the police lunacy continues, it will get worse before it gets better. As of now, you two belong to Homicide Special until further notice and answer to me. Got it?"

"Roger that," Drew said.

"Captain Mann also loaned us Jenkins and Ross from Open-Unsolved."

Drew nodded. "Who do we report to? Who's the lead on this?"

"You, Li, Jenkins, and Ross are the team for now. Since you're the senior D2, Drew, I'm making you the lead."

Drew hadn't expected that. He had assumed he and Li would work under the supervision of a Homicide Special detective doing grunt work.

"Okay, what have we got?"

"The body in the car is Connie Lynn Manley, a 45-year-old white female and the wife of William Lake, the actor. After dinner at the restaurant, the couple returned to Lake's car. He realized he left his revolver—which he has a permit to carry—inside the restaurant. He says he went back to retrieve the weapon he had left on the seat in a booth, and she waited in the car. When he returned, he says he found her slumped in the front seat and noticed blood coming from her nose and mouth. She was unresponsive, so he ran across the street to a house for help and to get someone to call for an ambulance."

Drew now understood why Homicide Special had the investigation. William Lake was a filmmaker and actor, although now pushing seventy, mostly retired. Still, he remained a fairly well-known Hollywood celebrity who had been popular in his time.

"Someone shot her?"

"Yes, twice. One in the right cheek and one in the right shoulder. Looks like the shooter walked up to the window and popped her while she sat in the front passenger seat. SID found one spent casing inside the car, a nine mil, probably from the murder weapon."

"Was Lake's weapon a nine?"

Moreno shook his head. "Colt 38 Detective Special. The lab will verify it, but the smell test says Lane hasn't fired the revolver recently. There are no spent casings in the cylinder."

An LAFD ambulance pulled away without emergency lights flashing or siren. Moreno and the detectives turned to watch it go.

"They're transporting her?"

"Already have. Paramedics found a weak pulse and were working on her. But I just heard from a patrol officer at the hospital a doctor pronounced her. That one was for Lake. After finding his wife, Lake got sick." Moreno waved toward the departing ambulance. "They came out to check him for shock."

"Okay, so where are we at, Lieutenant?"

"North Hollywood detectives transported Lake," Moreno said. "He's in an interview room there with his attorney."

"Why does he need an attorney?" Drew said. "Is he a suspect?"

Moreno shrugged. "You know how these things go. The attorney with him isn't a criminal lawyer. He's an entertainment attorney, a friend of Lane."

Drew was immediately suspicious. *Why had Lake lawyered up already? Someone had just murdered his wife. Why wasn't he still here at the scene, trying to help them find out who killed her?*

"I'll keep Jenkins and Ross here for now. They can impound the car and get it over to Hertzberg-Davis for processing. I want you and Li to go to North Hollywood to interview Lake. We've got North Hollywood detectives and uniforms canvassing the area for witnesses and looking for the murder weapon."

"Got it, Lieutenant. We'll just take a quick look at the car and then we'll be on our way."

"Keep me in the loop with regular updates, Drew. Lake and his wife have been fixtures in the tabloids recently. It seems their marriage wasn't one of Hollywood's great love stories. This one will get a lot of media attention. The tenth floor will expect daily updates from me, so I expect daily updates from you. Got it?"

Drew knew the tenth floor referred to the top floor of the LAPD Police Administration Building, where the chief of police and all the senior commanders had their offices. "Understood, Lieutenant."

"Good, then get to it. Look at what you want to see here and then get over to North Hollywood and see what's what."

Drew nodded. He and Li turned and headed over to the Challenger to examine the murder scene. It was almost 1:00 A.M., but reporters, photographers, and television camera people thronged behind the yellow crime scene tape. Several patrol cars, overhead LED light bars pulsing, blocked the street at both ends.

SID personnel and patrol cops stood around the parked Dodge on the dimly lighted street about a block from the restaurant. Next to the car was a large green dumpster filled with chunks of stucco and strips of lumber. The dumpster stood in front of an almost completely de-molished house encircled by a chain-link fence. Drew figured someone would soon rebuild it on a grander scale. The ranch-style houses lining the neighborhood street had carefully pruned shrubs and well-kept lawns. It was a warm night with the full moon and stars veiled thinly by a film of fog.

Drew and Li studied the ground around the car, littered with a bloody towel and ribbons of bloody gauze bandages the paramedics had left behind. Drew took his Pelican flashlight out of his hip pocket and held it up above his shoulder, illuminating the interior of the car. Both front windows were down.

"I see a glove in the car," Drew said to Li.

"A glove? Where? What kind of glove?"

"See it there on the floorboard?"

Li peered inside the car and saw a bloody latex glove where a paramedic had probably discarded it after working on the victim.

"I think it's O.J.'s glove," Drew said with mock seriousness.

Li chuckled.

"Well, if it doesn't fit, the jury must acquit," she said.

The two detectives studied the car's interior. There were reddish stains streaking the gray passenger seat upholstery and the center console.

Li pointed to obvious vomit dappling the car's exterior from the front passenger door to the taillight.

"Looks like someone got sick."

"The husband was throwing up," a nearby patrol officer said.

Drew didn't see Jenkins or Ross anywhere around. He expected they were interviewing witnesses from the neighborhood or searching for the murder weapon.

"I've seen enough," Drew said to Li. "You ready to head over to North Hollywood."

"Yup," Li said.

The detectives walked back to their cars. Once they crossed underneath the yellow crime scene tape, reporters and their camera people rushed toward them.

"Detectives, can you tell us anything about the victim?"

Drew held up a hand to ward them off, and the detectives kept walking. "No comment. You'll have to get with media relations."

"Seriously, I hope this doesn't turn into an O.J. thing," Li said.

"I hear you, partner.

Drew and Li got in their cars and drove away toward the North Hollywood station on Burbank Boulevard.

Three

WILLIAM LAKE'S RISE TO fame had been unusual. He began his career as a successful child actor but enjoyed little success as a young adult actor. With few acting prospects, he enlisted in the military, serving a four-year stint in the U.S. Marine Corps. After his enlistment expired, he returned to the motion picture industry and found regular work, but as a stuntman. But Lake never lost his desire to find success as an actor.

While working as a stuntman to support himself, Lake attended acting classes and improved himself professionally. Later, he landed a supporting role in a movie that did far better at the box office than anyone had expected. The movie was about two ambitious LAPD patrol officers, partners working in South L.A. Trying to make a big drug bust they hoped would get them promoted to detectives, the pair ran afoul of a drug-dealing street gang, and gang members ambushed and assassinated them. Because Lake out shined the better known lead actor in the film, he soon received supporting roles in several other major pictures. Then a television network signed him to play the lead role in a television drama where he portrayed a quirky San Diego private detective. The show became a hit that ran nine seasons, and the role cemented Lake's celebrity status. After achieving success as an actor, he then moved into directing and producing films.

When Drew and Li arrived at the station, North Hollywood Detectives Todd Sharp and Matt Lowe greeted them in the squad room. They were the first detectives to respond to the scene and had just finished interviewing Lake. The detectives gathered around Sharp's desk to discuss the investigation.

"Lowe and I talked with Lake at the scene until he said he wanted to call a lawyer. Then we brought him down here and interviewed him with his attorney present to lock down his story. Once we got word RHD was taking over, we shut down the interview and waited for you guys to arrive."

"What did he tell you?" Drew asked.

"He and his wife had a late dinner at Spirito's and then left at around 10:30. They walked back to his car, which Lake had parked on the street about a block from the restaurant. Lake said he had his snub-nose revolver inside his waistband, covered by his shirt when they arrived. He took it out and laid it on the seat when they sat down in his usual booth. When they got back to the car, he realized he had forgotten to pick up the weapon. So, he left his wife waiting in the car and jogged back to get it."

"Did he have the gun on him when you contacted him?"

Sharp nodded. "A Colt Detective Special. No one has fired it recently. The barrel still smells of gun oil, and it had six live rounds in the cylinder. He surrendered it voluntarily. I have it bagged and tagged inside my desk drawer. We don't think it's the murder weapon, but the lab needs to check it out just to cover all the bases."

Drew nodded, recalling the nine millimeter spent casing that SID had recovered from inside Lake's car. "Then he returned to the car after retrieving the revolver and found his wife shot?"

"Well, he returned to the car," Lowe said. "But he claims he didn't realize someone had shot her. He thought someone had mugged her or something because she was bleeding from the nose and mouth like someone had punched her."

"Okay."

Sharp continued the story. "Lake said she was breathing, but unresponsive. He said he forgot his cell phone and had left it at home, so he ran across the street to a nearby house to get someone to call for an ambulance."

"Was Lake alone with his wife when you arrived?" Li asked.

"No, a guy who lives across the street at the house Lake went to for help was with him," Lowe said, glancing at his notebook. "Bryant Riley. He told us Lake banged on his door and said someone beat up his wife and he needed an ambulance. Riley called 911, then he accompanied Lake back to the car and waited with him."

"What did you think when you talked to Lake?" Drew asked the two detectives. "Think he did it?"

Sharp shrugged. "Rumors say Lake and his wife have had a short and troubled marriage. And according to him, Manley was a star stalker who made her living as a grifter and selling nude pictures and sex videos on online porn sites. He said she also met lonely suckers, his words, online and conned them out of cash."

"A real sweetheart," Lowe interjected. "I don't know if you keep up with the Hollywood gossip, but the tabloids paint the same picture of Manley as Lake does. They claim he only married her because she trapped him by getting pregnant."

"Anyway," Sharp added, "Lake started seeing her. He knocked her up, and she gave birth to their daughter, Holly, about eleven months ago. Lake and Manley fought over custody because he considered her an unfit mother because she used the kid as leverage to coerce him into marrying her. They got married a few months ago."

"Sounds like a solid celebrity family," Li chuckled.

"What seems weird is instead of parking at the restaurant, Lake parked his car a block away on a dimly lighted street next to a construction site," Sharp said.

"Yeah, I wondered about that," Drew said. "Seems like a perfect location for an execution. You ask him about it?"

"Yes. He said the parking lot was full, and he didn't want someone opening their car door into his and dinging his fancy ride. So, he parked on the street as close as he could get."

"Lake has a carry permit," Lowe said, "When we asked him why he took his gun out inside the restaurant, he said it was digging into his side at dinner. He took it out to relieve the discomfort and laid it on the seat in their booth. Then, after dinner, he says he forgot all about it, paid the check, and they walked out without it."

Another North Hollywood detective walked into the squad room.

"Lake and his attorney are getting antsy," he announced.

"Tell them we're transferring the case downtown," Sharp said, "and that we're briefing the RHD detectives. We'll be with them in five minutes."

The recently arrived detective nodded and left.

"Only the one spent casing found at the scene?" Drew asked.

"Nope," Sharp said. "SID found one inside the car right away. But later, they found a second one in the grass between the car and the sidewalk. So, that supports the theory the shooter used a nine millimeter, but we won't know for sure until the medical examiner makes the cut."

The detective, who had come in earlier, interrupted again. "Lake and his attorney are ready to go. They're in the hallway."

"Okay," Drew said, getting up. "We'll finish this later. Li and I will go talk to him."

Four

THE DETECTIVES FOUND LAKE and his lawyer standing in the hall-way outside the interview room. Lake wore black jeans, a tight black T-shirt, and black cowboy boots. He had shaggy, unnaturally dark black hair which gave his pale, tautly stretched skin a ghostly pallor. Lake looked exhausted and a little sheepish as he glanced at the detectives and then stared at the floor.

"I don't want to be sixty-seven years old, but I am," Lake muttered disgustedly, standing in the hallway beside his attorney. "But I am sixty-seven years old. I'm tired, and just want to lie down."

Drew subtly scrutinized Lake's clothing, hands, and boots, looking for blood specks, but saw nothing.

"Can I ask your client a few questions before you take off?" Drew asked the attorney.

"Not tonight," the lawyer said. "But maybe in the morning."

"Can we search the house?" Drew said. "Mr. Lake can take a nap while we check out the house."

"Not without a warrant," the lawyer said. "Connie Manley lived in the guest house behind my client's residence. You can search it."

"Okay, I'll send someone out there," Drew said, feeling frustrated knowing he couldn't detain Lake unless he arrested him. And he didn't yet have the probable cause to do it. "Go home and get some rest," he said to Lake. "We'll talk in the morning."

Lake nodded, and the detectives watched him and the lawyer saunter down the hallway toward the exit.

"That's not how a man acts when someone has just murdered his wife," Li said. "Lake wasn't distraught, didn't ask how his wife died, or show any curiosity at all about the case. He was more worried about getting home to bed than finding his wife's killer."

Drew nodded, and the detectives returned to the squad room.

"Lake's attorney said we can't talk to him until maybe in the morning," Drew told the North Hollywood detectives. "They're gone."

"Are you going to search his house?" Sharp asked.

Drew shook his head. "The attorney said no. We'll have to get a warrant. But he said Manley lived in the guest house behind the residence and said we could search it. As soon as I get in touch with the other two detectives our boss assigned to the case, I'll send them to do it."

"Want me to call them?" Li said. "I know I have Jenkins' number on my contact list."

"Yeah, please do that," Drew said. "Tell them to go to the house and collect the clothes Lake is wearing first, before he gets rid of them. Then they can search the guesthouse."

Li nodded, got up, and walked away to make the call. Sharp resumed briefing Drew on the interview with Lake.

"We did a gunshot residue test on his hands as soon as we got here with him. But don't get your hopes up. Lake puked on himself after he discovered his wife in the car. He said he had chest pains, and the paramedics checked him out. One gave him a bottle of water and a towel to clean the puke off. I'm sure he probably washed his hands.

Lowe and I were talking to Bryant Riley, and didn't realize they had given him the water and towel to clean up with until it was too late."

"Well, the lab might get something from his clothing," Drew said.

"We've got a little more background on the victim," Lowe said. "She was from Arkansas and traveled back and forth. She still has family there. When I asked Lake when they married, he gave us that bullshit, crying without tears. Then he couldn't stop telling us how dirty she was. He seemed to love talking about it."

Li walked over, holding out her phone to Drew. "Jenkins wants to talk to you."

Drew took the phone and put it to his ear. "Drew," he said into the phone.

"We're wrapping things up here at the scene," Jenkins said. "Moreno sent us to the restaurant to interview the staff before they left. Lake lives close by, so we'll head over there in a few minutes. But I wanted to let you know that none of the staff remembers Lake returning after he paid the check and left with his wife. Moreno mentioned he claimed he returned to retrieve a gun he'd left on the seat of the booth where they had dinner."

"Interesting," Drew said. "I think he is using that story to establish an alibi. Did you interview any of the customers?"

"No, some North Hollywood detectives and patrol officers did that while we talked to the employees. I don't know what they found out."

"Okay, I have one more thing for you and Ross after you finish at Lake's house."

"Sure. What?"

"We don't have the murder weapon. I know it's a long shot, but there is a construction dumpster next to where Lake parked his car. Get it picked up and out to the landfill. Dump it and see if the shooter dropped the gun inside it. We're looking for a nine millimeter."

"Yeah, okay. I saw the dumpster when we were impounding Lake's car. I'll make sure someone stays with it until we get back."

Drew and Jenkins disconnected, and Drew turned back to the North Hollywood detectives. "You guys have anything from the interviews at the restaurant?" he asked.

"No," Sharp said. "Some of our guys interviewed people there, but no reports have come in yet. All I know right now is one of our detectives told me he verified the restaurant charged Lake's credit card at 10:28 when he paid the check, so that tracks with his claim he and Manley left the restaurant at around 10:30."

"Did you run him for guns?"

"Yeah, he has three or four registered," Lowe said. "I'll have to check my notes."

The phone on Sharp's desk rang. He picked it up and answered. After a few moments, he covered the received with a hand and glanced at Drew.

"The patrol guys at the hospital want to know what to do about Manley's clothes."

"If they are still on her, we can't take them," Drew said. "Might lose trace evidence. The coroner will handle it."

Sharp nodded. "I'll let them know." He spoke into the phone, relaying Drew's decision, and then hung up.

Drew glanced at Li. "Amy, while I'm thinking about it, call the coroner's office and tell them to hold all press releases for now. We need to control the flow of information, and I don't want the media getting anything except what media relations puts out."

Li nodded and walked away again to make the call.

"My guy told me none of the restaurant employees saw Lake return for the revolver," Drew said. "I've eaten there before, and I know they always have someone at the door to greet customers when they walk in. I don't think he could have gone back inside the restaurant without someone seeing him. Also, I meant to ask you if Lake explained why he was carrying a weapon."

"Yes, he told us," Sharp said. "Lake said his wife thought someone was stalking her, and she always asked him to carry a gun when they went out. He said she was paranoid."

"That's a convenient story," Drew said. "But his story about leaving his wife in the car and going back for the gun won't stand up. He needs someone to say they saw him come back into the restaurant before using that as an alibi to say he didn't shoot her. Everything circumstantial is pointing right at him."

"It was a dark street where he parked the car," Lowe said. "The nearest streetlight in the middle of the block is out, and there wasn't much light from the moon because of the fog. He told us she was paranoid, but leaves her there in the car alone on a dark street a block from the restaurant with both windows down. He's full of shit. Either he did her or got someone else to do it."

Drew smiled ruefully, nodding his head in agreement. "We need the recording from your interview. We'll never get another statement from him."

Sharp laughed. "That's for sure. Give me your address and I'll email the recording to you." Drew gave him his email address and Sharp copied it down.

"Manley was on probation for a scam she pulled back in Little Rock, Arkansas," Lowe said. "Lake told us it was probably someone she grifted that killed her."

"Sounds like he wants us looking at everyone except him," Drew said. "He never cried at all during the interview?"

"No," Sharp said. "He pretended to that one time, without tears. And he never once asked what happened to her." Sharp drummed his fingers on the table. "Good luck on this one. He did it, but he's a character. It might be hard to prove it."

"Like with O.J.," Lowe said. "Fucking celebrities."

"Maybe not that hard to prove," Drew said. "Killers are dumb. The only smart ones are on television."

"That's what I'm saying," Lowe said. "That asshole *was* on television."

The three detectives laughed.

Li returned to the table and confirmed she had notified the coroner's office not to release any information to the press.

"Let's head to the PAB, partner," Drew said to her. "We need to view the interview recording so we can ask Lake questions in the morning that Sharp and Lowe didn't already cover. If his attorney lets us talk to him. And we need to write a search warrant for his house and get a judge's signature on it."

"Okay," Li said. "We all done here?"

"Yeah," Drew said, standing up. "I think so."

After Sharp handed over Lake's revolver, Drew and Li shook hands with the two North Hollywood detectives, thanked them, and then left for downtown.

Five

DREW AND LI PARKED their personal vehicles in the underground parking structure beneath the 10-floor, 500,000 square foot Police Administration Building (PAB) on First Street between Main and Spring Street. Then they took the elevator up together to Open-Unsolved. While they now worked for Lieutenant Moreno until further notice, he had said nothing about the detectives moving over to Homicide Special. It was almost 4:00 A.M., on Saturday morning, so they had the office to themselves.

"Guess we're working all weekend," Li said.

Drew nodded. "At least the rest of today. We've got plenty to do." Drew switched on the computer on the desk inside his assigned cubicle. "Let's get coffee, then we'll watch the interview recording. After that, you can get started writing the search warrant for Lake's house while I call Moreno and update him."

Most detective pairings had a common division of labor. One investigator led the investigation, usually did the talking during interviews, and kept the case moving forward. The other often handled the paperwork because of their aptitude for it or because it suited their personality. Since Drew and Li had become partners, Li handled the paperwork and Drew led the investigations. Not that Li was any less skilled as an investigator or that Drew actively avoided paperwork.

Li was just better at writing warrants and complete summaries and maintaining a logical flow of reports. Using their respective strengths made them an effective team.

In the break room, Drew popped a pod into the single-serve coffee maker. The department had replaced the old school drip coffee makers with glass carafes and hot plates with the single-serve type similar to the one Drew had in his kitchen at home. Whomever made such decisions believed it was more cost effective and produced less waste. Also, in the name of saving a few bucks, the department ordered the cheapest and worst flavored coffee K-cups Drew had ever tasted. And every other cop he knew shared his opinion. Many of the detectives brought in their own coffee pods and kept them locked in their desk drawers to prevent pilfering. Since neither Drew nor Li brought their own coffee to work, they were stuck with the department supplied stuff when a coffee shop run wasn't an option.

When the brew cycle finished, Drew slid the cup across the counter to Li.

"Thanks, Howie," she said, stirring a packet of non-dairy creamer and two sugars into the coffee. "I needed this."

Drew dropped another pod into the machine and pushed the brew button. Then he glanced at Li, who took a sip of the hot brew and then made a face.

"Well, maybe I didn't need this," she said with a grimace. "It's awful. Still I need the caffeine boost."

Drew chuckled as he removed his cup from beneath the spigot when the brewer shut off. "Yeah, the only coffee worse than this is what they have in hospital waiting room machines."

· · • • • • • • · ·

Back in the squad room, Drew sat down at his desk and Li pulled her chair over so she could see the computer screen. After opening his email, Drew found the one from Sharp and clicked on the MP4 attachment. A video file player app opened on the screen and loaded the MP4. He clicked on the play button with his mouse and then clicked the icon in the corner for the full screen option.

The detectives watched the recording in silence. The North Hollywood detectives had already summarized the interview for them, but the video gave them the opportunity to observe Lake's demeanor while he answered the detective's questions. Drew had his notebook and pen ready to take notes he would use later to build a list of questions for when he and Li interviewed Lake at his home.

Sharp and Lowe sat on one side of the table in the interview room with Lake and his attorney seated opposite them, facing the camera.

SHARP: Thank you for coming in. I hope you don't mind, but we're recording this, so we will have a permanent record.

Lake slumped in his seat with his arms crossed, nodded along with his lawyer. After Sharp identified himself and everyone in the room for the recording, he continued.

SHARP: How are you managing, William?

LAKE: About as well as expected. I'm devastated by what happened. I still can't believe it.

SHARP: Who would want to do something like this? Is there anyone you know about who might have wanted to harm your wife?

Lake shrugged and sighed, but said nothing.

SHARP: We need verbal answers for the audio, William. You know a lot more about her than we do. Help us out here. You told us earlier she believed someone was stalking her.

Drew noticed the hint of impatience in Sharp's tone. Lake spoke up, relating a confusing story about a man named Ted—saying he did not know the guy's last name—that Manley had met online and dated for a while before she and Lake met. Lake's hit television series had been well before Drew's time, but he had watched a few episode reruns on late night television and guessed the series was still in syndication. So, he noticed immediately that Lake sounded like the private detective character he'd played on television, cursing and infusing his speech with a tough-guy inflection. With his attorney sitting beside him monitoring the interview, Lake provided the North Hollywood detectives some background on Manley after finishing his rambling story, then made a surprising statement.

LAKE: Ted tried to kill her about two years ago.

SHARP: Kill her how?

LAKE: They were in his car together, and he tried to crash it, telling her they were going to commit suicide together or something.

SHARP: Did she report it to the police?

LAKE: No, she told me she didn't.

SHARP: And this incident happened here? In L.A. or where?

LAKE: Yeah, somewhere in L.A., after Connie Lynn moved out here. I don't really know all the details. See, Connie made up stuff. You know, to get attention? So, I never really knew if the stuff she said was true.

SHARP: Can you tell us about what happened tonight? Take us through your activities this evening.

Lake said nothing for about ten seconds, and then finally responded.

LAKE: We decided to have a late dinner, so we went to Spirito's, my favorite restaurant. We parked... And things were going really good. We talked about bringing April, her daughter from a previous marriage, out here. When we sat down, the gun, which I don't always carry, but with her I always carry the fucking gun because she thought someone was stalking her. Usually, I leave it in the car, but I had it in my waistband, in a holster that slips inside my waistband and clips onto my belt. It was under my shirt and it was sticking me in the side. So, I took it out and put it on the seat. I've had the gun since I starred in *Quinn* in the late-eighties to early nineties.

SHARP: So, you put the gun on the seat? Then what?

LAKE: The server brought the check after we finished dinner, and we got up to go pay. After we left, I realized I'd left the gun in the booth on the seat. I was afraid someone might find it and I would lose my permit or something and that would be a bad scene.

SHARP: Did you realize the gun was missing before you got back to the car? Or were you sitting in the car in the parking lot and remembered you had left it on the seat in the restaurant?

LAKE: No, I parked on the street. The parking lot was too packed when we got there and I just took delivery of the Challenger a month ago, after waiting three months to get it. So, I parked on the street. I didn't want someone to open a car door into it and ding it up. You know? We got in the car and that's when I realized I'd forgotten to pick up the gun from the seat. So, I jogged back to get it. The gun was on the floor beneath the seat of the booth where we had been sitting. I only carried it when we went out. Connie was fearful and you might say hiding because she made many enemies because of her online scams.

"That gun is his alibi," Li said.

"Yeah," Drew agreed. "But it won't stand up without someone at the restaurant backing up his story about returning to get it."

On the video recording, Lake continued the story he was telling the North Hollywood detectives.

LAKE: Connie Lynn would connect with these guys online all over the country. Even guys in Canada, Australia, and who knows where else. She had been doing it for twenty or thirty years. She would call them on the phone and get them to send her money to go see them. But she never went, she just kept the money. They sent her cash, plane tickets, and credit cards. It was a whole mail fraud scheme behind something that looked legit. She would tell them she had maxed out her credit card or whatever and they would send her money or wire money to her bank account. She had a million different ways of doing it.

Lowe snorted derisively on the video.

LOWE: You're talking about everything except what happened tonight.

Lake ignored the remark and glanced at his attorney.

LAKE: I want to make out a will tomorrow. If those motherfuckers come after me next, I want to make sure Holly is protected.

Sharp interrupted.

SHARP: William, tell us what happened? You realized you didn't have the gun and went back to the restaurant. Did you say anything to anyone once you got back inside?

Drew and Li knew Sharp was trying to lock Lake into a story, so he could eventually use it against him that none of the employees or patrons that detectives had interviewed at the restaurant remembered seeing Lake return after paying his check and leaving with his wife.

LAKE: I just told the greeter I'd left something behind, and then hurried back to the booth and found the gun on the floor. Then I went back to the car.

Lake seemed to stifle a sob.

LAKE: And when I got back, it looked like Connie Lynn was asleep.

SHARP: So, during the time you went back into the restaurant, somebody came by and did this to her?

Sharp's tone was flat, with no hint of sympathy.

LAKE: Are you asking me? That's how it must have happened. Because she was perfect when I left her in the car.

SHARP: Why did you walk back to the restaurant? You were already in the car. Why didn't you just drive back?

LAKE: It was only about a block and I like to walk whenever I can. I like to stay in shape.

SHARP: Then what did you do?

LAKE: I jogged back to the car and opened the door to get in. Then I saw her slumped over in the seat. From the interior light, I saw blood coming from her nose and mouth. Oh my God, I thought someone robbed her or mugged her or something. I called out her name and shook her, but she seemed out of it. Unconscious. Since I had forgotten my cell phone at the house, I ran across the street to a house with the porch light on. I banged on the door and screamed for help. Dogs started barking. Finally, a guy came to the door.

Lake paused, as if stifling another sob.

LAKE: He recognized me and I told him to call 911, that someone had beaten my wife up and she was bleeding from the nose and mouth.

Lake paused and took a deep breath. His voice cracked as he continued.

LAKE: When I was a kid, maybe seventeen, I saw a young guy who owed money to some people for drugs, or gambling debts. I'm not sure. But anyway, I saw these people beat him with a hammer. When they left, I went over and looked at him. I do not know why, but when I saw her, that's what came to my mind.

SHARP: Meaning that's what she looked like to you and why you thought someone beat her. You didn't know someone had shot her?

Lake sobbed.

LAKE: It's just that thought came to me. I don't know if I consciously thought someone beat her and robbed her. I just didn't know someone shot her. That memory from when I was a kid came to me. I just lost it.

LOWE: You said your wife believed someone was stalking her. Did she or did you ever see anyone suspicious hanging around your house?

Lake nodded and told the detectives about a suspicious-looking man who had cruised by the house many times recently, driving a black pickup truck.

LAKE: Another time, he walked past the house. He wore an old plaid shirt, a windbreaker, jeans, a baseball cap, and sunglasses. It was like he didn't want anyone to recognize him. Earl, my bodyguard, nicknamed him Buzzy. Because of his hair. He had a buzz cut.

SHARP: Tell us about Earl. You said he's your bodyguard? What's his full name?

LAKE: Earl Lee. He helps around the house. I've used him as a handyman to fix things around the house. Then, when Connie Lynn told me she thought someone was stalking her, and we began seeing suspicious people hanging around, I hired Earl as a bodyguard. I can take care of myself, but it gave me peace of mind to have him around watching out for Connie Lynn and Holly when I had to be at the studios or meetings, or whatever.

Lake continued with another long, disjointed story about the times he had seen Buzzy lingering near his house. Finally, Lowe cut him off.

LOWE: Okay, so tonight when you went out to dinner, were you keeping a lookout for this guy you believed had been creeping your house?

Lake nodded.

LAKE: I've been looking over my shoulder since the day I met Connie Lynn and...

Lowe interrupted again.

LOWE: Given what you've told us, why would you park a block from the restaurant on a dark street and then leave your wife alone in the car there to go back after your gun?

LAKE: I told you. The lot was full. I've been going to Spirito's for almost fifty years. It's always busy and I usually have to find parking on the street. I had to park there because it was the closest spot to the restaurant available when we got there.

LOWE: If you were so worried about her, why did you leave her alone in the car when you went back to retrieve the gun?

LAKE: She was tired. She wanted to wait in the car. I wasn't gone for over five minutes, if that.

LOWE: Did you notice anyone suspicious hanging around when you parked the car, or on your way back after dinner?

LAKE: No, nothing usual.

SHARP: Okay, sometimes people see things, but it doesn't register at first. I want you to start again at the beginning, and recount the events of the evening. It might jog your memory, and you may recall something that could help us figure out what happened.

Lake sighed, and then began his story again, starting with the arrival at the restaurant. He paused midway through.

LAKE: I just remembered this. One night, maybe about a week ago, I saw two men inside a van parked in front of the house one night. It worried me because someone had burglarized a house down the street recently.

"See how he's always changing the subject," Li said to Drew. "He doesn't want to talk about what happened last night."

Lake finished the story by telling the North Hollywood detectives that he had gone outside and confronted the men, brandishing a pistol, and frightened them off. Lowe steered him back to the events at the restaurant. Lake again recounted what happened after he retrieved the gun and returned to the car.

LOWE: Let's go back to the van, the two guys in the van in front of your house.

LAKE: I hate to ask. But can we wrap this up? We've been over it again and again. I've told you everything I know, and I'm beat.

SHARP: What's holding it up now is the downtown detectives. The big shots from Homicide Special. They should be here any minute and they need to talk to you.

LAKE: Oh God.

He rubbed his face with his hands, then glanced at his attorney beseechingly.

SHARP: They will only need a few more minutes of your time. They will want to figure out what happened. It's because of your status as a famous person. That's why the big shots from downtown need to handle this case.

LAKE: I can't make it, man. Seriously, I can't. I'm sixty-seven years old and I'm beat.

Lake appealed to his lawyer, who had been silent during most of the interview.

LAKE: Tell them we've got to go. Tell them I'm sixty-seven years old.

Someone knocked on the interview room door, and a detective stuck his head in. Sharp got up and walked to the door. The detective whispered something to him that the recording didn't pick up. Sharp nodded, and the detective shut the door.

SHARP: Look, just a few more questions, William. We need you to hang in there just a little longer. The downtown detectives are here. Let's take a break. I'll brief them and then they will be in to wrap this up and you can go home and get some rest. Can I get you anything? Coffee? A bottle of water?

Lake looked at his attorney forlornly, and the lawyer spoke for the first time.

LAKE'S ATTORNEY: My client has suffered a great shock, and he isn't a young man. He has cooperated and answered all your questions. But he is worn out.

He glanced at his wristwatch.

LAKE'S ATTORNEY: Get the downtown detectives in here, and let's wrap this up. Unless you plan to charge my client, we're out of here in ten minutes.

SHARP: Okay. How about it, William? You want coffee or some water?

LAKE: I can't drink coffee this late at night. I won't be able to sleep. Let's just wrap this up. I want to lie down.

SHARP: Just a few more minutes.

Sharp and Lowe went out the door and the recording stopped.

"He will not talk to us," Li said. "He'll be lawyered up with an actual criminal defense attorney by the time we get there and won't answer our questions."

"I don't think so," Drew said. "He's playing games. We saw it on the video. Lake thinks he's smarter than the cops and we won't be able to put this on him." Drew stretched and yawned.

"Knock out the search warrant, partner. After we get a judge to sign off on it, we'll get breakfast on the way to see Lake."

Li nodded, rolled her chair back to her desk and switched on her computer.

···•••••···

Drew was about to pick up his desk phone to call Moreno with an update, but it rang just as he reached for the receiver.

He picked up the phone and answered. "Detective Drew."

"Drew, this is Jenkins." He sounded breathless on the phone. "We just got back to the restaurant after leaving Lake's place. SID was still here, and they said they would try to get the dumpster picked up. But when they called the number stenciled on the container, all they got was voicemail."

"If we can't get it picked up and out to the landfill, we'll have to search it there. Just throw the stuff out on the ground until it's empty enough to search."

"That won't be necessary. They had a ladder and a SID guy climbed up and looked over the side with his flashlight. They recovered a handgun. It was right on top of some building material scrap. It might be the murder weapon."

"A nine mil?"

"Yeah, the guy who found it says it's a Walther P38, an old one. Like those issued to the German Army during World War Two."

"Was it loaded?"

"Yes. Five live rounds in the mag and one in the chamber. Magazine capacity is eight, so assuming the shooter topped off the magazine, it's missing two rounds. The hammer was cocked and the safety off."

"Where is it now?"

"On the way to the lab. There was dirt and oil covering it when they found it. After they process it for prints, they will get it cleaned up and test fired and ready to make a comparison with the projectiles the coroner recovers at autopsy."

"Okay, good. You have anything else?"

"We collected Lake's clothing and searched the guesthouse. We've got a laptop, some paperwork, and found a next of kin notification card. No cell phone, though."

"She probably had it with her in the car," Drew said. "The coroner will have it."

"You're probably right. You have anything else for us?"

"Not at the moment. Thanks, brother. You and Ross take a break. You guys did good work. Amy is writing the search warrant for the house and then we'll get a judge out of bed to sign it. I need you and Ross to meet us at Lake's house to do the search." Drew checked his watch. "Let's say nine o'clock. Amy and I should have the warrant signed and be there by then. If that changes, I'll hit you back."

"Okay, we'll see you there at nine."

Drew and Jenkins hung up. Then Drew picked up the phone again and punched in the number Moreno had given him at the scene.

Six

Moreno answered, sounding like the call had awakened him. Drew, having been up all night, felt no sympathy for Moreno. He summarized the case status, ending with news of the recovery of the suspected murder weapon. He explained he was keeping an open mind and not looking at Lake with tunnel vision, but stressed everything circumstantial was pointing right at him as the shooter.

"I concur," Moreno said, "but we still need the evidence to prove it in court."

"We'll get there, Lieutenant."

"What's your next step?"

"Li is writing the search warrant for Lake's house and after we get a judge to sign it, we're going back to him to ask more questions. His attorney shut us down after the North Hollywood detectives interviewed him and we didn't get a crack at him."

"All right, it sounds like you have a handle on it. We need to make an arrest on this sooner rather than later, Drew. Lake may be a Hollywood has been, but he's still enough of a celebrity that the local press is already all over this and I expect the national press will be too by tomorrow. By Monday, the tenth floor is going to feel the pressure."

"Hopefully, we'll make more progress by Monday, Lieutenant. But it would help if Captain Mann would use his influence to expedite lab processing on the physical evidence. I'm not optimistic Lake will give us a confession, so the evidence is going to make or break the case."

"I'll speak with Captain Mann later this morning. Stay on it, Drew. Keep me in the loop."

"You got it, Lieutenant," Drew said, but Moreno had already disconnected.

After updating Moreno, Drew dialed the number for the LAPD media relations department and updated the duty officer. He hung up, shaking his head wearily, and said to Li, "Media relations says it's going to be an avalanche. The press is already going crazy. They are all asking: 'Is this an O.J.-type crime?'"

"I was afraid of that," Li said.

"But didn't you say the other day you hoped someday you could investigate a fresh homicide case again instead of a steady diet of cold cases?"

"Yeah, I wanted a fresh homicide case," Li said. "But not *this* homicide case. Investigating the murder of a celebrity's wife always comes with problems and pitfalls. Lake is no A-Lister, but no doubt this case will generate extensive press coverage anyway."

"Yeah, and the potential that they will subject us to the same criticism every member of Homicide Special endured who was directly involved in the O.J. case."

Li got up and walked to the printer shared by everyone in the unit. After the printer shut off, she returned to Drew's desk waving a sheaf of papers.

"I've finished the search warrant application," she said. "Want to look it over?"

"Nope. You write better warrants than I do. I trust your work implicitly."

Li nodded. "I focused on Lake's presence at the scene, his proximity to where the shooter tossed the murder weapon, and the strained relationship between him and the victim. I also included his demeanor at the scene and during the West Hollywood interview that was inconsistent with a man who had just learned someone murdered his wife. It should be enough, especially since we have the murder weapon."

"Sounds good," Drew said, looking at the clock on the wall that showed it was 6:18 A.M. "Let's wake up the judge and get the warrant signed. Then we'll grab breakfast on the way to Studio City."

"Got a judge in mind?"

"Yeah, someone I've used before for warrants. I've got her number on my phone contact list. She skips the boilerplate and goes right to the probable cause, and she is pro law enforcement."

Li nodded, and she and Drew left the office for the elevator. They collected their city ride from the parking structure. Li drove, turning onto First Street, driving away from the PAB. Drew called the judge on their way to her house.

· · • • • • • • · ·

Satisfied with the probable cause affidavit, the judge only asked a few questions before signing the search warrant. Li and Drew got back in the car. He told her she could choose the restaurant for breakfast. Li said she knew a good place in Studio City that was right on the way. Fifteen minutes later, Li turned off Tujunga Avenue, near to their murder scene, into the parking lot of the Aroma Café, a quaint, ivy-covered restaurant-coffee shop. Inside, they chose a table near a tiled fireplace with a brass chandelier overhead. Both ordered bacon, eggs, and coffee for their first meal of the day.

"This food sure beats eating breakfast tacos on the trunk of our car," Li joked. "That's what you would have picked, Howie."

As the detectives ate, they traded playful insults and then planned how they would approach Lake.

"Bet he has a real lawyer with him," Li said. "It won't be the entertainment attorney this time."

Drew shrugged. "I still think Lake might talk to us," he said. "But even if he doesn't, we've got the search warrant for the house."

After they finished breakfast, Drew paid the check, and then they got in the car and drove to Lake's house, located less than a mile from the crime scene, in a more upscale section of Studio City. The area was a mix of architectural styles——ranch, Spanish, Cape Cod, colonial, English Tudor——and the trees incorporated into the landscaping were a typical Southern California hodgepodge. Drew saw sycamores, live oaks, palm trees, and magnolias around the houses and shading the street. Rose bushes, Mexican sage, and jasmine edged the broad lawns of the neighborhood. Even in the eclectic neighborhood, Lake's house, just down the street from where Paramount filmed the old television series *The Brady Bunch*, was an eccentric anomaly. Constructed of rough hewn redwood planks with a rusted horseshoe hanging over the front door, a brass lantern and deer antlers affixed to the wall, the place looked more like a rustic lodge better suited to the Wyoming back country than suburban Southern California.

Jenkins and Ross sat in their unmarked car in front of the house when Li and Drew arrived. Li parked behind them and all the detectives got out.

"Get the warrant?" Jenkins asked.

"Right here," Drew said, patting his jacket over the warrant tucked inside.

Drew led the group to the front door and rang the bell. A house-keeper opened the door and then escorted the detectives through the house and out a sliding door to the patio.

The detectives saw Lake stretched out on a chaise lounger on the patio, with a cigarette in one hand and a coffee cup in the other. He wore black track pants, a gray sweatshirt, a black baseball cap, and white sneakers. Lake looked stoned and his eyes were glassy. Flanking Lake were two other men, a tall, slender guy with a receding hairline wearing a khaki untucked work shirt over faded denim jeans and a shorter man with shoulder length gray hair and a Palm Springs tan wearing an expensive suit. He introduced himself as Patrick Oberlin, Lake's newly hired criminal attorney. Oberlin introduced the third man as Lake's friend, Earl Lee.

"We want to ask you a few questions," Drew said to Lake, after glancing at the lawyer.

"I don't want to talk to you," Lake said without making eye contact. "I already told those detectives last night everything I know. I just lost my wife and I don't want to go over it all again."

"You're the only witness to your wife's murder," Drew said in an annoyed tone. "Don't you want to help us find out what happened?"

"My client has clearly stated he doesn't want to talk with you, Detective," Oberlin said. "And unless you intend to arrest him, it is his right to refuse."

"Okay," Drew said, not hiding his irritation. "The thing is, we need to exclude him as a suspect. His lack of cooperation will make that much harder."

"I know how it works, Detective," Oberlin said. "Anytime there is a female victim, the police immediately focus on the husband or boyfriend. My client has no intention of having something he might say misconstrued and becoming a suspect in his wife's murder. Something he had nothing to do with."

"Fine," Drew said. "Then we'll get started on the search."

"Do you have a search warrant?"

"We do," Drew said, offering the lawyer the warrant.

Oberlin took it and scanned the pages of the document while Drew talked to him about the terms of the search.

"Can't you make them leave?" Lake implored his attorney. "What am I'm paying you for?"

"The warrant is in order, and allows them to search the house," Oberlin replied.

Lake got up, flicking his cigarette butt onto the ground. "Tell me what you're looking for and I'll take you to it," he said. "Then we can get this done and you can leave my property."

"It doesn't work that way," Drew said. "You can wait out here or in the living room, but you can't follow us around or interfere."

"Wait here, William," Oberlin said. "I'll accompany the detectives inside and protect your interests."

Lake shook his head stubbornly. "I don't want to be here. Let's go get breakfast. Guadalupe is here and can make sure they steal nothing."

"But, William..."

"No buts," Lake interrupted. "I'm paying your fee and I want to go get breakfast. There's nothing here for them to find to frame me with."

"All right, William," Oberlin said, holding his hands up in surrender. Glancing at Drew, he said, "Leave an inventory of any property you remove on the dining room table."

Drew nodded and then Lake, the lawyer, and the third man, who hadn't said a word, walked inside the house, leaving the detectives alone on the patio. A few moments later, they heard a car start out front and drive away.

"I better update Moreno," Drew said. "Then we'll get started."

Drew took out his phone and called his lieutenant. He told Moreno that Lake and his attorney had been at the house, but had since departed and they were going to execute the search warrant. Then he ended the call.

"All good?" Li asked.

"Yeah, but I suppose I should have assured Moreno that even though Lake left, there will be no white Bronco chase."

Li chuckled. "You really should have told him that. But seriously, Howie, this is feeling more and more like an O.J. thing."

Drew nodded soberly, and then he and the other detectives walked into the house to execute the warrant.

Seven

As the four detectives donned their latex gloves to prepare for the search, the doorbell rang. Drew caught the eye of the housekeeper, still going about her duties, and nodded that she could answer the door. The woman opened the door, spoke briefly to two men dressed in casual clothes, and then stood aside to allow them to enter. Drew recognized the men immediately, Chris Beck and Scott Kelly, both Los Angeles County deputy district attorneys.

"Detective Drew," Beck said with a smile, offering his hand. "Long time no see."

"Chris," Drew replied, shaking the man's hand and nodding to Kelly. "What are you guys doing here?"

"Captain Mann called our boss and our boss called us in on a Saturday," Beck said. "Mann thought it was a good idea for representatives of our office to be here for the search since Lake and his attorney left the premises. No point in giving Oberlin ammunition to attack the search later on by suggesting any improprieties."

Drew nodded. "Can't argue with that. We are just getting started."

The detectives, accompanied by the two deputy district attorneys, fanned out and searched the house. The living room featured a wagon-wheel light fixture consistent with the rustic decor of the house. Dirty clothes and baby toys littered the room. A leather saddle on a wooden stand stood in one corner and a baby stroller in another. Other rooms suggested a homeowner trapped between old age and adolescence, with shelves and cabinets filled with vintage comic books, toy soldier figures, cowboy memorabilia, and several BB guns. Framed photos on the walls traced Lake's movie and television career from his first parts as a child actor to the present day. While most of the house was messy, the nursery was immaculate. Printed curtains with Disney characters adorned the windows. A crib occupied the center of the room and an upholstered stand stood against a wall next to a dresser with a neatly arranged row of stuffed animals on top.

The detectives spent hours carefully examining every closet, drawer, and cabinet on the property. When they finished the search, they felt disappointed that they had uncovered nothing linking Lake to the Walther they believed was the murder weapon. They did, however, come up with a few interesting finds. On a bathroom mirror, someone had scrawled with a marker: "I'm not going down." Ross turned up $20,000 in banded stacks of cash in a bedroom dresser drawer, and Jenkins found a suitcase packed with Lake's clothes in a bedroom closet.

"Maybe he intends to leave town," Jenkins said while showing Drew the suitcase.

Drew shrugged. "Everyone in L.A. has a go bag packed."

"What do you make of the cash Ross found then?"

"Could be his earthquake stash," Drew said. "It's not evidence of anything, since it would be too easy for him to explain it away. Photograph it and record a representative amount of serial numbers, then put it back."

Li found a hundred-count box of nine millimeter ammunition, missing eight cartridges, on a shelf in Lane's bedroom. Drew felt excited by the discovery since the capacity of the Walther, a nine millimeter pistol, was eight rounds. SID had recovered the handgun with one round in the chamber, and five in the magazine. The shooter had fired the weapon twice, so the numbers matched.

"Too easy," Li said, shaking her head. "I doubt this means what we wish it did."

The detectives loaded boxes with Lane's financial records, legal documents about a child custody suit his attorney had filed against Manley, and other documents. They seized several pistols and the box of ammunition. After Drew finished itemizing everything, the detectives loaded the boxes into the trunks of their cars, bid farewell to Beck and Kelly, and drove to a diner north of downtown to eat a late lunch and to plan their next moves.

·········

At the diner, over cheeseburgers and fries, the detectives discussed the case.

"I have one more thing for you and Ross," Drew said, looking at Jenkins. "After we drop off the evidence at the PAB, you can both go home to get some sleep. But this evening, I want you to go back to Spirito's to interview the staff again. Most of the same crew from Friday night will probably be working. I want to make damn sure no one remembers Lake returning to the restaurant after he paid the check and left with the victim."

"To make sure we can knock down his alibi?" Jenkins asked.

"Yes, because if he didn't go back inside the restaurant as he claims, he could have instead gone somewhere nearby to retrieve the Walther from where he might have stashed it earlier."

Jenkins and Ross nodded.

"Amy and I will go back to Bryant Riley, the guy Lake contacted to call 911. North Hollywood interviewed him, but I want to hear his story straight from him."

"What are we doing tomorrow?" Li asked. "I have plans that I need to cancel if we're working."

"I think we'll take tomorrow off," Drew said. "We've been at it going on fourteen hours since the call out last night. And we all have a few more hours left to go this evening. We've accomplished enough for the weekend. So, we'll all have a restful Sunday and hit it hard again Monday morning."

"Sounds like a plan," Jenkins said. Li and Ross nodded in agreement.

"Good," Drew said. "Then let's get out of here and finish the day."

Eight

AFTER THE DETECTIVES HAD secured the property that they had collected from Lake's residence, Jenkins and Ross left for home. Li suggested to Drew that they head directly to Bryant Riley's home to interview him.

"It's Saturday and Riley might have plans for the evening," Li said. "Plus, we'll have our day finished afterward."

"Agreed," Drew said. "I'd rather do that than nap and have to get up and go out again a few hours later."

Leaving the office, they drove back to the scene in their personal vehicles to avoid a trip back to the PAB. Riley lived three houses down the street from where Lake had parked his car the previous evening, in a modest single-story stucco house with an air conditioning unit jutting from a front window. The detectives walked along a cement sidewalk bracketed by rose bushes leading to the front door. Drew knocked on the door. A man who looked to be in his mid-thirties, wearing jeans, a T-shirt, and a baseball cap, along with a dazed expression, opened the door.

"LAPD," Drew said, holding up his badge case. "Bryant Riley?"

"That's right."

"We would like to ask you a few questions about the incident that happened across the street last night if you can spare us a few minutes of your time."

"Some detectives talked to me last night. I already told them everything I know."

"We understand, Mr. Riley," Drew said. "But we're from downtown and have taken over the case. We would like to hear your story firsthand to make sure we miss nothing."

"Okay, sure," Riley said. "Come on in."

Riley stood aside so the detectives could enter, then after closing the door, he led them to the dining room and they all sat down at the table.

"Would you care for coffee or anything?" Riley asked.

"No, we're fine," Drew said. "We don't want to take up too much of your time this afternoon."

Riley nodded.

"First, I'd like for you to run through the story for us real quick about what you saw and heard last night," Drew said. "If you don't mind, we're going to record the interview. Later, we'll get it transcribed as a witness statement and we'll circle back to get you to sign it."

When Riley signaled his agreement with a nod, Li took out her phone and cued up an audio recording app. Laying the phone on the table, she told Riley he could begin.

"I was in the back on my computer," Riley said. "I'm a film director and was reviewing a screen play. Anyway, I had just taken a shower and was wearing a bathrobe when I heard someone banging on the front door. It was like, well, crazy. Knocking and banging and shouting. I opened the door and the first thing I heard was: 'You've got to help me! You've got to help me. She's bloody and beaten! Oh my God!'" Riley had imitated the cries of someone in a panic as he related what Lake had said. "Then, I said, William Lake? William? And he said, 'Yeah, yeah. It's me.'"

"Then what happened?" Drew asked.

"I asked him to come inside and asked what was going on. But he shook his head and said, 'She's bloody! She's bloody! My wife is bloody. They beat her up. She's been beaten!' So, I'm like, where is she? What do you mean? He says, 'She's in the car. Across the street.' So, I looked down at his hands. That was the first thing I thought of. Had he beaten her up? You know, a domestic situation? His eyes were totally dilated. He seemed a little inebriated, but also like he was in shock. Then he begged me to call 911."

"When you looked at his hands, did you see anything? Blood or anything suggesting he'd been in an altercation?"

"No, like I said. It was just the first thing I thought of. But I saw nothing. No blood or anything."

"Okay, so you called 911?"

"Yes. I ran to the bedroom, grabbed my phone, and called. The dispatcher asked me some questions and told me to grab a clean towel to apply pressure if there was a serious wound. I put on some shorts and a T-shirt and we rushed outside to the car with the towel. I saw her slumped over in the seat and opened the car door. William got sick and then stumbled away toward the restaurant down the street. I found that odd. Like why wasn't he going to help me help her? You know?"

Riley described how he tried to staunch the bleeding. "All I saw was blood coming out of her nose. Like a lot of blood. But it was thick, not completely runny, and it didn't look completely fresh. Then I noticed what looked like a bullet wound on her cheek. I've seen bullet wounds. As a director, I've done a lot of research and stuff. And she was totally catatonic. I looked into her eyes. They were all over the place. No focus, no anything."

"So, he just took off and left you alone with her?" Li asked.

"At first, but he returned a while later. I tried to console him, talking to him while I kept pressure on her wounds. Then the paramedics arrived, and William broke down and cried." Then Riley continued in a confidential tone. "What I found odd was he was crying, but there were no tears. I'm a director, so I'm looking at him as an actor and observing his emotions. It's really weird to see someone making these heart-wrenching sobs and nothing is coming out. I don't know if being in shock shuts that off. I have no clue."

"You think he might have been faking it?" Drew asked.

"I just don't know. Maybe. But could it have been because of going into shock?"

Drew shrugged. "Okay, so then what happened?"

"While the paramedics worked on his wife, I hugged him and tried to comfort him. Then an LAPD sergeant arrived and asked who was related to the woman. William told him she was his wife. Then he said: 'I knew this would happen. I knew it. She was afraid. And I'm carrying my piece.' Then he took out a revolver and handed it to the sergeant. William said he was so thirsty, so I ran back here and got a glass of water and took it back over to him."

"Okay," Drew said. "Let's go back to the beginning."

Riley again described how he had called 911 after Lake showed up at his door and how Lake had wandered away toward the restaurant after they got to the car.

"And you thought that seemed odd?" Drew asked.

"Absolutely. If it had been my wife or girlfriend, I wouldn't have left her alone for a second." Then Riley again mentioned seeing the bullet wound to the side of Manley's face.

"Did you get any sense of what direction the shot came from?" Drew asked.

"This occurred to me, as a director, like if I was shooting a scene in a film. I think she totally trusted the person who did it. You know what I'm saying? He comes up to the car. He says something to her. And then, boom! Because it looked like she just... you know, slumped over in the seat without even raising her hands."

"Tell me something," Drew said. "Did you notice if Lake walked all the way back to the restaurant? Or did he like walk that way and then change his mind and come right back to the car?"

"I can't say," Riley said, shaking his head. "I mean, I saw him wandering toward the restaurant, but when he walked away, I just focused on what I could do for his wife until the paramedics arrived."

"Do you think he was gone long enough to walk a block away and then a block back?" Li asked.

Riley shook his head. "Sorry, I was so stressed by the whole thing. I wasn't thinking about time other than hoping the paramedics would hurry and get there before she bled to death. He walked away and the next thing I knew, he was back looking over my shoulder."

"Did you hear any gunshots before Lake knocked on your door?" Drew asked.

"No, but I was in the back of the house and I have an older window unit back there. It's sort of loud. So, I'm not positive I could have heard shots even if they came from my front yard, much less across and down the street."

"Okay," Drew said. "Anything else you saw or heard that we should know?"

"No, I think I've told you everything I can remember."

Drew took out a business card and laid it on the table in front of Riley. "Well, if you recall anything else, call me, yeah? Even if it doesn't seem important. Sometimes it's the minor details that make the difference in an investigation like this."

Riley nodded. "Honestly, I have thought of little else since it happened and I'm sure I've told you guys all I know. But sure. If anything comes to mind, I'll call you."

Drew and Li thanked Riley for his time, then they left the residence.

"That's the first we've heard that Lake might have gone to the restaurant after the shooting," Drew said. "If he made it all the way there before turning around and returning to the car."

"Maybe he was heading to the restaurant to wash up after getting sick and puking," Li said.

"Or to wash his hands after shooting his wife to get rid of the gunshot residue," Drew said.

Li nodded. "There is that."

After they got back in their cars, Drew and Li said their farewells and then left for their respective homes. On the drive to his apartment, Drew reviewed what Riley had told them. *Maybe Lake left Riley alone in the car while he dumped the Walther into the construction dumpster.* All Howard really knew was he felt more and more certain that William Lake had murdered his wife.

Nine

DREW HAD JUST WALKED into Open-Unsolved Monday morning and sat down for a team meeting when his phone rang. When he picked up the phone, it was Lieutenant Moreno.

"I expected an update yesterday, Drew," Moreno said. "I didn't hear from you."

"Sorry, Lieutenant. I planned to get with you this morning after meeting with my team. After the long day Saturday, I gave them Sunday off, so I had nothing except the search results from Lake's house and didn't want to bother you on a Sunday."

"You got nothing accomplished yesterday, Drew? Is that what you're saying?"

"Well, Lieutenant, I expected we would have many long days ahead of us this week, so yes, I told everyone to take a breather Sunday so everyone would feel rested and good to go this morning."

"Drew, are you unaware of how important it is that we get a quick resolution of this case?" Moreno said in an exasperated tone. "When Captain Mann told me to give you the lead, I assumed you knew how to run a homicide investigation. I can't believe you thought it was appropriate to waste an entire day."

It irritated Drew that Moreno had blatantly questioned his judgement, and he felt the anger building. But he stopped himself from mouthing the angry retort that almost spilled out. "I'm sorry, Lieutenant. I felt like we were in a holding pattern after covering everything we could on Saturday and were waiting to submit evidence to the lab for analysis."

"Fine, it's water under the bridge, Detective. But there will be no more days off until we have handcuffs on a suspect for this homicide. Am I clear?"

"Crystal," Drew said.

"Bring your team over to Homicide Special. You can have your meeting here in the conference room and maybe I'll get the update I should have received yesterday."

"Yes, sir. We're on the way."

Moreno disconnected. Drew, still flushed with anger, collected Amy Li, Jenkins, and Ross, explained the change in plans, and they all headed over to the Homicide Special conference room. Sure, Drew had intentionally not called Moreno on Sunday. He hadn't wanted to risk the lieutenant countermanding his decision to give his team the day off. But Moreno had his phone number and hadn't reached out on Sunday. If he had been so impatient for an update, why not?

·· • • •• • • • ··

Despite the reduced staffing, Homicide Special was thrumming with activity when Drew and his team entered. Howard nearly collided with a uniformed officer on his way out as he walked in, someone Drew hadn't seen in a long while, someone it wouldn't have bothered him to never see again. The officer in the crisp, tailored uniform with two silver stars on the collars was none other than Drew's old nemesis, Deputy Chief Greg LaChasse. Drew last saw the deputy chief when LaChasse had visited him in the hospital months before.

When a murder suspect ambushed Drew in his own apartment, Howard suffered a gunshot wound and other injuries that almost ended his law enforcement career. LaChasse had visited Drew and pressed him to accept a disability retirement. Ever since Howard, while assigned at West Bureau, had made the mistake of confronting a murder suspect alone, a confrontation that ended with Drew fatally shooting the suspect, LaChasse had tried his best to force Drew out of the LAPD. He had pressed for Drew's termination over the incident, but the department had exonerated him. And since then, the deputy chief had made getting rid of Drew his special project.

While investigating the cold case that had culminated with the suspect shooting him, Drew had uncovered evidence of LaChasse's involvement in corruption where the deputy chief had tried to bury the investigation to cover up past misdeeds stretching all the way back to when LaChasse had been a lieutenant in RHD. Instead of exposing LaChasse's corruption, Drew had held onto the evidence to use as leverage to get LaChasse off his back. That had led to a standoff between them and an uneasy truce. Howard believed the evidence of corruption had moved him beyond LaChasse's reach, yet he always knew that the man was back there on his six, biding his time, looking for any opportunity he might use as leverage to drive Drew from the ranks of the LAPD. They remained bitter enemies.

"Chief," Drew said with a curt nod.

"Detective," LaChasse replied with a wry grin. "How's the leg?"

"Good as new," Drew said, willing the conversation to end.

"Yes, I heard you passed the physical and returned to duty," LaChasse said. "Now it seems you've even got your shot at Homicide Special." LaChasse's grin widened into a smile, the kind that didn't reach his eyes. Looking at LaChasse's teeth made Drew think of a shark. "Too bad it seems you've already stepped on it again, Detective.

I suspect your big chance will be short-lived and you will have occasion to regret not taking the disability retirement when you had the chance." With that, the deputy chief turned and strode away without waiting for a riposte. *Smug bastard, Drew thought.* Then he continued to the conference room with Li, Jenkins, and Ross in tow.

Lieutenant Moreno was already sitting at the head of the conference table, drumming his fingers on the tabletop. When Drew entered, he sat down on one side of the table next to Moreno. Amy Li sat down beside Drew. Jenkins and Ross took chairs across from them on the opposite side. The frustration over Moreno's earlier call and anger at LaChasse's comments still flooded Drew. He took a deep breath and tried to focus on getting through the meeting. Sensing her partner's dark mood, Li spoke up.

"Want me to cover the results from the search warrant?" she asked Howard.

"Sure," he said, opening up the murder book in front of him and handing Li the itemized list of property they had seized under the warrant.

"It's already a media circus," Moreno said with disgust before Li could start. "Lake's attorney is already dirtying up the victim, telling the press all about her shady past. He's really spinning it. On the way in this morning, I heard him say on the radio that it was a professional hit because of the scams she had been running."

Drew had expected the murder would attract some media attention, but because the victim had been an aging grifter and Lake was best known for a television series canceled years in the past, he had not expected a firestorm of publicity. Maybe Amy Li had been right. It seemed the specter of the O. J. Simpson debacle hovered over this investigation.

When Drew didn't respond to Moreno's comments, and after Li had glanced at him, she briefed the others on the property she and Drew had collected on Saturday from Lake's residence. Moreno perked up at the mention of the recovered nine millimeter ammunition.

"That would sink Lake if it matches the ammunition recovered with the Walther," he said. Then he gave Drew a pointed look. "If you had called me, I could have got with the captain and had someone called in at FAU and we would already know the answer by now."

Drew lifted his hands, palms up, in surrender. "I was waiting until the autopsy, so we would could get everything to FAU at the same time."

Moreno shook his head, snorting in disgust. "I want no more delays, Detective. Anything you get from this point on, I want you to run with it. Understood?"

"Yes, sir."

"Okay, what else?"

Drew cleared his throat. Everyone sensed the mood of the room was tense and subdued. "Detective Li and I interviewed Bryant Riley."

Howard summarized the interview, pointing out as he went through it what he felt were the most salient points. While he spoke, the door opened and Captain Mann, Commander of Robbery-Homicide Division, entered the room and took a seat at the far end of the table.

"More crocodile tears?" Moreno asked. "I saw the same thing on the North Hollywood interview recording."

"That was Riley's impression," Drew said. "As a film director, he knows acting when he sees it, so I believe he knows what he is talking about."

"Except he also said Lake seemed to suffer the effects of shock," Li offered. "And he speculated maybe that explained why Lake was sobbing, but with no tears."

"Bullshit," Moreno said. "I've seen plenty of people suffering from shock and it makes tears more likely, not less, when an individual is actually upset and sobbing."

Li shrugged. "Just reporting what the man said."

"Did he verify whether Lake returned to the restaurant when he left him alone with the victim?" Moreno asked.

"Riley couldn't say," Drew said. "He focused on trying to staunch the victim's bleeding and didn't notice. He just said Lake left and then returned sometime later. Maybe he was dumping the murder weapon, not going back to the restaurant."

"We could run down that North Hollywood sergeant Riley mentioned," Li said. "Sounded like he arrived at the scene about the time Lake returned to the car. Maybe he passed Lake on his way to the scene and knows if he was walking back or towards the restaurant."

Moreno pointed a finger at Drew before growling, "That's something else you could have done yesterday instead of taking the day off."

"We'll do it today," Drew snapped, anger showing on his face. *What the hell was going on? Had Moreno missed the boss-employee paradigm class at the LAPD supervisor school? Praise in public, criticize in private. Why was Moreno ripping him every chance he got in front of the others? It was as if he was intentionally undermining the team's confidence in their lead investigator.*

Amy Li's cell phone, on the table beside her, vibrated. Looking at the screen, she looked at Moreno apologetically. "I need to take this," she said, grabbing up the phone. "It's the medical examiner's office." Then she got up and hurried out of the room, answering the call on the way.

"What's your plan for today, Detective?" Moreno asked.

Looking at Jenkins and Ross across the desk, Drew said, "Get Lake's clothing and the ammunition we collected from his house out to Cal State and the victim's laptop over to Piper Tech to access it. Find out if FAU has come up with anything on the Walther, and run down that patrol sergeant. We've also got some documents to go through."

"Did we at least verify with the employees whether Lake went back to the restaurant after the gun, like he claims?" Moreno asked.

"I can answer that," Jenkins said.

"Let's hear it then, Detective," Moreno said.

"Ross and I went back to Spirito's Saturday evening and interviewed the owners and staff. No one recalled seeing Lake return after he paid the check and left with his wife. Not only that, the waiter who served them dinner told us he cleared and wiped down the table and booth seats as soon as they left to pay the check. He didn't see a gun and said he would have noticed if he had wiped a gun off the seat onto the hardwood floor."

"So, the alibi is dead in the water?"

"I'd say so," Jenkins said. "We also learned something else interesting."

"Well, don't keep us in suspense, Detective," Moreno snapped.

"A customer recognized us as cops and asked if we were investigating the murder. When we told him we were, he said he was at the restaurant Friday night having drinks with a friend at the bar. Shortly after Lake passed by them on his way to the restroom the second time, this guy went to the restroom and noticed someone had vomited in the trash can. He said he'd gone to the restaurant for at least a dozen years and had seen nothing like it before."

"And he believed it was Lake who vomited in the trash can?"

"Yes. The guy said he noticed bits of spinach and pasta in the vomit. Later he tracked down Lake's server and asked what Lake had ordered for dinner. The server told him it was Lake's regular dish, *Fusilli e minestra*. It's corkscrew pasta with garlic, olive oil, spinach, and tomatoes. So, the guy said he found it significant and maybe showed Lake was very nervous about something."

"Like he was about to kill his wife?" Moreno said, stroking his chin.

"Exactly."

After Jenkins finished, Drew turned back to Moreno. "Detective Li and I are hopefully going to attend the autopsy today, assuming that's what her call is about."

Moreno nodded. "Captain Mann called the medical examiner's office and asked them to expedite it. Now, Detective, make sure you document who is doing what and when. I don't want to see you all end up on the stand later saying, 'We all did a lot of stuff, but don't know exactly what.'"

"Roger that," Drew said, seething.

Captain Mann spoke for the first time, looking at Moreno. "Sounds like you need to tighten up this investigation, Lou. You need to make sure Drew here clearly understands your performance expectations."

"Don't worry, Captain," Moreno retorted. "I intend to do exactly that." Turning to Drew, he continued. "When we finish here, you and I will talk privately, Detective."

Before Drew could reply, Li reentered the room. "Post time is 11:00 A.M., Howard."

Drew glanced at the clock on the wall and saw it was 10:18 A.M. Then he looked at Jenkins and Ross. "Get the evidence we've collected out to Cal State and then drop the laptop at Piper Tech," he said, pushing away from the table and standing up. Then, we'll meet back here and go from there. Turning to Moreno, he said, "We need to get to the autopsy."

"Okay, Detective, but you get right back here afterward and we'll have that conversation."

Drew nodded and gathered up his files.

"Anything you need from me in the meantime?" Moreno asked as Drew turned to leave.

"Now that you mention it," Drew said, turning back. "We could use more people on this. Even some uniforms in plain clothes would help. They could handle getting evidence where it needs to go, and would free up Jenkins and Ross for investigative work." Opening a folder, he took out a printed document and slid it across the table to Moreno. "Detective Li and I need to fly to Little Rock, Arkansas, tomorrow morning to interview the victim's close family and associates." Drew knew submitting the travel request through normal channels would mean he would be lucky if they approved it by the end of the week. He was in no mood to wait after Moreno's rebuke.

Moreno stabbed the tabletop with his index finger several times. "I want you here in L.A., Detective, running the investigation. Use Jenkins and Ross as the travel team."

"You said you want a speedy resolution, Lieutenant," Drew said in a more sarcastic tone than intended. "You said you wanted us to run with whatever we have. I've already planned an assignment schedule for Jenkins and Ross. You want me to scratch everything, start over, and send them to Little Rock?"

Moreno flushed. Drew's sarcastic tone hadn't escaped him. He snatched up the travel request. "Fine, leave it with me. I'll expedite the request, Detective. But, as you know, we have severe staffing issues. Don't get your hopes up about getting more people."

"Roger that, Lieutenant," Drew said. Then he and his team filed out of the room, leaving Mann and Moreno sitting at the table alone.

On the way back to Open-Unsolved, Li exclaimed, "What the hell? Moreno ripped you a new one every chance he got back there. I thought we were all on the same team."

"This is a jackpot," Drew muttered. "I don't need that. I've got enough pressure as it is."

"What do you mean, this is a jackpot?"

"I'll tell you on the drive over to the autopsy."

Ten

JENKINS AND ROSS ROLLED into Hertzberg-Davis and went directly to FAU, the Firearms Analysis Unit, deciding to drop off the clothing at the Trace Analysis Unit afterward. Captain Mann had already called and secured expedited processing of all evidence for the high-profile case. So as soon as the detectives walked in to FAU, a firearms technician met them and escorted them back to the lab. Ross handed over the box of ammunition collected from Lake's house to the criminalist, Tom Vega. When Jenkins asked about the Walther, Vega shook his head and delivered the bad news.

"TID couldn't lift a single print from it, not even a smudge," Vega said. "It came in covered with motor oil and that obliterated any prints. Then after we cleaned it up, we tried running it through the system every way possible, but got nothing. We figure it's unregistered."

"Damn, that's disappointing," Jenkins said. "We'll have to ask the ATF if they can trace it."

Vega nodded absently while he examined the box of ammunition the detectives had brought him. "This will probably not help you guys either," he said.

"Why not?" Ross asked. "Can't you compare it to the rounds recovered with the Walther?"

"It wouldn't prove anything," Vega said. "This is a box of gangsta loads."

"Shit," Jenkins said, understanding Vega's meaning. The criminalist had explained the box contained a variety of rounds. Looking at the cartridges Vega had spread out on the table, Jenkins saw a mixture of ball ammunition and hollow points.

"There might be some cartridges here from the same manufacturer and even of the same type," Vega said. "But all the rounds in this box would have to be the same and be what came in with the weapon for you to link it to the location you got this ammunition from. Since that isn't the case, the lot number printed on this box is also useless."

"Were the rounds in the gun all the same?"

"Yes, Federal 124 grain FMJ. You have spent projectiles for comparison?"

"Not yet, but we will later today. They're doing the cut this morning."

Vega nodded. "I can test fire the Walther using the ammunition that came in with it, so I'll be ready to make the ballistics comparison."

"I understand it's an old weapon," Ross said. "Is it in good shape?"

"Oh, yeah," Vega said. "Once I cleaned it up, I found it was in great condition. They made Walthers to last and someone has taken good care of it."

"Guess we'll leave it with you then," Jenkins said. "We've got to make a stop at TAU."

"Okay," Vega said. "Good luck with ATF, gentlemen."

· · · · · · · · · ·

In good traffic, passing through Los Angeles by car takes under an hour. However, the same trip easily takes three to five hours during rush hour. Weekday mornings L.A. rush hour lasts roughly from 7:00 A.M. to 10:00 A.M., but residents know they can't count on it when needing to arrive at a destination at a specific time. As Li and Drew inched along the 101 toward the medical examiner's office, it was one of those days when rush hour had extended past 10:00 A.M. In good traffic, the trip from the PAB, a little less than three miles, took around ten minutes. On this Monday morning, it would take closer to twenty, which was still better than the forty-five minutes it would have taken had the detectives opted for the surface streets.

"Spill it, Howie," Li said as she guided the unmarked car through the congested freeway traffic. "What were you talking about when we walked out of Homicide Special?"

Still miffed that Moreno had publicly second-guessed his handling of the case, Drew was in no mood for conversation. Suddenly, without looking up from his phone screen, he loosed a string of expletives.

"What?" Li asked.

"I can't believe this," Drew said in disgust, reading the online version of the *Times*. "Media relations told reporters that Lake is a witness, not a suspect, not even a person of interest. I wish they could have been a little more vague instead of making him look as clean as a shiny new penny."

"Well, initially, North Hollywood only interviewed him as a witness."

"Some witness. Now he has lawyered up and won't talk to us."

"Come on, Howie. You said you would tell me what you meant earlier when you said this investigation is a jackpot."

Drew relented and put away his cell phone. "You ever wonder why they picked us to run this investigation?" he asked.

"They told us, didn't they? Moreno said Homicide Special was short-staffed because of the budget cuts, the pandemic, and vacations."

"Yeah, but why us? There are plenty of veteran murder cops in the bureaus they could have brought in for it. Why us?"

"Well, I guess because we're in Open-Unsolved and our unit is a part of RHD, so we aren't like outsiders."

"I don't think so. I don't think that's the reason at all."

"What does it matter, Howie? We've both wanted a shot at Homicide Special forever. And now we've got it. We wanted a fresh murder investigation real bad. It's not ideal, but now we've got one."

"Yeah," Drew said, shaking his head. "But I wanted a regular one. I don't want to be the LAPD's sacrificial lamb."

"What are you talking about?" Li asked, glancing at her partner, eyebrows raised.

"You heard LaChasse's comments," Drew said. "Before we left the office, I looked up the command staff roster on my computer. I'd wondered why I hadn't seen LaChasse since I returned to duty. Know why I haven't? He isn't on the tenth floor anymore. LaChasse transferred. He's now the commanding officer of Operations-Valley Bureau. He is over North Hollywood and Valley Bureau homicide. I think LaChasse is behind our temporary assignment to Homicide Special and this case."

"First, LaChasse hates your guts, Howie. Why would he have recommended us, specifically you, to take on a high-profile case that might lead to your permanent assignment to Homicide Special? And besides. It is a celebrity case, so it had to go downtown. LaChasse had no say in the decision."

"Sure, but that doesn't mean he might not have persuaded Mann to give us the case. And everyone in the LAPD knows about the pandemic and staffing issues. Depending on how tight Mann and LaChasse are, LaChasse could have known Mann couldn't staff an investigation like this in house."

"Still, I don't get your reasoning, Howie. The last thing LaChasse would do is help you get assigned to Homicide Special."

"Unless he saw it as the means for finally shoving me out of the department," Drew said. "LaChasse had plenty of time to get a reading on the case before Mann called me. Maybe he understood this case was going to be a charlie foxtrot just like O. J. was. He could have convinced Mann that Homicide Special and RHD would take it on the chin again in the press and court of public opinion if things broke bad. So, Mann took LaChasse's advice and dropped the case on us."

"I'm not buying it," Li said. "Come on, Howie. You think Mann doesn't want this murder cleared by arrest? Isn't he going to look bad if it isn't, even if he wanted to make us scapegoats?"

"Oh, I'm sure he'd be happy for us to clear it with an arrest," Howie said. "But if it doesn't happen, he can control the damage by pointing the finger of blame somewhere outside Homicide Special. If he spins in just right in the press, putting the blame on us, the department could use it to its advantage. The brass could tell the city council that the budget cuts and staffing issues forced them to hand the case to a less qualified detective who previously worked nothing but cold cases."

"Sounds too much like a tinfoil hat conspiracy theory to me, partner," Li said. "Just saying."

Drew's phone rang. He took it out and answered. "What have you got?" He listened for several moments. "Terrific," he muttered. "Okay, well, get the laptop out to Piper Tech. Then, get with ATF and see if they can do anything with the Walther." After listening another moment, Drew said goodbye and disconnected the call.

"Jenkins?"

"Yeah, the box of ammunition was a bust. It's a box of gangster loads. About half of the cartridges are hollow-points and half ball ammunition. So it doesn't give us a link from the gun to Lake's house. Also, FAU got no prints off the gun and believes the Walther is unregistered."

"That's not surprising," Li said. "It's probably a war souvenir some G.I. brought back after the second world war. Dealers don't have to register guns manufactured that long ago."

"Yeah, I know."

Li turned into the parking lot of the Los Angeles County Medical Examiner-Coroner and parked. The detectives got out of the car and went inside the building.

Eleven

DREW HAD NEVER GROWN accustomed to viewing autopsies. It seemed yet another indignity heaped upon the indignities victims had already suffered. He'd attended many, but to Drew, autopsies represented reminders of human inhumanity, something he had witnessed far too many times. The pathologist, Nina Garraway, a petite blonde, hunched over the steel table, her hip pressed against the side to gain leverage. After making the iconic Y-shaped chest incision, she had removed, weighed, and bagged Connie Lynn Manley's organs and intestines. Now she had her gloved hands deep inside Manley's gutted torso, working with forceps in one hand and another long-bladed instrument in the other.

Garraway blew out a breath that temporarily fogged her face shield, and she dropped from her tiptoes back onto her heels to rest. "Almost there," she said. "It's lodged in the spine." After dropping the long-bladed instrument into a stainless-steel sink where the running tap kept the water at the overflow drain level, Garraway selected a slender stainless-steel pick from the instruments spread out on the table atop a green cloth. Then, back on her tiptoes, she again thrust her hands into the torso. "Got it," she said a few moments later, blowing out another breath. Pulling her hands out, she dropped the pick into the sink and rinsed the forceps beneath the running faucet.

The pathologist then held up the forceps and examined the object of her efforts.

Tapping the floor button with her foot to activate the recorder, she said, "A projectile recovered from anterior T-five vertebra. Severe mushrooming observed. I will photograph and mark it with my initials before turning it over to Detective Howard Drew of the Los Angeles Police Department." Garraway tapped the button again to end the recording.

Taking the bullet over to the counter, she photographed it and marked it with an indelible pen before dropping it into a small plastic evidence bag, which she also initialed before handing it to Drew. Drew took the pen and added his initials to the bag to establish the chain of custody. Studying the flattened projectile inside the bag, Drew felt sure there was enough of the shaft with stria visible for the criminalists at FAU to make a comparison.

Garraway picked up a Stryker, a small electric rotary saw, and used it to cut away the skull cap. After carefully prying off the cranial cap with a skull chisel, she removed the brain and then examined it. "Here it is," she said, removing with forceps a second projectile from the brain tissues. After rinsing the forceps beneath the running trap, she repeated the previous process with the recorder before photographing, marking the projectile, and bagging it. Then she handed the evidence bag to Drew, who initialed it and then examined the bullet through the plastic. It was in about the same condition as the first and again he thought usable for comparison.

"Will you stay for the rest?" Garraway asked.

Drew held up the evidence bags. "We better get these over to Cal State," he said. "We're getting pressure on this case and our boss wants verification that we have the murder weapon."

"Right, well, let me give you the unofficial summary before you go. It will be a few days before you get the full report. The first projectile entered the right shoulder area, severed the carotid artery, and perforated the aorta, causing severe internal bleeding and then lodging in the spine. Trajectory was almost level, with a slight upward tilt. The second projectile entered the right cheek area, six inches below the vertex, and four inches to the right of the anterior mid-line. It lodged in the left temporal lobe of the brain. There was no stippling present at either wound site, so neither were contact wounds. But given the depth of penetration, I'd say the shots came from close range."

"You know which was the kill shot?" Li asked.

"Either would have been fatal," Garraway said. "Cause of death was exsanguination. She bled to death."

"Okay, thanks, Doc," Drew said.

As Drew and Li stripped off their protective gear at the autopsy suite exit, Garraway called across the room. "Detective Drew, take down my cell phone number. You can call me if you have questions before you get the report." The pathologist had lifted her face shield and pulled her surgical mask down so Drew could see the wide smile on the face of a very attractive woman. "Or you can also call if you just want to meet for a drink or a bite to eat."

Drew blinked in surprise, but hastily grabbed the notebook from his shirt pocket and a pen. "Shoot," he said. After Garraway recited her cell phone number and Drew had copied it in the book, he looked at her and returned her smile. "Got it, thanks."

"Thank you," Garraway said, continuing to smile. "I'll look forward to your call."

"You got it," Drew said, also still smiling, and then he and Li walked out of the suite.

"Look at you," Li chuckled. "You've still got it, partner. You're definitely going to call her, aren't you? She's a cutie."

"Who knows?" Drew said, trying to appear noncommittal but unable to suppress his grin. "Maybe."

Twelve

FROM THE MEDICAL EXAMINER'S office, Li and Drew headed directly to FAU at Cal State, with the projectiles recovered during the autopsy.

"As long as you're disregarding Moreno's instructions to return straight back to the PAB for your meeting, you think we can get lunch after this?" Li asked.

"Sure," Drew said. "After we finish at FAU, we'll grab something on the way back."

"Moreno won't be happy with you, partner."

"Too bad," Drew said. "We need to build momentum on this murder, and wasting time at headquarters talking with Moreno will not get it done."

"It's your butt, Howie," Li said. "But I think Moreno already has you on a short leash. And I'm getting that same vibe from you as the time you tried to pick a fight with that special agent in charge at the FBI."

Drew grinned. "Can I help it if I have a low tolerance for bullshit? Anyway, the only way out of the jackpot is closing this case by arrest. So, that's my solitary focus. Not to make nice with Moreno."

Li shook her head as she drove into the lot at Hertzberg-Davis and parked. Once inside the FAU, Vega, the same firearms examiner

Jenkins and Ross had seen earlier, met them and walked them back to the lab.

"What have you got for me, Detectives?" Vega asked.

"We have projectiles for ballistics comparison recovered at the autopsy of Connie Lynn Manley." Drew recited the case number.

Vega nodded, took the two evidence bags, and pulled up the case on his computer screen. "Leave it with me. I'll call when I get to your case."

Drew shook his head. "This is a hurry-up thing. We need you to do the comparisons now."

"We don't do hurry-up anymore," Vega said, sounding bored.

"This is a high priority case," Drew said with an impatient tone.

"Everything we have is high priority now," Vega countered.

"I guarantee the chief of police will tell you to drop everything else to work on this one," Drew said, growing frustrated. "We need to know if we have the murder weapon or not. We need you to make the comparisons right now."

"No," Vega said flatly.

"The chief will call your supervisor."

Vega shrugged. "I can't do anything until I'm told to."

"Hold that thought," Drew said, pulling out his phone. He called Robbery-Homicide and asked for Captain Mann.

When Mann came on the line, Drew explained the situation. "The criminalist says he can't get to the comparisons right now unless his supervisor tells him to do it. Please call his supervisor so we can get this started."

"What's the supervisor's name?" Mann asked.

Drew asked Vega for the name of his supervisor and then relayed it to Mann. "We're dealing with Tom Vega."

"Give me five minutes and I'll straighten it out," Mann said and then he disconnected.

Vega picked up the evidence bags one by one and examined the spent bullets through the plastic. "I can work with this if my supervisor tells me to drop what I'm doing now and do the comparisons." Then Vega looked at his computer screen again. "We have four nine millimeter handguns on this case."

"Yeah, we're interested in the Walther right now. It came from the scene. We collected the others from the residence of a suspect on a search warrant doing our due diligence."

"Yeah, okay. I remember now. Two other detectives brought those in this morning with a box of nine millimeter ammunition. I've already test fired the Walther, so I have the exemplars ready."

The phone on the desk rang. Vega picked up, listened, said "Okay," and hung up. "Hang on," he said to the detectives. "Let me go get the projectiles from the test firing." Then he left the room.

"This is turning into an ordeal," Drew said in exasperation. "I don't need that."

"Calm down, partner," Li grinned. "You're getting what you want now."

Vega returned with a plastic evidence bag containing two tiny cardboard boxes. He picked up the evidence bags the detectives had brought in and carried everything over to a table holding a comparison microscope. He clamped one spent evidentiary bullet and one exemplar projectile to the platforms beneath the microscope's twin objective lenses to make the side-by-side comparison. After peering into the eyepiece, and making adjustments for several minutes, Vega replaced the first evidentiary bullet with the second and clamped it into place. Then he repeated the process. After several minutes, he turned and looked at the detectives.

"My supervisor told me to take a quick look since I had already test fired the Walther and had the exemplars. We have definite matches. Both of the spent bullets you've brought me came from the Walther. You have your murder weapon. I'll make the official comparisons when I get to it on the schedule and you should get the report within a few weeks. We good?"

"We're good," Drew said. "Much appreciated, Vega."

Vega nodded. "There is something else I discovered about the box of ammunition after the other detectives left."

"What's that?" Drew asked.

"The cartridges are all reloads. None are factory loads."

Drew's pulse quickened. "That means the cartridge cases all have extractor tool marks on them, like any other spent cartridge cases," Drew exclaimed. "Can you do comparisons between those and the spent cartridge cases we collected at the scene?"

Vega pursed his lips. "I could do that, but it wouldn't give you anything. The cartridges that came in with the Walther aren't reloads. They're factory."

Drew groaned. "Yeah, okay. Got it."

"Good job thinking outside the box, anyway," Vega said with a chuckle.

"Thanks again," Drew said and he and Li left the lab.

"You were a little hard on the guy," Li said as the detectives walked outside and back to the car.

"Tough," Drew said. "We're getting pressure, so I'm spreading the wealth. Besides, I only asked him to do his damn job."

Li chuckled and slid behind the wheel as Drew climbed in on the passenger side. "Where do you want to get lunch?"

"Any burger place suits me."

Li made a face. "Howie, I'm not eating burgers and fries every single day that we're on this case."

"Noted, but that's all we have time for today."

"Whatever," Li said, putting the car in gear and driving out of the parking lot.

Drew's phone rang. He took it out, looked at the screen, and answered.

"Detective Drew, this is Carl Sloan at North Hollywood. We've got a guy here who says William Lake solicited him to kill his wife."

"Hang on to him. We're leaving Hertzberg-Davis and will get there as quick as we can."

"You got it," Sloan said and then he disconnected.

"Lunch will have to wait, partner," Drew said. "Someone just walked in to North Hollywood saying Lake solicited him to kill his wife."

"Seriously? We going there now?"

"Yes, if this turns out the way I hope it does, William Lake's life is about to end in a prison cell."

Li took the ramp onto the I-10, put her foot down on the accelerator, and the detectives sped north toward the North Hollywood Station. Drew's phone rang again. He looked at the screen and then turned the phone off before putting it away.

"Moreno?" Li asked.

"Moreno."

"Sucks to be you, Howie."

Thirteen

CARL SLOAN, THE DETECTIVE supervisor at North Hollywood, was waiting in an interview room with a man named Grayson Cohen, who had walked in the station with the revelation that Lake asked him to kill Manley. Sloan stepped outside into the hallway to meet Drew and Li. After introductions, he quickly briefed them.

"The guy is Grayson Cohen. He's a retired stuntman and says he met Lake about thirty years ago while working on the set of Lake's television show, *Quinn*. He claims Lake called him out of the blue recently and asked to meet him in a restaurant. Then, eventually, Lake solicited him to kill his wife."

"Let's hear what he has to say," Drew said.

"I'll introduce you and then I'll videotape the interview for you."

"Sounds like a plan," Drew agreed.

Li and Drew followed Sloan into the interview room.

"Grayson, this is Detective Drew and Detective Li. They are the downtown detectives I told you about."

Cohen stood up and shook hands with the detectives, and then sat back down. Li and Drew took the seats across the table from him while Sloan set up the video recorder.

"We're from Homicide Special, downtown," Drew explained. "Because of William Lake's status as a celebrity, we're investigating the case."

Cohen nodded his understanding. He was stocky and weather-beaten and looked to be in his sixties, but Drew thought the man still looked fit enough to perform stunt work.

"Well, I'm a little late in revealing this, but I've got so many personal problems," Cohen said sheepishly. "I just went through a messy divorce and am dealing with some difficulties with some property I own. But it finally reached the point where I didn't want to lead you guys down a wrong trail. And I might be able to tighten things up for you. So, I thought I better come in and tell you what I know."

"I'm glad you did," Drew said in a reassuring tone. "We appreciate it."

"That woman didn't deserve what she got."

"No one does," Drew said.

"William knew I'd killed a guy a while back. I suppose he figured because of that and that I got off, and everything, he reached out to me."

After the detectives nodded, speaking in staccato bursts and sometimes breaking off in mid-sentence as if losing his train of thought, Cohen told the detectives briefly how he had killed an ex-convict in self defense who had raped a family friend.

"The DA agreed it was a case of self-defense and didn't charge me. Anyway, I hadn't seen William until recently in over twenty years, not since we worked together the last time on a movie set. Then, about six weeks ago, a mutual acquaintance, another old stunt man everyone calls Squeaky, called me. He asked me to meet William for lunch at Du-Par's in Studio City."

"Did he say why?" Drew asked.

"He just said it was about a job. I figured it was a stunt job, a movie job. So, I went."

"What happened when you met?"

"We just bullshitted some about the old days and made a little small talk at first. Then William talked about this gal he wanted something done with. I thought…" Cohen stopped talking abruptly, as though he forgot where he was going with the story.

"Did he specify who this woman was?" Drew asked.

"He said it was a girl he met at a party and had sex with one night, and then she got pregnant. It turned out it was his kid, and she was bilking him out of a lot of money. To keep the kid here in L.A., he was giving her a couple of thousand a month and was tired of it. That's why he wanted to get her bumped off, I guess."

Detectives always pray for that golden moment when someone comes forward with critical information that helps break a case. Drew and Li attempted to remain poker-faced, but struggled to conceal their excitement, believing they were in one of those moments. Unwilling to jinx it, they kept quiet and allowed Cohen to keep talking.

"He took me to his place and showed me the backyard and layout like I might come in through there and do it. He took me to a guesthouse out back and opened the sliding back door. William told me she lived back there."

"Quick question," Drew said. "Why do you think William didn't call you directly? Why would he go through a third party and have this Squeaky call you?"

"Because that motherfucker is smart," Cohen said. "He always was. He didn't want to leave a trail in case I did it for him by calling me direct, so he set it up through Squeaky. That's how smart he is."

Drew nodded. "Okay, take me back to Du-pars and the meeting. What did he say exactly?"

"We just shared some small talk about movies. I thought he wanted me to do a stunt coordinating job or double or something. But it turned out he wanted me to kill his wife." Cohen sounded incredulous when he spoke the last sentence.

"Did he say how he wanted you to do that?"

"I can't really tell you what William said, word for word. But that's what it boiled down to. I understood clearly he wanted me to kill her for him."

"Did he mention something about killing her specifically at the restaurant? Is that why you felt sure that was what he wanted you to do?"

"No, it was just the vibe I got from the conversation. I think he wanted to get me to the house first and show me what a bad person she was. To convince me to do it, you know?" Cohen shook his head. "Oh man," he said breathlessly. "The reality of it all was overwhelming, to say the least."

"What do you mean by he wanted to show you what a bad person she was?"

"Oh, yeah. When we got to the house, William showed me stacks of emails she had sent to lonely guys around the country, and naked pictures she had emailed them. William said she was a con artist and had bilked them out of money."

"Okay, tell me exactly how Lake proposed you kill Manley."

"He showed me where she slept in the guesthouse and suggested someone could slide open the door at night and sneak into her bedroom and pop her while she slept."

"Were those his exact words?" Drew asked. "Pop her?"

"Something to that effect."

"Anything else happen while you were at the house?"

"We left the house and walked around the neighborhood for a while. William told me he was planning a trip to Arizona. He said he could stop at a restaurant and someone could walk up and kill her while she sat in the car in the parking lot. Just like what happened. When I heard that on the news, I thought…" Cohen paused and whistled, looking amazed. "I thought that sounded awfully coincidental."

Drew and Li nodded.

"Then he talked about maybe someone could do it on the highway. He could pull over, pretending he needed to take a leak. And after he walked away from the car, someone could walk up and do it."

"What were you supposed to be doing all that time?" Drew asked.

"William suggested someone could follow them. So, when he pulled over to take a leak or whatever, they would be ready to walk up to the car and pop her. Like I said, it's pretty overwhelming. He had so many scenarios in mind for how to do it."

"So, you felt sure he was serious about it? He wanted you to kill her."

"I knew that's what he wanted. It was clear as day. After we got back from the walk, William drove me back to my car at Du-pars. He asked if I wanted to call him when I was ready. 'You call me,' I told him. Then I asked him what he was talking about money wise. I had no intention of killing his wife, but I was just making sure he was serious."

"And?"

"William asked me how twenty thousand sounded."

"Did he call you?"

Cohen nodded. "He called about a week later and asked me if I would do the job. I told him I wanted nothing to do with it at all."

"What did he say to that?"

"He asked me why. I told him that number one, I didn't want to do anything like that. And I told him another reason was because he was a celebrity and the police would be all over it. Then, William just hung up without another word."

"What did you think when you heard someone killed his wife?"

"I thought, oh man, William found someone to do it. I know I should have picked up the phone right then and called the police. But I let it go. And let it go. And let it go. Finally, I told myself I couldn't let it go any further."

"Did Lake ever come right out with exact words asking you to kill his wife?"

"It was more like you walk over and pop her."

"That's what he said?"

"Yes. And when we were at his house, he showed me a gun. William said he was thinking about getting a silencer for it."

"What kind of gun?"

Cohen couldn't describe the gun in much detail, explaining he knew little about guns. "I know you pull the trigger and it goes bang. That's about it."

"Was it a revolver?"

"No, there was no cylinder. It was sort of boxy looking and black, an automatic, I guess."

"Anything else you can tell us?" Drew asked.

"No, I think I've covered it. I know I should have come in sooner, but I've had a lot going on with the problems I mentioned. Anyway, I was talking to a friend this morning about it and he persuaded me I should contact the police. Hiding something like this would just be ridiculous."

"You did the right thing, and we appreciate it," Drew said, handing Cohen his card. "If you think of anything else, call me. And if we need anything more, we'll circle back to you."

"Okay," Cohen said, slipping the card into his shirt pocket. "Hope I've helped you."

After escorting Cohen out the front doors, Drew and Li exchanged a high five. "We have to do a lot of work to confirm his story," Drew said. "But there's no doubt we just caught a big break."

"We sure did," Li agreed. "And suddenly, that twenty thousand we found at Lake's house seems relevant. Now, can we get lunch, please?"

"Sure, partner," Drew said with a grin. "We'll get something on the way back downtown and I'll even let you pick the place."

Fourteen

IT WAS 3:48 P.M. by the time Drew and Li got back to the PAB. The moment they walked into Open-Unsolved, their boss, Ed Howard, jumped up from his office chair and hurried out to meet them. Howard was less than a month away from retirement. The last thing he wanted was Drew or anyone else stirring up trouble that might interfere with that.

"Drew, why is your phone turned off?" Howard growled. "I've called you a dozen times."

"What's up, Lieutenant? We're working the case for Homicide Special. Remember?"

"Save it, Drew," Howard said. "Why are you stirring up trouble with Lieutenant Moreno?"

"I'm not."

"He's called me every fifteen minutes since noon asking where you were. You were supposed to meet with him as soon as you got back from that autopsy."

"I'll tell you what, Lieutenant. Things come up during a murder investigation. I'm trying to build momentum on this case and I can't drop everything every time Lieutenant Moreno wants to have a meeting."

"You don't have a choice, Drew. He's your supervisor for the time being. You'll do whatever the hell he tells you to do." The lieutenant's tone invited no debate. "You're a loose cannon. You have been since the day you got here."

"That's bullshit and..."

Howard cut him off. "Shut up for once, Drew, and listen."

Drew held his hands up in surrender.

"Get over to Homicide Special and see Lieutenant Moreno right now. And a word to the wise. Because of the budget cuts, the department is closing down Open-Unsolved. If you get yourself kicked off the case they assigned you, you won't have any place to come back to. So, unless you're eager to go back to patrol and wearing a uniform, I suggest you find a way to get along with Moreno."

"Roger that," Drew said, sobered by the news Open-Unsolved was shutting down. Without another word, he turned and left for Homicide Special.

· · · • • · • • · ·

"Sit down, Detective," Moreno said, red-faced, anger transforming the muscles in his clenched jaws into hard lines.

Drew sat down without comment.

"What part of getting back here as soon as you finished with the autopsy did you fail to understand?"

"Sorry, Lieutenant," Drew said. "I only intended to get the two slugs the pathologist recovered to FAU as soon as possible so we could confirm we had the murder weapon. Then on the way back, North Hollywood called..."

Moreno held up his right hand for quiet. Then he held up the hand with his thumb and forefinger almost touching.

"Save the excuses," Moreno said. "I'm about this far from going to the captain and asking to take you off this investigation. Care to give me one good reason I shouldn't?"

"Let me ask you something, Lieutenant. Why did I get this case?"

"Because I made you the lead on it, Detective. And you seem determined to make me regret that decision every single day."

"No, I mean, why did Detective Li and I get the case to begin with? If Homicide Special is so short-handed, why didn't Captain Mann pull someone in from one of the bureaus? There are many more senior murder cops he could have chosen."

"What's the matter, Drew? You don't feel up to investigating this case?"

"Not at all. I think we're making good progress, considering we only have four detectives working on it. And I believe we are building momentum. I'm just curious."

"Curious? Why?"

"This morning I ran into Deputy Chief LaChasse coming out of Captain Mann's office. I'm curious to know if he had anything to do with me getting the case?"

"What does any of this have to do with your insubordinate conduct, Detective? That's what we're discussing here."

"It's just that the deputy chief and I have some history. I'm suspicious he is behind the assignment because he knew this would be a difficult case to solve. I think he wanted to set me up to fail."

"To what purpose?"

"I'm a project for Deputy Chief LaChasse. He has tried to shove me out of the LAPD since an OIS review board I was involved in didn't go the way he thought it should have."

Moreno leaned back in his chair and looked up at the ceiling for several moments. Then he looked back at Drew.

"So, you're saying a member of the command staff is pursuing a personal vendetta against you? Sounds a little like paranoia to me."

"That's what I'm saying, Lieutenant. And I'm not paranoid. The deputy chief has told me more than once he wants me out of the LAPD."

"All right, let's assume for a moment you aren't paranoid and Deputy Chief LaChasse is out to get you. Captain Mann is my boss, and he doesn't explain himself to me. So, I don't know why he chose you and Li for this case or whether Deputy Chief LaChasse had input into the decision. But even he did. Whatever his reason for it, he has no control over how it turns out that I can imagine. If you do your job and you clear the case, I cannot see how that would put you at any disadvantage."

"Unless he has found a way to make sure I can't clear it. It was before my time, but I've heard the stories about what happened to a lot of the guys that worked the O. J. case. I just don't care to see my partner and me end up as the department's sacrificial lambs if this case goes sideways like that one did."

"You can request me to relieve you of responsibility for the investigation, Detective. But I don't see that helping your career any if the captain approves your request."

"I'm not asking to get relieved, Lieutenant. I only want to know what game I'm playing and what the rules are."

"First, I'd caution you about casting dispersions on a senior officer unless you have some very compelling proof of this vendetta you claim to be a victim of, Detective. Second, if you plan on staying on the case, my advice is you better find out who killed that woman and come up with the evidence the prosecutor needs to charge them for her murder. You do that and you shouldn't have anything to worry about."

"Don't worry, Lieutenant. I intend to do that. I'd just rather not have to look over my shoulder all the time I'm doing it."

Moreno rubbed his face with his hands. "I'll tell you what, Detective. Let's get back to the purpose of you being here. I get the sense you feel I'm micromanaging you and you resent it. Am I right?"

"That sums it up pretty well."

"All right, then let's clear the air. I didn't choose you to lead this investigation. Captain Mann did. And unlike you, judging from your recent behavior, I follow my supervisor's orders. That said, I have nothing against you. I've heard uncomplimentary things about you, but also some good things. I believe you're a competent detective. So, I was willing to give you every benefit of the doubt about the less positive things I've heard. But so far, you haven't impressed me. I don't care how good an investigator you are. I won't tolerate any more of your insubordinate attitude. Are we clear?"

Drew nodded. "We're clear."

"When I tell you to do something, you will do it to the best of your ability and in a timely manner. I'm expected to provide daily updates to my superiors. That's why I expect daily updates from you. And I don't see that as micromanaging you."

"Lieutenant, I intended nothing I've done or failed to do as any disrespect or as a challenge to your authority. I only planned to drop off those slugs at the TAU and get right back here like you said. But a witness walked into North Hollywood and it seemed too important to blow it off. Maybe he would have walked right back out and wouldn't have cooperated with us later if we hadn't gone there right away."

"I'm not unreasonable, Drew. If you had called and told me what was going on, I'd have agreed you needed to get over there to talk to your witness. But you didn't call. You did it your way. Then you ignored my call, and you turned your phone off. That's going to stop. Right now."

Drew nodded.

"It's water under the bridge. I'm willing to give you a second chance to get off on the right foot. But I don't give third chances as a rule. If you're subordinate again and disregard another direct order, I will initiate formal disciplinary action and I'll yank you off the case."

"Fair enough."

Moreno nodded. "Now tell me about this witness you interviewed at North Hollywood."

Drew summarized the interview with Grayson Cohen.

Moreno stroked his chin. "Sounds like we're getting somewhere finally. Did you have a good feeling about Cohen?"

"Yes. We need to vet him and see if we can corroborate what he told us. But he seemed credible."

"Did FAU check the slugs against that Walther?"

"The firearms expert did a preliminary examination while we were there. He confirmed the bullets came from the Walther, so we have the murder gun."

"Now if we could only tie that gun to Lake, we would have him."

"That will be difficult. FAU ran it every way they could think of and found nothing. They believe the Walther is unregistered. Some soldier may have brought it back from Europe as a souvenir after World War Two."

"You said Cohen told you Lake showed him a handgun when he solicited him to kill his wife. Was it the Walther?"

Drew shrugged. "Cohen said he knew little about guns. All he could say for sure was the gun Lake showed him wasn't a revolver, so it was probably a semi-automatic. I doubt he can positively identify it as the gun Lake showed him."

"Well, keep digging. Maybe you'll find the source of the gun."

"We will. While Li and I are in Little Rock, I'll have Jenkins and Ross track down and interview the guy Lake used to reach out to Cohen. If we talk to everyone around Lake, we might find someone who knows where the Walther came from."

"You mean that Squeaky character?"

"Yes. Cohen gave us his phone number. Jenkins and Ross can find him with that."

Moreno nodded. "How long do you expect to be in Little Rock?"

"We'll arrive before noon tomorrow morning. It looks like there are three or four people there we need to talk to, so I think we can be on a plane back here Thursday morning at the latest."

"Okay. I want you to talk to everyone you need to because I don't want you making another trip back there later. But unless something comes up after you get there, I want you and Li back in L.A. Thursday. If you feel you need more time there, call me and we'll discuss it."

"Roger that."

"You have anything else?"

"The ammunition we found at Lake's place was a bust. It was a box of gangster loads, so it doesn't link Lake to the Walther. The cartridges SID recovered with the gun were all factory loads."

Moreno picked up an envelope and tossed it on Drew's side of the desk. "That's your travel documents. Call me with an update tomorrow afternoon."

"You got it, Lieutenant."

"Fine. You can get out of here and get back to work."

Drew left Moreno's office and headed back to Open-Unsolved.

Fifteen

WHEN DREW ARRIVED IN Open-Unsolved, he found Li at her desk combing through a stack of documents and saw that Jenkins and Ross were back from Piper Tech. He stopped at Li's desk first.

"What have you been working on?"

"I've been going through the documents we seized from Lake's house."

"Anything interesting?"

"Yes, a lot. One thing I found was an invoice from a private investigator Lake hired, Mark Nash. I called him. He wasn't very forthcoming until I threatened to send a patrol unit out to bring him in for questioning. Finally, he admitted Lake hired him to dig up dirt on Manley so he could get her declared an unfit mother. He also gave up the names of Manley's next of kin in Little Rock. The people we need to talk to there."

"That's great," Drew said. "I wanted us to work up a list before leaving this afternoon so we could hit the ground running when we get to Little Rock. Moreno wants us back here Thursday."

"It looks like we only need to interview two people. I reached Connie Lynn Manley's sister, Regina Manley. She told me their mother suffers from Alzheimer's disease and lives in a nursing home. According to the sister, Connie Lynn and their mother were estranged, and

Connie never confided in her before the mother became ill. So, no point in trying to interview her. Also, Regina said their brother, Dean, lives in Mexico. She suggested the only other person in Little Rock we might want to talk to is Connie's ex-husband, Paul Hudson."

"Did she know about her sister's death?"

"Yes. Lake called her. He told her the coroner hadn't released the body, but he would call her back about the funeral arrangements when they did. So, she and the brother plan to fly to L.A. when she hears back from Lake."

"You get any sense about whether she will talk to us?"

"She's eager to talk to us. She wanted to get into it on the phone, but I told her it would be better if we talked to her in person and would be there tomorrow."

Drew nodded. "Okay, then I guess we should go as planned instead of waiting until she comes here for the funeral."

"I think so. We should probably talk to the ex-husband too, and Regina said he didn't plan to come out for the funeral."

"Yeah, I agree. So, why don't you go home and pack? I'm leaving after I've talked with Jenkins and Ross."

"Great," Li said. "I need to pick up some clothes from the dry cleaners and take care of a few things that won't wait until we get back."

While Li returned the documents to the boxes and prepared to leave the office, Drew walked over to see Jenkins and Ross at their cubicles. He found them both hovered over a laptop on Jenkins' desk.

"That Manley's laptop?" Drew asked.

"Yeah," Jenkins said. "It's a PC, so the guy at Piper Tech got into it easily and changed the password for us. We're reviewing it now."

"Anything interesting?"

"She was definitely a con artist," Jenkins said. "There are lots of homemade porn images on here and lots of emails to and from the guys she reached out to on the Internet and talked out of their money."

"Find anyone else with a motive to kill her?"

"Nah, I don't think so. Manley went for quantity instead of quality. So far, it looks like she never got more than a couple of thousand from any of them, and only a few hundred from most. We're not seeing the kind of money that might have caused someone to want her dead."

"My money is on Lake," Ross said. "He's the asshole who killed her."

Jenkins turned to his partner, raised an index finger, and said primly, "I don't approve of calling a murder suspect an asshole. You should refer to him as an anachronism, someone whose primal instincts are not moderated by the more intellectual parts of his brain."

"Bite me, Jenkins," Ross retorted before all three men burst into laughter.

"Listen," Drew said finally. "Li and I should be back from Little Rock on Thursday. I have a couple of things for you guys besides digging into the laptop."

"Sure," Jenkins said. "What is it?"

Drew told them about the interview with Grayson Cohen.

"Dig into Cohen's background so we can see whether he'll make a credible witness. Also, I want you guys to track down that Squeaky character and interview him. Maybe he will corroborate Cohen's story."

Drew handed Jenkins a page from his notebook with Squeaky's phone number on it.

"All I've got is the nickname. Cohen couldn't remember his actual name."

Jenkins and Ross both nodded. "We'll find him, and that should keep us busy until you're back."

"And I need you to call me with a progress report tomorrow afternoon," Drew said to Jenkins. "So I can include it in my update for Moreno."

"No problem. One of us will call you."

"Okay, Li and I are leaving for the day, so we can pack and get ready to travel. We have an early flight in the morning."

"Sure, Howie. See you when you get back. Try not to have too much fun in Arkansas." Both Jenkins and Ross laughed.

"Well, Little Rock isn't exactly Vegas," Drew said with a grin.

"Okay if we check out at the usual time today?" Ross asked Drew.

"Sure. You have something going at home?"

Ross nodded soberly. "I'm taking my wife to Spirito's tonight. I'm going to tell her to wear her best clothes and put on all her jewelry. Then I'm going to park by that big dumpster, throw all my credit cards on the dash, and leave her there."

"If that doesn't work and you want to be single again," Jenkins said, "hire Earl Lee as her bodyguard."

As Jenkins and Ross burst out laughing again, Drew shook his head and walked away without saying a word.

· · • • · • • • · ·

Li was gathering her things to leave when Drew got back to his desk. So, they walked out together and took the elevator down to the parking structure.

"How did it go with Moreno?" Li asked.

"We reached an agreement about his expectations," Drew said with a grin. "I promised to do better at keeping him updated."

"Probably time to make nice with him, Howie. Lieutenant Howard's news earlier floored me. I had no idea the department was shutting down Open-Unsolved. Maybe if we close this case and make everyone happy, they will move us to Homicide Special permanently."

"Yeah, I have no desire to return to uniform."

"Me either. I don't think I could do it."

"Well, we'll see what happens," Drew said as they exited the elevator and walked to their cars.

"See you at LAX in the morning, Howie. Five sound about right?"

Drew groaned. "Yeah, see you at five, Amy."

Sixteen

A LITTLE UNDER FOUR hours after departing LAX, the flight carrying Howard Drew and Amy Li touched down at Adams Field in Little Rock, Arkansas. Neither had checked a bag, making do with a carry on, so they headed straight to the car rental counter and then the shuttle stop in front of the terminal to catch a ride to the rental car lot. There they picked up their reserved economy car and Drew drove them directly to the headquarters of the Little Rock Police Department's Major Crimes Division on West 12th Street with the help of the GPS app on Li's phone. The detectives didn't need local assistance, but intended to make the time-honored and expected courtesy notification visiting cops typically made to the locals.

Arriving at the police department, Drew found parking, and the detectives went inside. After checking in at the front desk, a uniformed officer, who seemed unimpressed by their LAPD badges, ushered them upstairs to the office of Major Thomas Macreedy, the division commander. Dressed in full uniform with gold oak leaves on his shirt collars, Macreedy rose from his desk to greet them.

"Tom Macreedy," he said affably, shaking hands with Drew and Li. "All the way from Los Angeles, huh? I expect you're here in connection with the Connie Lynn Manley murder. It's been in the paper here and on all the local television news stations."

Macreedy invited the detectives to sit and took his place behind his desk.

"How can the Little Rock Police Department assist you, Detectives?"

"Actually, we only stopped by to let you know we were in town, Major," Drew said. "We're just here to visit with our victim's next of kin to get some background on her."

Macreedy nodded and smiled. "Seems Connie Lynn got to be famous, though maybe not in the way she had hoped. Anyway, if you don't mind, I'd like one of our own to tag along with you and help you find your way around our city."

"That's kind of you, Major," Drew said. "We don't want to be an inconvenience, but it's fine with us if you think it best."

Macreedy nodded, "I do. Excuse me for a moment, Detectives." Macreedy picked up the phone, spoke into it for a moment, then hung up.

"So, you think that movie star killed Connie Lynn?" Macreedy asked.

"He's a person of interest," Drew admitted. "But it's still early in our investigation."

Macreedy seemed poised to ask another question when a man wearing a suit knocked and then entered the office through the open door. He was mid-thirties and in good shape, his dark hair in a buzz cut. He looked like a capable and experienced detective.

"Come on in, Detective," Macreedy said. "Meet Detectives Drew and Li from Los Angeles. They are here to meet with Connie Lynn Manley's folks. I'd like you to go along and facilitate for them."

"Of course, Major, Happy to," the detective said. After the major introduced the detective as Dean Erickson and shaking hands all around, Drew and Li said their goodbyes to Major Macreedy and left the office with Erickson.

"Hadn't heard you were coming," Erickson said. "Did y'all call ahead?"

"No, we just showed up," Drew said. "We only came in to give a courtesy notification, following our protocol."

"Did you take a taxi from the airport?"

"No, we have a rental. We parked on the street downstairs."

"Well, I'll direct you to long-term parking, and we can take my car and save you some gas. Y'all had lunch yet?"

"No, we came straight here from the airport."

"Do you like barbecue?"

"Sure," Drew said. "Who doesn't?"

Li winced.

"Great. I know a good place nearby. We'll get some lunch and then I'll drive you to see the people you're here to talk with."

"Sounds like a plan," Drew said.

· · · · · · · · · ·

After getting the rental parking situated, Erickson drove the detectives to a place called Corky's Smokehouse that was about a ten-minute ride from the police station. The detectives grabbed a table and ordered.

"So, who are you here to see?" Erickson asked as they sipped ice tea and waited for their food.

"Regina Manley, our victim's sister and her ex-husband, Paul Hudson. You know anything about Connie Lynn Manley?"

Erickson nodded. "She came up on our radar a few times. Mostly petty stuff. But a while back, she passed a forged six-hundred-thousand-dollar check. She was lucky she didn't get prison time over that.

Once one of our patrol units pulled her over for running a stop sign. When they searched the car, they found sixteen stolen credit cards and five social security cards, all under different names. Another time, she bilked a rich kid out of tens of thousands of dollars and that scam attracted the attention of the FBI. Connie Lynn was a con artist all the way."

"Interesting," Drew said. "But Connie Lynn isn't under investigation. She's the victim and we have to be sensitive to that."

"You think the actor she married out there in L.A. killed her?" Erickson asked. "In my experience, about sixty percent of the time, it's the husband or boyfriend."

Drew understood the man's curiosity, but he wasn't comfortable sharing too much with someone he didn't know well, even if Erickson was a cop.

"He's a person of interest until he's not," Drew said. "But we're still early in the investigation and we've learned Manley made more than a few enemies."

Erickson seemed to understand he would not get much from the two tight-lipped LAPD detectives, and so the trio made small talk while they concentrated on finishing lunch.

Seventeen

While Drew and Li were having lunch in Little Rock, Arkansas, Detectives Jenkins and Ross were at their desks in Open-Unsolved, digging into the documents they had printed from Connie Lynn Manley's laptop. Printing everything out allowed them to divide the workload instead of both working with the computer. The detectives learned Manley had been a meticulous record keeper. And the documents they found gave a detailed account of her business. There were addresses, amounts, post office boxes she had used as drops, and copies of emails she had sent. Hundreds of emails, along with her marks' responses, and how much they had paid. Most of the emails sounded like language Manley had cribbed from trashy paperback novels. Ross picked up one from the stack and read it.

I was on my way to your place, but my car broke down. The mechanic said he has to go to the junkyard to get me another drive shaft. With the labor, tax, and towing, it's going to cost $800. Do you have a credit card?

"Get this," Ross said. "In this email she asked a total stranger to hand over his credit card details. What guy would do that?"

"Guys will do crazy things for the promise of sex," Jenkins said. "Judging from the figures on this spreadsheet, a lot of guys gave her whatever she asked for."

"Here's another one," Ross said.

"Why not just send me a plane ticket? I can get there quickly and be your very own love slave. Or if you send me $200, I can drive there. But please, don't send a check. They are hard to cash on the road. Cash is best. Money orders are fine."

Jenkins shook his head in disbelief and continued poring over the figures on the spreadsheet he held in his hands.

"Most of the amounts are small potatoes," he said. "But when you add them up, Manley was raking in some serious cash."

"Still, it sounds like she didn't scam any single mark for an amount large enough that would have provoked them to travel across the country to L.A. to kill her," Ross said. "I think this is a waste of time."

"I agree," Jenkins said. "I think we both know who killed her. But as Drew said, we have to do our due diligence. Otherwise, Lake's attorney will claim we just zeroed in on his client as our suspect from the start and didn't even look at anyone else."

Jenkins' phone rang, and he picked it up. It was an officer at the front desk on the first floor telling him there was a Roy Cooper in the lobby to see him. Jenkins told the officer he'd be down to get Cooper and hung up.

Jenkins had reached Roy "Squeaky" Cooper that morning at the number Grayson Cohen had given Drew. Cooper had agreed to come to the PAB to talk to him.

"Roy Cooper is downstairs," Jenkins said to Ross. "I'll go get him and we'll meet you in the interview room."

Ross nodded, and Jenkins left the office to retrieve Cooper.

·········

Jenkins and Ross sat across the table from Roy "Squeaky" Cooper in the Open-Unsolved interview room. Cooper, a retired stuntman, was in his sixties.

"What's this about, anyway?" Cooper asked.

"As I told you on the phone, we're investigating the murder of Connie Lynn Manley," Jenkins said.

"What's that got to do with me?"

"That's what we want to find out," Ross said.

"How well do you know William Lake?" Jenkins asked.

"We've been friends for a long time," Cooper said.

"How did you meet?"

"We worked together when Bill was a stuntman," Cooper said. "Then, many years later, he got me the job as the stunt coordinator for the *Quincy* television series he starred in."

"So, you're still close friends?" Jenkins asked.

"Sure we are," Cooper said. "But I don't know a thing about what happened to his wife. That's why I don't know why you called me down here."

"Tell us about Grayson Cohen," Jenkins said.

"What about him?"

"You know him, right?" Jenkins asked.

"Yeah, Gray is another stuntman I've worked with. Why?"

"Did he work with you when you coordinated stunts for *Quincy*?" Jenkins asked.

"Yes, he did."

"So, William Lake knows Grayson."

"Yeah. So what?"

"Did you phone Grayson Cohen on William Lake's behalf to set up a meeting between them at Du-Par's in Studio City?" Jenkins asked.

"I may have," Cooper said guardedly. "What of it?"

"We're just curious about why Lake went through you instead of going direct to Cohen," Jenkins said. "They knew each other, right? Why did Lake ask you to set up the meeting?"

"Well, Bill called and asked me if I had Gray's number. I didn't, but I told him I could call the guild and get it."

"The guild?"

"Yeah, the Screen Actors Guild. All stuntmen belong to the union."

Jenkins nodded. "Did Lake tell you why he wanted to meet with Cohen?"

"Yeah, Bill said he had a script he was going to produce, and he wanted to use Gray for some stunt work."

"You sure that's all Lake wanted to discuss?" Jenkins asked.

"That's what Bill told me."

The answer disappointed Jenkins, but considering the friendship between Cooper and Lake, it didn't surprise him. And his gut told him Cooper was lying. But he couldn't prove it. At least Cooper had confirmed he had contacted Cohen on Lake's behalf, which would give Cohen some credibility with a jury.

Jenkins thanked Cooper for coming in to talk with them, and then he escorted the old stuntman back downstairs.

·······

Jenkins had just walked back into the squad room when his phone rang. He picked it up and answered.

"Jenkins."

"Jenkins, this is Gardner in Homicide Special."

"Yeah, Gardner. What's up?"

"I've got a San Bernardino County sheriff's department deputy on the line. He asked to speak to someone investigating the Connie Lynn Manley murder. I heard Drew was out of town. Can you take the call?"

"Sure, transfer it to me," Jenkins said. The detectives hung up and immediately Jenkins' phone rang again.

"Detective Jenkins."

"This is Deputy Stan Perkins, San Bernardino County. Are you investigating the Connie Lynn Manley murder?"

"Yeah, I'm on the team," Jenkins said. "Our lead, Detective Drew, is traveling today. What can I do for you?"

"One of my confidential informants, a handyman from the high desert, called me about the Manley murder. You guys will probably want to talk to him."

"What did he say?"

"A guy he knows, an old retired stuntman out here, told my informant that William Lake offered him a hundred thousand dollars to kill his wife, Connie Lynn Manley."

"You better believe we want to talk to your guy," Jenkins said. "Did he tell you the name of the individual who told him Lake solicited him?"

"Yes. His name is Ronald Saunders. He lives out here. My informant does handyman work for him occasionally."

"Can you set up a meeting for us with your informant?"

"Sure, just say when."

"Where are you located, Deputy Perkins?"

"Victor Valley Patrol Station in Adelanto?"

"Give me the address there and we'll get there as soon as we can."

Perkins gave him the address.

"Depending on traffic, it will probably take you around ninety minutes to get here from downtown Los Angeles," Perkins said. "I'll pick up my guy and have him here at the station in two hours."

"Okay, see you then. And thanks."

Jenkins hung up, stood up, and grabbed his jacket off the back of his chair.

"Come on, partner," he said to Ross, shrugging into the jacket. "We're heading to San Bernardino County."

"What's in San Bernardino County?"

"Another stuntman claiming William Lake solicited him to kill his wife," Jenkins said. "Come on. I'll fill you in on the way. This could wrap up the case."

The detectives rushed out of the squad room and headed for the elevators.

Eighteen

ERICKSON DROVE. THE ADDRESS Li had given him for the home of Regina Manley was an apartment house about a twenty-minute drive north from downtown Little Rock. The street they turned off of was wide with a grassy median. Along the way, they had passed houses, churches, and businesses with space around them. Drew saw a Little Rock patrol car parked at the entrance to the apartments.

"So," he said. "This is the place?"

"This is the place," Erickson said.

Drew was in the backseat of the unmarked car, having given Li the front. It was two o'clock in the afternoon and the parking lot was half full. Erickson parked and the black-and-white patrol car parked next to him. Having realized Drew called the shots in the partnership with Li, Erickson looked in the rear-view mirror at him.

"How do you want to handle it?" he asked.

"We have your uniformed officers make contact at the door. Then we'll all go in together. She might feel more comfortable having a local officer inside while we talk to her."

Erickson nodded.

"Sounds good."

The detectives got out of the car. Erickson relayed the plan to the two uniformed officers, a male and a female. He didn't bother to introduce Drew and Li, other than to explain they were detectives from Los Angeles. The officers said they were good to go and walked to the door of the ground-floor apartment after Li gave them the apartment number. After they knocked on the door, a woman opened it. The officers spoke to her for a few moments, then the male officer turned and motioned the detectives forward.

"Ms. Manley?" Drew asked when they got to the open door.

"Yes, I'm Regina Manley. Are you the detectives from Los Angeles?"

"Yes," Drew said, holding up his badge. "I'm Detective Drew and this is my partner, Detective Li. And this is Detective Erickson from the Little Rock police."

"You're the one I spoke to on the phone?" Manley asked Li.

"Yes, ma'am. That's correct."

"Well, come on in," Manley said, standing aside to allow the detectives to enter.

Regina, four years younger than her sister, was heavyset and pasty-faced. She had on black stretch pants, a coral-colored T-shirt, and brown leather sandals. After everyone had sat down in the cluttered living room, Drew began the interview.

"What can you tell us about your sister's relationship with William Lake?" he asked.

"Oh, gosh, I'm not sure where to begin."

"I've always found the beginning a good place," Drew said.

"Okay. Well, Connie Lynn met Lake at a jazz club out there in Los Angeles. They had sex for the first time that same night inside his car parked outside the club. Then they saw each other off and on. But even when they had sex at Lake's house, he wouldn't allow Connie Lynn to spend the night or even sleep in his bed."

"You seem to know a lot about their relationship," Drew said.

"She had to talk about it," Manley said. "She was so elated. Some of our phone conversations lasted six or seven hours. I'd fall asleep or hang up."

"You said your sister was elated?" Drew asked.

"Yes, Connie Lynn moved to Los Angeles intending to meet and marry a celebrity," Manley said. "She first met a guy named Christopher Daugherty. She had a much better relationship with him than with Lake."

"Christopher Daugherty, the actor?" Drew asked.

Manley nodded. "He was nice," she said earnestly. "For a murderer."

"Nicer than most murderers?" Li asked dryly.

Manley looked flustered and then said, "I don't know how to put it."

Drew knew about Christopher Daugherty. His fame stemmed less from his own limited success as an actor than from the fact he was the son of Jeremy Daugherty, a major Hollywood actor and celebrity who had starred in many blockbuster films during his career. Like many with famous Hollywood parents, Christopher had some issues. He had a history of alcohol and drug abuse, and about ten years before, he had shot and killed his sister's boyfriend. Kourtney, his sister, had told him earlier on the day of the killing that her boyfriend had physically abused her. So, Christopher confronted the boyfriend that evening at the Daugherty family home in Malibu, and shot him to death.

While the prosecutors had charged Daugherty with murder initially, Jeremy Daugherty had admitted his daughter Kourtney into a psychiatric hospital in Tahiti to prevent her from testifying against her brother. After the prosecutors made several unsuccessful attempts to get her to return to California, a judge had eventually quashed all efforts by the prosecution. Without Kourtney's testimony, prosecutors felt they could not prove premeditated murder, so they offered Christopher a plea deal. After heavily publicized pre-trial proceedings, Daugherty pleaded guilty to manslaughter and spent five years in prison.

"Let's talk about the baby," Drew said.

"Connie Lynn timed her visits to Los Angeles when she was ovulating," Manley said. "And to enhance her chances of getting pregnant, she took the fertility drug Clomid."

"Why did she want to get pregnant?" Li asked.

"She wanted to marry Lake, and she knew she couldn't get him unless she got pregnant. She read an article about how to take a tampon, put shrink wrap on it, insert it afterwards, and then stand on your head so the sperm wouldn't leak out." Manley sat with her hands together as if praying.

"That's what she did?" Li asked, looking incredulous.

"Yes," Manley said, her face flushed.

"Did she do that for a while, or did it work the first time?" Drew asked.

Manley smiled. "I think it worked the first time." She primly folded her hands on the coffee table, leaning forward. "Connie Lynn missed her period the next month. But she waited another few months until she was sure she wouldn't miscarry before she told Lake."

"How did Lake react?" Drew asked.

"She called and told him over the phone. First, he asked her to take the morning-after pill. When Connie Lynn told him it was way too late for that, then he kept going on about her having an abortion."

"And she refused?"

Manley nodded. "When Lake realized Connie Lynn wasn't enthusiastic about ending the pregnancy, he told her he had a terminal illness and probably wouldn't live to see the child grow up. When she still wouldn't agree to an abortion, he asked her to visit his daughter's gynecologist for an amniocentesis. But she refused because she knew there was a slight chance the procedure could cause her to lose the baby. She got what she wanted, pregnant by a movie star, and she wasn't giving it up."

"Then what happened?" Drew asked.

"Lake called and told her he wanted her to take the test so he could get the fetus's DNA. When she still refused, he told her the baby was probably not his and hung up on her. Then he changed his phone number so she couldn't reach him."

Manley shrugged and said casually, "So she went back to Christopher Daugherty and told him the baby was his, because she didn't want to risk losing another star."

Sipping from a bottle of Diet Pepsi, Manley told the detectives a convoluted story about how her sister eventually pressed Lake to accept responsibility for the baby, their drawn-out negotiations, and his threats.

"She told me all the time, 'He's going to kill me, he's going to kill me.'" Manley said. "Connie Lynn once told me that Lake said, 'I'm going to blow my brains out, but don't worry. You're coming with me because I've got a bullet with your name on it.'"

"Do you believe Lake might have carried out his threat?" Drew asked. "At least as far as it concerned your sister?"

Manley nodded. "In April, five months after the wedding, Lake invited me to join him and Connie Lynn and Earl Lee, his bodyguard, on a vacation to Arizona. This was supposed to be the honeymoon Lake and Connie Lynn never had. I drove partway, but then turned around and returned home."

"Why did he want you to come?" Drew asked.

"Because he knew I knew everything. It was a chance for him or his bodyguard to kill me and her at the same time. I would not let that happen. It was Connie Lynn's game, not mine."

"Was your sister in fear for her life?" Drew asked.

"Yes, absolutely. Lake asked her to sign some papers, so if anything happened to them on the trip, the baby would go to his daughter. She wouldn't do it. Connie Lynn said, 'I'm not signing my death warrant.' When she moved in with Lake after the vacation, just weeks before her murder, she was still frightened. She was so afraid for her life that she wanted me to record everything she said."

"When did you last speak to your sister?" Drew asked.

"On that Friday morning, the day Connie Lynn died. She called me. While we were talking, she heard a loud bang and said, 'Oh my God. The burglar alarm is going off. My God. I think he's coming to kill me now. If I scream, hang up and call the police.' One bang freaked her out. I told her maybe the idiot blew his own brains out. She said, 'No. He said he was taking me with him.'"

At the end of the interview, Manley held up a scrap of paper with a phone number scrawled on it. "She left me this number for a tabloid reporter. Connie Lynn said he'd always done good stories on her and for me to call him when it happened. She said, 'Call him and make sure he has a nice picture of me.'"

Manley sobbed and dabbed her eyes with her knuckles. "I think it was revenge." She paused to compose herself, then said softly, "Just revenge. That's why he killed her."

Nineteen

JENKINS AND ROSS HEADED for the San Bernardino County patrol station in Adelanto in the Victor Valley area of the Mojave Desert, nearly two hours from downtown. As they drove through the city streets on the way to the freeway, they passed stands of jacaranda trees in full bloom, the vivid lavender blossoms heralding the end of spring. Jenkins drove east on the freeway, inching along in the L.A. traffic. As the traffic thinned and the housing tracts gave way to verdant foothills, he cut north, and the car climbed four thousand feet over the crest of the San Bernardino Mountains, and the detectives cruised down into the dusty, dun-colored flatlands of Southern California's high desert.   Saunders' property, encircled by a chain-link fence, was cluttered with more than a dozen cars, trucks, and motorcycles in varied states of disrepair. Rowe stopped at the gate and bumped the siren. A few moments later, the front door of the house swung open and a man, the San Bernardino County detectives confirmed was Ronald Saunders, walked out to the gate. Saunders, in his mid-sixties, was an atypical desert rat, a wrinkled, grizzled character with a bushy mustache and a fringe of gray hair. Because Rowe and Evans knew the man and had established rapport, they opened the conversation. Rowe introduced Jenkins and Ross as LAPD detectives who wanted to ask Saunders a few questions about a case they were investigating. Saunders reluctantly let them in through the gate and he led the detectives into the squat, ranch-style house.

Jenkins stared out at the limitless horizon and said, "After we talk to the C.I., we need to go talk to Ronald Saunders while we're out here."

"Yeah, and we need him to fess up," Ross said. "If Saunders levels with us, combined with what Grayson Cohen told Drew and Li, Lake is bought and paid for."

The detectives finally reached the patrol station, where they found Deputy Perkins and two detectives waiting for them.

"How much faith do you have in this C.I.?" Jenkins asked.

"He's solid," a detective named Rowe said. "He's helped us build several good drug cases."

"Will you need his testimony in court?" the other detective asked. "We'd hate to burn him by putting his name out there."

Jenkins shook his head. "Nothing for him to testify about concerning our case. What he told you guys would only be hearsay. We don't even need to know his name. We only want to hear his story firsthand before we go out to see Ronald Saunders."

"Great, then let's go talk to him," Perkins said. "He's waiting in the meeting room."

Jenkins, Ross, and the others walked back to the meeting room, and Detective Rowe introduced the L.A. detectives to the C.I., a wiry, tanned man of average height with dark brown hair that he had pulled back into a ponytail.

"All they need is to hear the story you already told us," Rowe told the man. "They won't need you to testify in court or anything."

"Okay," the man said, turning to Jenkins and Ross. "What do you want to know?"

"Just tell us how you know Ronald Sanders and what he told you," Jenkins said.

The man nodded. "I'm a handyman, self-employed. Ron pays me to work out at his place when he needs something done. The other day I was out there helping him build a fence. I'd heard on the television news about someone killing William Lake's wife outside that restaurant. Anyway, I knew Ron had worked as a stuntman in the movies, so I asked him if he knew William Lake. He said he did and that they had worked together back when Lake was a stuntman before he made it as an actor. Then out of the blue, Ron tells me that Lake had offered him a hundred thousand bucks to kill his wife, just a few weeks before someone shot her."

"Did he say he did it?" Jenkins asked.

"No, nothing like that," the handyman said. "Ron told me he turned Lake down, and Lake told him he guessed he'd have to do it himself."

Jenkins nodded. "Good enough. Your guy knows Ronald Sanders and understood what Saunders told him as far as who was involved. That's all we need. Now we'd like to go see Saunders if you can tell us where to find his place."

"How about we show you?" Rowe asked. "Sanders is a cantankerous old cuss, and he hates trespassers. I know he has a rifle and if you two show up at his place alone, he might shoot first and ask questions later. Seeing cops he knows should keep him calm."

"Okay, sounds good," Jenkins said.

"We can take our car," Rowe said. "The roads out to Sanders' place are pretty rough. This is my partner, Danny Evans."

The four detectives piled into the San Bernardino County unmarked car, with Jenkins and Ross in the back. After leaving the patrol station, Evans turned to Jenkins and Ross.

"Are you guys hungry?" he asked. "We've been out on a dead body somebody found in the desert since early this morning and we haven't had lunch."

Jenkins glanced at Ross, who nodded affirmatively.

"Sure, we could eat," Jenkins said. "We haven't had lunch either. You know a good place here?"

"Yes, there's a good Chinese place that's right on the way," Evans said.

Jenkins and Ross looked at him skeptically. But Evans assured them the food was excellent.

"Okay, Chinese it is," Jenkins said, still doubtful there could be decent Chinese food found in the middle of the desert.

Rowe drove about a mile down a stretch of desert road and then stopped the car in front of a small restaurant, its windows coated with dust. They all got out and ventured inside. The owner seemed excited to see customers. After taking their orders, he hurried back to the kitchen. And ten minutes later, he returned with heaping plates of kung pao beef, beef with snow peas, and almond chicken. The detectives took a few bites and then Rowe and Evans looked at Jenkins and Ross for their culinary assessments.

"Not bad," Jenkins said.

"Actually, it's surprisingly good," Ross said.

· · · · • · • · · · ·

After the detectives finished their Chinese food, they got back in the car, and Rowe drove them to Saunders' house. The afternoon was warm and a bone-dry breeze kicked up clouds of dust when Rowe pulled off the highway onto a long, serpentine dirt road, the car bumping over ruts and rocks. Finally, they reached Saunders' isolated compound, which Rowe said encompassed around four acres. Hours before, Jenkins and Ross were in urban Los Angeles, and now felt as if they were at the ends of the earth with a barren landscape boasting only a few jagged Joshua trees standing on the perimeter like lonely sentinels.

Twenty

DETECTIVE ERICKSON TURNED OFF a city street into a dilapidated mobile home park at the address Regina Manley had given them for Paul Hudson, her ex-brother-in-law. Erickson followed the circular road inside the park until the detectives arrived in front of a mailbox displaying the number they were looking for and probably the most decrepit trailer house in the park. The sun-faded paint on the outside metal skin was now an indecipherable color and a couple of sheets of metal were missing along the side that was visible from the road. An old beat-up Ford F-150 with a crash at every corner and big tires sat on the concrete driveway in front of the trailer.

"Can't believe Connie Lynn left all this for L.A.," Li said dryly, as the detectives got out of the car.

Before they reached the wooden porch steps, the door opened. A tall, thin bearded man, probably mid-forties, with red hair stood framed in the doorway. He had on a wife-beater that might have been white once and faded jeans. The man held a cigarette in the fingers of one hand and a Budweiser can in the other.

"You the L. A. cops?" he asked.

Drew held up his badge. "We are. I'm Detective Drew and this is my partner Detective Li. And this is Detective Erickson with the Little Rock police. Are you Mr. Hudson?"

"Yeah, I'm Paul. Gina called and told me you were on the way over."

Drew said, "We would like to ask you a few questions about your ex-wife, Connie Lynn, if you can spare us a few minutes, Mr. Hudson."

"Okay, as long as you're quick about it. I have to pick the kids up from school in half an hour. You arrest that guy who killed her yet?"

"We haven't made an arrest," Drew said. "We're still investigating."

"What's there to investigate?" Hudson asked. "Everybody knows Lake killed her. Seems you could do more good back in L.A. than running around here in Arkansas."

"We're getting background information about Connie Lynn," Drew said. "We need to know about her and the people she knew to make certain we arrest the right person, the person who killed her."

"Okay, what do you want to know?"

"We're interested in learning more about her business dealings," Drew said. "Her sister Regina said you helped operate the business and knew more about it than she did. Some individuals we've talked with felt Connie Lynn may have made enemies among her... clients."

Hudson laughed. "Clients? That's one way to put it. Sure, maybe some of those losers got a little bent out of shape when they didn't get exactly what they expected for their money. But there wasn't enough money changed hands that anyone of them would have gone to the trouble of tracking her down in Los Angeles to get even. Lake is your man. He's the one who killed Connie Lynn."

"So, you helped her with the business?" Drew said.

"I sure did. Connie Lynn made so much money I quit my job so I could stay home and help her run the business full-time. I know about cameras and video equipment. So, I took pictures, made videos and helped her put them on the Internet. Once lonely men started emailing her through the various websites, she emailed them back.

Then we sold pictures and videos direct. Connie Lynn would promise to visit them to get them to buy the content we produced, but she rarely did. She just kept the money or cashed in the plane tickets they sent."

"How would you describe the business?" Drew said.

"It was all legitimate, Detective," Hudson said. "We provided content and services to people who wanted them and paid us. But I'll tell you what. I will not try to put lipstick on a pig. Connie Lynn was an Internet whore. She mostly persuaded lonely old men to pay her for nude pictures and videos and let them think they were going to get sex out of the deal. And once in a while she had to put out to get the money."

"Did you have contact with Connie Lynn after she moved to Los Angeles?" Drew asked.

"Yes, we talked on the phone regularly. That's why I know Lake killed her. She told me after she married Lake that if she was killed to call the L. A. police and tell them Lake did it and not to let him get away with it."

"When did she tell you that?" Drew asked.

"Maybe a month before he killed her."

"Did she say why she thought her husband planned to kill her?"

"Yeah, she believed Lake, and a guy named Earl Lee, his bodyguard, had intended to kill her during a vacation a few weeks before her death. After they visited Arizona, they drove to some national park in California. Connie Lynn said she and Lake had sex in the woods for the first time during the trip and she heard a noise. She looked around and saw Earl Lee holding a gun and throwing up in the bushes. She said Lake walked over to Lee and comforted him and Connie Lynn heard Lake say, 'It's okay. Don't worry about it. I'll have someone else do it.' What does that sound like, Detective?"

"Suspicious," Drew said in agreement. "You don't feel one of the angry individuals she got money from through the Internet business could have killed her in revenge?"

"I do not," Hudson said. "Lake did it. Or he hired someone to do it. I just hope you L.A. cops don't let him get away with it."

Drew nodded. "We don't plan to let her killer get away with it. Thanks for your time, Mr. Hudson. I think you've answered our questions. If anything else comes up, we'll circle back to you."

"No problem, Detective. I'm happy to help anyway I can."

"Have you ever been to Los Angeles, Mr. Hudson?" Li asked.

"No, ma'am. Never saw the need to see California. We have enough crazies right here in Little Rock."

Drew thanked Hudson again, who then went inside and closed the door. The detectives got back in the car for drive back to downtown Little Rock.

"I think y'all will have a hard time finding a jury sympathetic to Connie Lynn if all that comes out at a trial," Erickson said.

"We're talking L.A., and you can be sure it will all come out," Li said. "Besides, I suspect most of Connie Lynn Manley's immediate family and close friends have already sold their stories to the tabloids."

"None of that matters," Drew said. "Everybody counts. If that ever stops being true, there will be no justice for anyone. It will only be an illusion."

Twenty-One

SAUNDERS' CLUTTERED HOUSE WAS a bachelor's residence with a dartboard on one living room wall and a coffee table covered with stacks of National Enquirers. Tacked on another wall, beside a window shaded by threadbare drapes, was an article clipped from a newspaper about how the police could not protect witnesses.

Jenkins handled the questioning. Saunders admitted meeting William Lake at Du-Par's in Studio City and in response to a pointed question from Jenkins, also acknowledged that the old stuntman, Squeaky, had called him to set up the meeting. He then frustrated Jenkins and Ross by sticking to the same story Squeaky had spun them about the purpose of the meeting the man had set up between Lake and Grayson Cohen.

"Bill discussed a movie project with me he was planning to produce," Saunders said. "That's all we talked about."

"Okay, we'll come back to that," Jenkins said. "What I want to know about now is a conversation you had with a handyman who worked for you recently. He claims you told him Lake offered you a hundred thousand dollars to kill his wife, Connie Lynn Manley."

"I only made up that story," Saunders insisted. "I wanted to seed that gentleman, to determine if he was a snitch, as I suspected. The way I figured it, if the story came back to me, then he was a snitch.

And I don't like snitches around me. I figured, well, I'd find out if he was a yackety yacker. Now I know he is nothing more than a snitch. That's why we're talking now."

"Don't you think it's kind of odd that you met with Lake and a few weeks later, someone killed his wife?" Jenkins asked dismissively.

"Yes, it was," Saunders said earnestly.

"Isn't it true that Lake got in touch with for one reason, to ask you to kill his wife? And you turned him down? Isn't that the reason you met with him, not over some bullshit movie project?"

"It was specifically about a movie project," Saunders insisted.

"Are you willing to take a polygraph?" Jenkins asked.

Saunders shook his head. "I'm not familiar with polygraphs and I don't trust them."

After a few more minutes of back and forth, Saunders finally acknowledged he was afraid to cooperate with the police because he associated with members of the Hell's Angels and the Mongols motorcycle gangs.

"They hate snitches," Saunders said. "I know for goddamn sure if I go and testify in a huge case of this nature, I know the collar I'd be wearing and I know my life wouldn't be worth a shit."

"How do you know we would ever need you to testify in court?" Jenkins asked. "You don't know that for sure."

"If you guys give me an affidavit that says I don't have to testify, I'll be happy to tell you what I know."

"We can't do that."

"Then I know nothing," Saunders said sullenly.

"What would it take to get you to tell us the truth?" Ross asked. "Would it take a relocation out of state?"

Saunders considered the question for a few moments. "You guys can prove the case without me getting involved. I have no doubts about your capabilities. You guys are sharp as a tack. It isn't worth it to me to put myself in a dangerous position."

"You didn't answer my partner's question," Jenkins said. "What would it take?"

"I don't know," Saunders said wearily.

"You're not being truthful with us," Jenkins said.

Saunders chuckled. "I think I've copped to that. I think that's pretty well established."

The man's mood changed quickly, and his voice strained in frustration. "For crying out loud. I'm trying to be righteous. But I'm over a barrel."

Feeling convinced Saunders would not voluntarily change his story, Jenkins asked, "If you were on your deathbed, would you tell us the truth?"

Saunders chuckled again. "I imagine on my deathbed I would."

"Well, I could shoot you and put you on your deathbed," Jenkins said wryly. "But I won't go that far to make you tell us the truth. But I'll tell you what. You've just lied to the police. Your story about the movie project is bullshit. That's obstruction of justice. But a woman is dead, so we're talking about murder and that's a whole different thing. That's what we call an accessory after the fact. Accessory to murder."

A pained expression moved across Saunders' face.

"Did Squeaky tell you why Lake wanted to meet with you when he called to set it up?" Jenkins asked.

Saunders shook his head. "No. He told me he didn't know what it was about, but speculated it was probably about a movie project or something."

"You think he didn't know what Lake wanted to talk about?"

"Bill and Squeaky are tight, have been for a long time," Saunders said. "If I had to guess, I'd say he probably knew the score, but didn't tell me on the phone because he was covering his own ass. I'm telling the truth. He said it was probably about a movie deal."

"But when you got to Du-Par's, Lake didn't talk to you about any movie project, did he?"

"No," Saunders said glumly.

"Just be truthful with us and keep yourself out of a jam," Jenkins said. "I can't promise the prosecutor won't call you to testify, but I give you my word we won't do that unless we have to do it. We might get a more direct connection to Lake and might not need your testimony."

"Okay, goddamn it," Saunders said with frustration. "Bill offered me a hundred grand to kill his wife."

Jenkins turned to Ross, snapped his fingers, and pointed to his partner. "Get your phone out and record this."

Hastily, Ross pulled out his phone and cued the recording app. He spoke into the phone, identifying everyone present, and then recorded the location, date, and time. Afterward, he nodded to Jenkins.

"Okay, Ronald," Jenkins said, turning back to Saunders. "Start at the beginning, and tell us about the meeting with William Lake at Du-Par's in Studio City."

Saunders told the detectives his story, admitting he had met with Lake three times during the days leading up to the murder of Connie Lynn Manley. He acknowledged that, beginning with the first meeting at Du-Par's, Lake had repeatedly asked him to kill his wife.

"'Snuff' is the word he used," Saunders said. "He never came right out and said kill her or shoot her. He said he couldn't think about or do anything until someone took care of her. Then he offered to pay me the hundred grand if I would 'snuff' her for him. Of course, I understood what he meant by it."

Recalling what Drew had told him and Ross about Grayson Cohen's statements, Jenkins asked, "Did he suggest how you might do it?"

Saunders nodded. "Bill offered several scenarios for killing his wife. He must have outlined at least a half dozen different plans."

"Where did he want you to do it?" Jenkins said. "At his house?"

"That was one scenario, but he had other ideas. Bill suggested I could do it in her bedroom, in his camper, while she was walking with Bill down a street, at a motel, or in one of several secluded areas anywhere from near the Grand Canyon to somewhere between Memphis and Los Angeles. But here is the scenario that will interest you guys the most."

"What was it?"

"When I met Bill the second time, he drove me to the street Spirito's sits on. Bill stopped in front of a house someone was tearing down about a block from the restaurant. He discussed how someone could wait nearby to kill Manley. I think it was the same day he told me he could ask some mob guy he knew to kill her, but said he didn't want to be beholden to organized crime."

Saunders' story about accompanying William Lake to Spirito's, the actual murder scene, almost floored Jenkins. What he had learned from the man had exceeded his wildest expectations.

"But you turned him down, didn't you?" Jenkins asked.

"Of course I did," Saunders blustered. "I'm no killer. I told him when we met the third time, just a few days before the woman died, that I wanted no part of it. When asked why, I told him it was because he was too well known and the cops would be all over it like the O. J. thing."

"Why did you take so long to turn him down?"

"Because Bill scared me at our first meeting. I had already heard too much information to feel safe and secure, and well... I felt very locked in, very concerned primarily because of the way he had presented it to me. It was not a question of will you.... It was a question of you will. And Bill often mentioned my grandchildren and children, remarks I interpreted as threats against them."

"What did he say when you told him you wouldn't do it?"

"Bill said if I wouldn't do it, he would."

·········

After the San Bernardino County detectives drove the L. A. detectives back to the patrol station, Ross drove them back to L. A. so Jenkins could use his phone. He called Howard Drew's cell phone number to brief him about Saunders' story.

Twenty-Two

ERICKSON DROVE DREW AND Li back to their rental car outside the downtown police station.

"When are you heading back to Los Angeles?" he asked when they arrived.

"Our flight back is tomorrow afternoon," Drew said. "But since we've already interviewed the individuals we came here to talk with, I'm going to try to get us on a morning flight back."

Erickson nodded. "I'll let the Major know. It was nice meeting you both." The detectives shook hands all around.

"Good meeting you," Drew said. "We appreciate your help. If you're ever in L. A., call us and we'll show you around."

Erickson smiled. "I doubt I'll ever be out to L. A. because Hudson was right about one thing. We have enough crazies here in Little Rock."

Drew chuckled. "Well, take care Detective Erickson, and you be careful out there."

"Always. You two do the same."

After Erickson drove away, Drew tossed Li the keys to the rental. "You drive, partner," he said. "I want to make some phone calls on the way to the hotel."

Li nodded. When they got in the car, she plugged the address of their hotel into her phone's GPS app and then they left the police station.

"Who you calling?" she asked.

"I'm going to try to reach Jenkins and Ross first to see what they accomplished today. Then I'll check in with Moreno and give him his update."

As Drew paged through his contact list looking for Jenkins' cell phone number, his phone rang. He looked at the screen.

"Speak of the devil," he said as he answered.

"How's Little Rock?" Jenkins asked.

"Well, it's not Vegas," Drew said. "I was just about to call you."

"We're on our way back to L.A. from San Bernardino County," Jenkins said.

"What are you doing out there?"

"Interviewing another old stuntman."

Jenkins quickly told Drew about the phone call they had received from the San Bernardino County deputy and how, after he and Ross had interviewed the deputy's C.I., they had gone out to interview Ronald Saunders.

"He was a tough nut to crack, but he finally leveled with us," Jenkins said. "After Cohen turned him down, Lake upped the ante. He offered Saunders a hundred thousand dollars to kill Manley."

"Did Lake go through Squeaky to set up the meeting like he did with Cohen?"

"Yeah, same deal. Saunders met Lake for the first time at Du-Par's in Studio City. Then they met two more times before Saunders turned him down. But wait until you hear this."

"What?"

"Lake discussed various scenarios about how Saunders could kill her. And when they met the second time, Lake drove him over to Spirito's and suggested the exact scenario used for the actual murder."

Stunned, Drew said, "You're kidding me."

"I kid you not, brother."

"This is big," Drew said.

"Yeah, the timeline's perfect," Jenkins said. "The case is good, and it keeps getting better."

"Did you interview Squeaky?"

"Yeah. His actual name is Roy Cooper. We had just finished interviewing him when the deputy called."

"What did he tell you?"

"He admitted setting up the meeting between Lake and Cohen at Lake's request. But he claimed Lake wanted to talk to Cohen about a movie deal. Based on what we learned from Saunders, I'm sure the story was bullshit. And unfortunately, we didn't know about Saunders then, so we weren't able to ask him about setting up that meeting for Lake."

"Well, it disappoints me he didn't come clean about what the Cohen meeting was about, but at least it supports part of Cohen's story and gives him some credibility."

"Think we should pull Cooper back in and take another shot at him?"

"We probably do that, but not now. I learned something here we need to follow up on. Tomorrow, I want you and Ross to reach out to Christopher Daugherty and interview him if he will agree to it."

"Christopher Daugherty, the actor?"

"Yes, that Christopher Daugherty," Drew said.

He summarized the information he and Li had got from the victim's sister about Connie Lynn Manley's relationship with the actor.

"This gets better and better," Jenkins said. "She tried to shop the kid to Daugherty after Lake froze her out?"

"Yes. She was determined to marry a celebrity, and I guess cared little about which celebrity."

"I know Daugherty killed his sister's boyfriend and did time for it," Jenkins said. "You think he did Manley?"

"I think it was Lake," Drew said. "Especially after what you guys learned today. But Daugherty is another big name and someone who had opportunity and maybe a motive. We can use him to deflect any claims by Lake's attorney that we didn't look seriously at anyone but his client as a viable suspect. So, I want to interview him and document it thoroughly."

"Got it. Then maybe we don't have to waste time following up on the marks Manley conned on the Internet. We also went through more of her business information and emails this morning. She raked in a lot of cash, but not a lot from any specific individual. It was all small potatoes. Nothing I believe would have motivated anyone to kill her."

"We will still probably have to reach out to some of them," Drew said. "But maybe only a handful now that we have Daugherty."

"Okay," Jenkins said. "We will continue digging into her computer files in our spare time and try to identify the most likely suspects we need to get alibis from. When are you and Li back in L.A.?"

"Our flight is tomorrow afternoon. But we're finished here so I'm going to reschedule us on a flight for tomorrow morning if possible. If it works out, we should be back in L. A. before noon tomorrow."

"Great. I will make some calls now and get a number for Daugherty. Then I'll call him and try to set up an interview for tomorrow morning. We might have something for you on that when you get back."

"Sounds like a plan," Drew said. "And good work on your end. I appreciate your efforts."

Drew and Jenkins disconnected, and Drew filled in Li on the conversation.

"What is it with this case and all these elderly ex-stuntmen?" Li said incredulously. "Do a lot of stuntmen do hits for hire to finance their retirements? Why did Lake go to stuntmen when he was looking for someone to kill his wife?"

"Well, finding someone to hire to kill your wife isn't as easy as they make in look in the movies," Drew said. "It seems that was he crew. Maybe he thought stuntmen were tough enough to do the job and knew they could use the money. And he probably only wanted to solicit people he knew and believed he could trust."

"Still, you have to admit it's pretty wild," Li said.

"That's Hollywood, partner," Drew chuckled. Then he picked up his phone and called Moreno with an update.

Moreno was still in his office. Drew summarized what he and Li had accomplished in Little Rock, including what they had learned about Christopher Daugherty. Then he told the lieutenant about the interview with Ronald Saunders by Jenkins and Ross that afternoon.

"Sounds like you're about to close the case, Detective," Moreno said after Drew had finished. "You ready to take a charging packet to the DA?"

"Unless we get pressure from the tenth floor, I want us to continue working the case instead of going to the DA with the bare minimum," Drew said.

"But you've got two witnesses who can testify Lake solicited them on multiple occasions to kill his wife and at least one he told he intended to do it himself when they turned him down."

"I don't want this to turn out like O. J., Lieutenant."

"With O. J., it wasn't because the detectives got him charged prematurely," Moreno said. "It was the way they popped him that was the problem. It turned public opinion against them, and that's why the jury let him off."

"Yes, but this case is opposite from O.J.," Drew said. "They had a lot of physical evidence and with this one, we have very little, just some witness statements. I'm still hoping the crime lab will come up with something that will strengthen the case before we take it to a prosecutor."

"I understand your point, Detective. But trust me, we will soon get the pressure from upstairs to close this case with an arrest. Especially once they learn what you've got already. And the media circus is about to explode. Besides the local press, we have trucks from all the national cable news networks out front now. When you are you getting back here?"

"Hopefully sometime tomorrow morning. We're finished here and I'm going to reschedule our afternoon flight tomorrow to an early morning flight, if possible."

"The sooner the better," Moreno said. "Lake's attorney, Patrick Oberlin, has scheduled a press conference in front of the PAB for noon tomorrow. He is ready to put his case on before the court of public opinion and you can be sure he is going to dirty up the victim and question the competence and integrity of the LAPD. I want you there if humanly possible."

"Terrific," Drew said dryly. "Well, hopefully the airline cooperates and can get us on an earlier flight. I'll call as soon as we hang up."

"All right, Drew. Unless I hear differently, I'll expect to see you sometime tomorrow morning."

Drew and Moreno disconnected, and Drew punched in the number for the airline's reservation center to ask about getting him and Li on an earlier flight back to Los Angeles.

Twenty-Three

JENKINS HAD GOT A number for Christopher Daugherty the previous afternoon and had reached Daugherty at his Malibu home. After identifying himself as an LAPD detective, Jenkins explained he wanted to interview Daugherty about Connie Lynn Manley and why. Daugherty, initially noncommittal, finally reluctantly agreed to speak to the detectives. But he insisted the police talk to him at his attorney's office on Stuart Ranch Road, about nine miles east of Daugherty's beach house off the Pacific Coast Highway.

After phoning Daugherty's attorney at his office and confirming the interview was on, the detectives left downtown in their unmarked city ride for Malibu. Jenkins merged onto the 10 and they drove along the freeway, passing through Culver City, Santa Monica, and Pacific Palisades. For once, the traffic cooperated. About an hour later, the detectives passed Topanga Beach and entered eastern Malibu. Minutes later, they exited the highway, turning onto Civic Center Way and then Stuart Ranch Road. They arrived at Malibu City Hall, a modern, concrete and glass multi-level building that housed the law office on the first floor at 10:50 A.M., for their eleven o'clock meeting with Daugherty and his lawyer. Jenkins parked the car, and the detectives went inside.

A legal assistant escorted Jenkins and Ross to the conference room where they found Christopher Daugherty flanked by his criminal defense attorney, Del Pierce, waiting for them. After introductions, Pierce asked a few questions to verify his client wasn't a suspect in any criminal matter, and then established a few ground rules. Then everyone sat down around the mahogany conference table. Pierce's assistant brought in coffee and then Jenkins began the interview.

"We understand you and Connie Lynn Manley dated for a while," Jenkins said.

"We did," Daugherty said.

"How long did the relationship last?"

"Let's see. I met Connie about five months after I got out of prison... I guess we dated on and off for about a year."

"On and off?"

"Yes, we were never in an exclusive relationship. She traveled back and forth between L.A. and her home in Arkansas. We were both free to see other people."

"When did the relationship end?"

"When Connie became involved with someone else and got pregnant."

"We also understand that Ms. Manley told you that you fathered her infant daughter after the child was born."

"That's true."

"How did you feel about that?"

"Naturally, the news shocked me. I had believed Connie took precautions."

"Were you willing to accept responsibility for the child?"

"I was initially on the condition that we got a paternity test to prove I was the child's father."

"Did you subsequently learn Ms. Manley hadn't been truthful with you and that someone else fathered the child?"

"Oh, yes. Indeed, I did."

"And did you learn the identity of the child's father?"

"I did."

"How did you find out the truth? Did Ms. Manley level with you?"

"You could put it that way. She emailed me, admitted she had lied to me, and told me who the father was. She even attached a photo."

"A photo?"

"Yes, a photo of William Lake holding the baby."

Jenkins understood Daugherty had a reason to be angry. But was it reason enough to kill her?

"How did you feel about the picture?" he asked.

"I felt Lake was sitting there holding the kid with a, you know, sort of smirk on his face. It was insulting. But I wasn't angry enough about it to get violent with anyone. Since you gentlemen are LAPD detectives, I'm sure you know I got into trouble about six years ago, and did five years in prison because of it. Believe me. I learned my lesson."

"Who do you think did this to Connie?"

Daugherty was silent for several moments. "Well, she played hardball with a bunch of people, and I guess that was the payoff. You know what I mean? Just wrecking people. Taking all their money."

"Where were you the night of the murder?" Jenkins asked.

"What was the date?"

Jenkins recited the date. "It was last Friday night, around eleven o'clock in the evening."

Daugherty nodded. "I was at my beach house here in Malibu. But I have an alibi. I wasn't alone. And she is waiting in Del's office if you want to ask her about it."

"Who is she? A new girlfriend?"

"If I might interject," Del Pierce said. "Christopher suffered from drug and alcohol addictions for many years. Addictions that culminated in the trouble he mentioned. When he got out of prison after serving his sentence, his father hired a woman named Emily Baxter to keep an eye on him and help him stay clean and sober."

"I see," Jenkins said, glancing at Daugherty.

Daugherty appeared nervous, but it didn't stop him from offering the detectives a little advice.

"I'm not a detective or in law enforcement. But if I was investigating this, I'd be looking at William Lake pretty closely."

Jenkins nodded. The evidence they had pointed at Lake, but they needed to eliminate Daugherty as a suspect to show they had looked at others who may have had a motive and opportunity to shoot Connie Lynn Manley. If this Emily Baxter corroborated Daugherty's story, they could scratch his name off the suspect list.

"Thank you for your time and cooperation, Mr. Daugherty. I believe we have all we need from you." Turning to Pierce, he continued. "And thank you, counselor. Now, if we could have a few minutes alone with Ms. Baxter, we can get out of your hair and let you get on with your day."

"Certainly, Detectives," Pierce said. "I'll bring her in." Turning to Daugherty, Pierce said, "Christopher, would you mind waiting in the lobby for a few minutes?"

"Glad to," Daugherty said, rising from his chair. He left the conference room without offering to shake hands and without a backwards glance.

Pierce followed his client out, and then returned a minute later with an attractive woman in her mid-thirties, casually, but nicely dressed. Pierce introduced her to the detectives as Emily Baxter. She sat down at the table across from the detectives and Pierce left the room, closing the door quietly behind him.

"How can I help, Detectives?" Baxter asked. She felt a little jittery, but Christopher's lawyer had prepared her the previous evening when he had called, telling her she had to do only three things. Keep Christopher sober before the interview, not bring up anything about his drug or alcohol use or violent tendencies, and corroborate his alibi. She hoped that's all there was to it.

Jenkins turned on the recording app on his phone and Ross conducted the interview.

"How would you characterize your relationship with Christopher Daugherty?" he asked.

"Strictly professional," Baxter said, explaining she was Christopher's caretaker. She had briefly considered saying she was his adult babysitter, but that would have made him sound like a toddler. Although that wouldn't have been inaccurate. "I live with Christopher at his beach house, in my own room, but we share the common spaces."

"So, you're with him all the time, twenty-four seven?"

"Except for my weekends off. I get every other weekend off when a colleague substitutes for me."

Ross nods and gets to the point.

"Were you with Christopher Daugherty last Friday evening?" he asked. He then recited the date to be precise for the recording.

Emily was prepared for the question. Now she just needed to answer it. She needn't say anything about his hallucinations or meth-fueled tantrums. Or about how he turned over his refrigerator, broke windows, and punched holes in the wall.

"I was with Christopher at his house that night," she said. "We barbecued out on the deck, finished dinner around seven o'clock, and we both went to bed around eleven." All of that was true.

"Does Christopher Daugherty own a handgun?" Ross asked.

"Absolutely not," Baxter said. "His status as a convicted felon prohibits him from possessing a firearm. And I wouldn't tolerate a gun in the house, anyway. That would breach of our agreement."

She waited while Ross made some notes and Jenkins turned off the recording app. Then Ross looked up at her and smiled.

"We're pretty sure we have our man," he said.

The implication was clear to Baxter. The man wasn't Christopher Daugherty. Emily felt relieved. If the police knew who did it, the interview had only been a formality. The things she had feared the detectives might ask her no longer mattered. Ross and Jenkins thanked her, and she left the conference room to meet Daugherty in the lobby. The detectives thanked Del Pierce, and then left the law office and headed back downtown.

Twenty-Four

AFTER DEPARTING LITTLE ROCK at 9:10 A.M., Drew and Li's plane touched down at LAX three hours and twenty-eight minutes later at 10:38 A.M., Los Angeles time. Both detectives had driven their own cars to the airport the day before. So, twenty minutes after their arrival, they caravanned toward downtown and the PAB. Drew and Li had gone directly to their rooms after checking into their hotel the previous evening and hadn't talked again until they met in the lobby to drive to the airport. On the flight, Drew had brought his partner up to speed on what they would face when they got back to Los Angeles, Patrick Oberlin's presser. He also told Li that Jenkins and Ross were supposed to interview Christopher Daugherty that morning if they could persuade him to talk to them.

After parking their cars at the PAB, they took the elevator upstairs. Li went to Open-Unsolved and Drew went directly to Homicide Special to talk with Moreno about the press conference.

Moreno told Drew that Jenkins had given him a heads up before he and Ross left the PAB, and they were on the way to Malibu to interview Daugherty at his attorney's office.

"The rumor is, Oberlin plans to present the LAPD with several boxes of evidentiary documents that will assist us in identifying

Manley's killer," Moreno said with disgust. "It's going to be a media circus."

"What are we supposed to do?" Drew asked.

"Just stand by while Oberlin gives his speech and look serious. Then you will accept custody of the documents."

"What documents?"

"I assume it's stuff they dug up about the victim that will supposedly point us toward the marks she ripped off who have motives to commit murder in revenge. It's just a way to dirty her up in the press to get the public on Lake's side when it goes to court."

"So he wants to bury us in paperwork, hoping we'll have less time to find the actual evidence we need to charge his client?"

"That's it, Detective. You've got it. This morning he told CNN that the gunshot residue test on Lake and his clothing came back negative."

"What? We haven't even got the results back from the lab yet."

"Get used to it, Detective. That's only the beginning. There's no law against lying to the press and Oberlin will take full advantage of it."

"We only have four investigators on the team," Drew said. "If I put people on Oberlin's documents, it's going to slow us to a crawl."

"Don't worry about it, Drew. We can't ignore the stuff. But I'm giving you four uniformed officers from Central in plainclothes. They can work on Oberlin's documents and your team can continue taking care of business."

"Thanks, Lieutenant. I appreciate it."

"I'm only sorry I can't give you more investigators, Drew," Moreno said earnestly. "But with the staffing situation, giving you the four plainclothes patrol officers is the best I can do for now. Now get back to work. And give me an update on the interview with Daugherty when Jenkins and Ross get back."

"You got it, Lieutenant," Drew said. Then he left the office for Open-Unsolved. Drew began believing Moreno wasn't part of whatever conspiracy had got him and Li assigned to the Manley case and maybe Moreno could be trusted.

·•••••••·•

Fifteen minutes before the noon hour, Drew and Li went downstairs to the Civic Center plaza, where Lake's attorney would hold his press conference. The plaza and street beyond teamed with dozens of photographers, camera crews, and local and national television, radio, and newspaper reporters. At two minutes after the hour, Patrick Oberlin, driving a silver Mercedes and trailed by his private investigator in a black Chevrolet Tahoe, pulled up and parked on the street next to the plaza. As LAPD Property Division employees wheeled out large dolly carts, the private investigator opened the rear hatch of the Tahoe and began removing and stacking cardboard boxes on the sidewalk. Television reporters shouted to their camera crews, "Get the boxes! Get the boxes!" Oberlin strode to the podium someone had set up in advance for the press conference. The crowd grew quiet as he spoke into the microphones.

"My duty as a criminal defense attorney is to turn over to the police department evidence that might be relevant to the investigation. I've had many dealings with the LAPD over the past years. In the past, the LAPD has been obstinate. On this investigation, I hope they will fairly evaluate the situation and show a flexibility they haven't shown in the past."

When Oberlin finished his prepared remarks, the reporters' mostly softball questions included, "Is Mr. Lake getting support from the Hollywood community?" and "How is the baby?" Once Oberlin signaled the end of questions, Drew walked forward to the podium and signed the legal paper to accept the transfer of the documents. The formalities concluded, Drew instructed the property division employees to take the boxes upstairs to Open-Unsolved and then he rejoined Li at the PAB entrance.

"What's next, Howie?" Li asked.

"We will talk about it when we get back upstairs," Drew said. "You go ahead. I'm going to grab us some coffee and I'll meet you in the office."

"Great," Li said. "I'll take a latte, please."

Drew nodded and headed to the onsite café called LA Reflections.

·· • • • • • • • ··

Inside the café, Drew ordered and paid for a large black coffee and Li's latte. As the server put the cups in a cardboard carrier for him, Drew felt a presence next to him at the counter. He turned and looked at the smiling face of Deputy Chief LaChasse.

There had been no love lost between Drew and LaChasse. The chief had often been Drew's adversary and had done his best to oust Drew from the LAPD after Howard had violated department policy by confronting a murder suspect alone. The confrontation ended when the suspect pulled a weapon and Drew had fatally shot the man. But Drew had dirt on LaChasse and the chief was no longer on the tenth floor. Howard had thought he was beyond the reach of LaChasse until he had run into the chief in Homicide Special earlier in the week. LaChasse had clarified that things between them were far from over.

"I thought that was you, Detective Drew," LaChasse said. "I'd buy you a cup of coffee but see you already have some. Would you care to sit down for a minute anyway?"

Drew held up the drink carrier.

"I'm kind of in the middle of something, Chief. And my partner is waiting for one of these."

"It will only take a minute, Detective," LaChasse said, a stern tone entering his voice. "The coffee will still be hot when you get back upstairs. I promise."

Without waiting for a reply, LaChasse turned and walked to a nearby table. Drew followed, noticing the chief was wearing a suit rather than his usual smartly tailored uniform. Howard wondered if LaChasse had shown up for the press conference and hadn't wanted to stand out in the crowd. The man's muscular jaw and his shock of silver hair were his most prominent features. He took a seat at the table, sitting ramrod straight and looking somewhat uncomfortable. He didn't speak until Drew placed the drink carrier on the table and sat down. The pleasant tone returned to his voice.

"All I wanted was to welcome you back to the department," LaChasse said, smiling like a shark. Drew hesitated like he had back in Iraq before entering an alley he assumed held concealed IEDs.

"It's good to be back, Chief."

"I thought the Open-Unsolved Unit was an appropriate place for someone of your temperament and skills. But I'm sure you must have heard by now the department is shutting down the unit because of the budget crisis. I hope you're making the most of your shot at Homicide Special, Detective."

Drew removed his cup from the carrier and took a sip of the steaming coffee. He didn't know whether LaChasse had complimented or insulted him. All he knew was he wanted to leave.

"Well, we'll see, Chief," Drew said. "I hope so. Now, if you'll excuse me, I think..."

LaChasse held out his hands, spread wide as if to show he wasn't concealing anything.

"That's it, Detective," he said. "I just wanted to welcome you back officially after your serious injury. And to thank you."

Drew hesitated, but then he bit.

"Thank me for what, Chief?"

"For restoring me to my rightful place in the department."

Drew shook his head and smiled uneasily, not understanding.

"I don't get it, Chief," he said. "How am I supposed to have done that? I mean, you're no longer on the tenth floor, right? I heard you're the commanding officer of Operations-Valley Bureau now."

LaChasse folded his arms on the table and leaned forward. All pretense at civility, false or otherwise, evaporated. He spoke sternly, but quietly.

"Yes, that is where I am. But I guarantee you that is temporary. Especially with the likes of you leading such a high-profile murder investigation as a temporary member of Homicide Special."

LaChasse leaned back in his chair and adopted a casual manner and then continued.

"You know something, Drew. The city council's support for Chief Sandoval is waning because of incidents like that patrol officer fatally shooting the store manager in Silver Lake recently. Many of the council members feel the department is slipping back into its bad habits of the past and believe it's time for a change of leadership."

"If memory serves, Chief, Chief Sandoval and the police commission ruled that those officers acted within the department's policy, and the district attorney's office declined to charge them criminally."

"All that's true, Detective. Chief Sandoval again showed poor judgement by making another poor decision, similar to the one he made about your OIS. And he persuaded the outgoing district attorney to decline charging those officers. However, it is your assignment to your current case that will be his ultimate undoing."

LaChasse nodded silently as he let Drew think about that.

"You see, Drew, you are my ticket to the COP's office. You will fuck up, please excuse my language. It is your history. Your nature is what it is. It is a guaranteed result. When you fuck up and your case turns into another debacle rivaling the O. J. case, our illustrious chief fucks up, too, for allowing you to lead the investigation."

LaChasse gave Drew another of his patented shark-like smiles.

"And when his stock with the city council goes down, my stock goes right back up. I'm a patient man. I've waited some forty years for my chance to run this department. And thanks to you, Detective Drew, I won't have to wait much longer."

Drew expected the chief to say more, to gloat more after making his revelation. But LaChasse only nodded and stood up. Then he pivoted and walked away. Drew felt the bile and anger rise in his throat. He felt like an idiot for having sat there as if defenseless and just took it while LaChasse landed one verbal punch after another. The chief's meaning had been clear. He intended to replace Chief Sandoval, and if that happened, Drew understood there would be no place for him in the LAPD. Finally, he got up, grabbed the drink carrier, and headed back to Open-Unsolved.

Twenty-Five

Drew walked in to Open-Unsolved with the unease of the LaChasse confrontation still lingering. He had intended to pull Li aside and to tell her about it, but found Jenkins and Ross were back from Malibu. They were both standing beside Amy Li's desk and Ross was telling another of his ridiculous jokes. As Drew approached his team, Jenkins looked at him, smiled, and held out his hand.

"One of those for me, Howie?"

"Only if you want to fight Li over it."

"Forget it then," Jenkins said with a fake frown. "I could take her, but if it's for her, then it's probably a latte and I'm a more black coffee kind of guy."

Drew laughed and handed the latte to Li. "How did the interview go?" he asked.

Jenkins filled Drew in and then summarized.

"So, Daugherty has a solid alibi, and I think we can cross him off our suspect list."

Drew nodded. "Listen, Jenkins. Amy and I heard something interesting from our victim's sister about Earl Lee, Lake's bodyguard, in connection with a trip he took with Lake and Connie Lynn Manley."

"Yeah? What did you hear?"

Drew summarized the story about a trip the trio made to some California national park where Manley had told her sister that she and Lake had engaged in sex in the woods, and afterward Manley had seen Earl Lee vomiting in some bushes nearby while holding a gun.

"Manley told her sister that Lake went over to comfort Lee and told him everything would be okay. That he would get someone else to do it, which she interpreted to mean he would get someone else to kill her."

"That is interesting."

"Yeah, I agree. So I want you and Ross to go out to Earl Lee's house and see if you can convince him to come back here with you for an interview."

"That won't be necessary," Jenkins said with a grin.

"You're entitled to your opinion, Jenkins," Drew said, his face coloring. "But I still want you to do it."

Jenkins chuckled. "No, I mean, it won't be necessary for us to go out and bring Earl Lee in. He's already here. He walked in with his attorney about five minutes ago. We stashed them in the interview room until you got back to see who you wanted to do the interview."

"Oh," Drew said, feeling foolish for thinking Jenkins had been bucking his authority as the lead investigator. "Okay, then why don't you and Ross interview him? There is someone else Amy and I need to interview. Call my cell when you finish. We will be away from the PAB for a while."

"Sure thing, boss." Jenkins looked at his partner and jerked his head toward the direction of the interview room. Then he and Ross headed that way.

"Where are we going, Howie, and who are we interviewing?"

"Another lawyer," Drew said. "Assuming Lake killed his wife, what do think his motive was?"

Li thought for a moment. "Well, her sister said she thought it was revenge. Lake was angry because Connie Lynn trapped him with her pregnancy and forced him to marry her. I guess that seems as good a motive as any."

"I think that's part of it," Drew said. "But my gut tells me that maybe the kid was part of it too. I think we need to dig a little deeper into the custody battle Manley and Lake were having. That might turn up something to support my theory."

Li nodded. "So, you want us to talk to the attorney who handled Manley's side of the custody dispute?"

"Exactly. We might learn something that firms up the motive part of it before we take the case to the district attorney's office."

·· • • • •· • • • ··

Li plugged the North Hollywood Lankershim Boulevard address for the Zelda Alvarado law offices into the GPS app on her phone. They had got the lawyer's name and address from some copies on legal documents on Connie Lynn Manley's laptop. Then the detectives left the PAB in their unmarked car. On the twenty-minute drive from downtown, Drew told his partner about his encounter with Deputy Chief LaChasse.

"For real?" Li exclaimed. "Did he admit he was behind our assignment to investigate this case?"

"Not in so many words. But he made it easy for me to read between the lines. He will not say it out in the open. He expects us to fail, and he wants the city council to blame Chief Sandoval for another O. J. disaster."

"Then he expects to get the chief's job?"

"Exactly, and then he'll have the power to shove me out of the department. I think he wants that almost as much as control of the department."

"Then we better not fail, partner," Li said firmly.

"Damn right."

When they arrived, the detectives found the law offices occupied a suite in a high-rise office building. Li found parking, and they went inside and took the elevator up to the seventh floor. Entering the office suite, Drew showed the receptionist his badge and asked if he and his partner could have a few minutes of Zelda Alvarado's time. The receptionist phoned the attorney's office with the message. When she hung up, she pointed toward a hallway and told Drew and Li they could go in. The detectives followed the hallway and found Alvarado standing in the open doorway of her office, waiting.

"Come on in, Detectives," Alvarado said. "I'd expected the LAPD would want to talk to me at some point."

Li and Drew followed the lawyer into the office and sat down at her invitation.

"What can I do for you?" Alvarado asked.

"I'm not sure how much you can tell us about it," Drew said, acknowledging the ethics of the legal profession. "But please tell us what you can about the custody dispute in which you represented Connie Lynn Manley."

Alvarado leaned forward, putting her arms on the desk. "Ethically speaking, the attorney-client privilege survives the death of a client and I can't talk to you about the case," she said. "But the things Patrick Oberlin has been telling the press about my former client and William Lake's treatment of Connie before her murder have got under my skin. So, I'd decided if the police came to me, I would tell them everything I know that might help put that bastard in prison."

"I think what you know would be very helpful to our investigation," Drew said.

"I think Connie was misguided and also a little naïve," Alvarado said. "But she didn't deserve to lose her life."

"We couldn't agree more."

"How much do you know about the custody dispute?"

"Very little. Our victim's sister told us William Lake wasn't happy when Connie Lynn told him she was pregnant and that he was the father. That makes his attempt to get full custody difficult to understand."

"He wasn't happy about the baby at first. But it seems his feelings changed about it. By the time he sued to have Connie declared an unfit mother and gain sole custody of the child, he seemed obsessed with taking the baby from her and excluding her from any contact with their daughter."

"Any idea why he changed his mind?"

"Yes. Connie and I both believed that William Lake wanted to gain custody so that he could give the baby to his adult daughter Miranda to raise. Miranda Lake is in her mid-thirties and apparently was desperate for a child. But she couldn't conceive. So Connie's child was a way William Lake could give his daughter what she wanted. And, I don't discount that he also truly believed Connie was an unfit mother because of her rather colorful past."

"Does Miranda Lake have custody of the child now?"

"Yes, she has had physical but not legal custody for a long while, so long that it precedes Connie's marriage to William Lake."

"Connie Lynn allowed that?"

"No, she never approved of the arrangement. Essentially, William Lake kidnapped the baby, gave the child into his daughter's custody, and then only allowed Connie to see her daughter occasionally and always under supervision."

"How did he do that?"

"William Lake pulled a sneaky stunt. After he had rebuffed Connie when she told him she was pregnant, she moved back to Arkansas and delivered the baby there. When the child was a few months old, Lake called Connie and asked her to bring the baby out here for a paternity test. He told her if the test proved he was the father, then he would marry her and support them."

"Well, that sounds like he did what she wanted all along."

"That's how he made it sound. But it was only a ruse. Once Connie arrived, they took the baby and had the paternity test. Afterward, when they arrived at his house, Lake introduced Connie to a full-time nanny he claimed he hired. Then he convinced her to leave the child in the nanny's care while they went back to her hotel to have lunch. After lunch, Lake assured Connie the child was safe with the nanny and convinced her to stay at the hotel and relax after her long flight with the baby while he took care of some movie business. He said he'd pick her up later that evening. Reluctantly, she agreed. Then Lake had the so-called nanny meet him somewhere. He took the baby directly to his daughter's house, and Connie never had custody of her daughter after that day."

"What did you mean when you said the so-called nanny?"

"The woman Lake introduced as a nanny wasn't a nanny at all. The woman, named Gale Tyler, was one of Lake's former assistants."

"Why didn't Connie Lynn file a kidnapping complaint with the police?"

"She couldn't," Alvarado said. "The kidnapping was only Lake's opening gambit. He then tricked Connie into getting arrested back in Arkansas."

"Arrested for what? And why did she return to Arkansas without her baby?"

"Connie was on probation for passing a rather large bogus check in Little Rock and couldn't legally leave the state. But she came out to L.A. with the baby anyway, at Lake's request. After he left the hotel that afternoon, he sent a private investigator he had hired, Mark Nash, to her hotel. Nash is a retired LAPD detective. He contacted Connie at the hotel, flashed a badge, and identified himself as an actual LAPD detective. Nash told Connie her probation officer had called the LAPD, told them she had violated her probation by leaving Arkansas, and had asked them to arrest and extradite her back to the state."

"He pretended to arrest her?" Drew asked in disbelief.

"Oh, no. When Connie explained she had only come to L. A. to introduce her baby to the child's father and to get a paternity test, Nash pretended to be sympathetic. He told her he didn't want to arrest her, and if she would go straight to the airport and fly back to Little Rock to square things with her probation officer, he wouldn't."

"So, she left the baby here and went back?"

"Only after she called Lake, told him what happened, and he convinced her to leave the baby here with the nanny until she went home and cleared things up. Then he said she could come back. So, that's what she did. She got on a plane and flew home."

"Then Nash called and dropped a dime on her with her probation officer and that's when she got arrested," Drew said.

"Precisely. The Arkansas authorities were waiting at the Little Rock airport and arrested her for violating her parole as soon as she got off the plane."

"It sounds like Mark Nash has some explaining to do," Li said. "He could lose his license for impersonating a cop."

"I expect it would be hard for you to prove it now," Alvarado said bitterly. "The only witness is dead."

"Did Connie tell you what hotel and where Nash spoke to her at the hotel?" Drew asked.

Alvarado nodded and named the hotel.

"Lake had suggested that she spend some time relaxing by the pool. Probably to make it easy for Nash to know where to find her. So, that's where she was when Nash approached her."

"We might use that," Drew said. "Depending on how long the hotel preserves security video recordings, a camera might have captured Nash flashing the badge. That would be all we need."

"That would make my day if that scummy private detective lost his license," Alvarado said.

"So now William Lake has full custody by default since Connie Lynn is dead?" Drew asked.

"For now. But Connie's next of kin in Arkansas could contest it. I don't know if you're aware, but William Lake has plenty of skeletons in his closet I've found out. When he was a big television star, he used to make the late-night show circuit, and he practically bragged during those appearances about his history of drug and alcohol abuse. In one video I saw on the Internet, he even bragged about punching out some director. A court might find him an unfit parent, and his daughter, Miranda, has no legal claim to custody."

"We appreciate your candor, Ms. Alvarado," Drew said. "I think this strengthens our motive theory."

"I hope you nail that sneaky son of a bitch. Just between us, I know he murdered Connie. That removed her from his life permanently, and his daughter gets to keep the baby. Yes, I agree. That sounds like a solid motive."

Drew and Li thanked Alvarado for her time and left her office. In the elevator, Drew said, "Let's find out where his office is and go see if we can catch Nash there and have a chat."

Li grinned and opened a browser on her phone. She found Nash's website. "His office is in Van Nuys."

Drew nodded. "Let's go to Van Nuys."

Twenty-Six

EARL LEE HAD WALKED into the PAB accompanied by a lawyer, paid for by William Lake. When Jenkins had gone downstairs to collect them after the first-floor front desk had called Open-Unsolved, Lee had told him he had come in voluntarily because he figured it was only a matter of time before the LAPD came looking for him. Jenkins had escorted the men upstairs and put them in an interview room while he waited for Drew to return from the Oberlin press conference. Now Jenkins and Ross sat across the table from Lee and the attorney. Lee, unshaven and balding, about six feet tall, slender and fit, didn't have the physical presence of a bodyguard in the opinions of either detective. Yet they had heard others refer to Lee as Lake's handyman and bodyguard more than once.

"How and when did you first meet William Lake?" Jenkins asked.

Lee told the detectives that he had worked at a car stereo and alarm shop in Studio City and met Lake when he brought his car in. He eventually began working at Lake's house as a handyman, and Lake had hired him full time the previous year. As Lee described Lake's relationship with Manley, Jenkins' tone turned confrontational and incredulous. He believed Lee's comments were scripted, slanted, to protect Lake and condemn Manley. Several times the attorney prompted Lee, or he simply said, "I'm supposed to tell you this," before he recounted an anecdote.

"When Connie Lynn lived in the guest house, she and Bill were lovey-dovey," Lee said.

"Don't you think that's odd when they were sleeping in separate residences?" Jenkins asked sarcastically.

Lee didn't respond. Instead, he changed the subject.

"When Connie Lynn visited, I served as her bodyguard," he said. "I noticed she constantly looked over her shoulder, as if she feared someone was following her. I know she was afraid of an old boyfriend. Connie Lynn told me one day that the guy's attitude was if he couldn't have her, no one could."

Lee then recounted a story similar to the one Lake had told to North Hollywood detectives about a man they called "Buzzy," who appeared to have been stalking Lake's house.

"He only showed up whenever Connie Lynn was visiting," Lee insisted. "Otherwise, we never saw him hanging around."

"Describe him," Jenkins said.

"He was in his late twenties, I guess, average build, and he always wore a baseball cap and sunglasses. Like a disguise, you know?"

"If he always wore a baseball cap, how did you know he had a buzz cut?"

"Well, I mean, he took the hat off sometimes. Besides, you could tell anyway from the hair on the sides and back of his head. It was very short."

"Did you and Lake believe he was the boyfriend you just mentioned, or what?"

"We figured he was some guy Connie Lynn conned out of money on the Internet. Maybe looking for a little payback, you know?"

"We've already checked out a lot of those guys," Jenkins said. "None of them were in their twenties or even anywhere close. Most of them were senior citizens. So, this Buzzy character doesn't fit the profile of the men the victim exchanged emails with."

Again, Lee made no reply.

"Okay, tell us about the trip you, Lake, and Ms. Manley took together to a national park."

"You know about that?"

"Yeah, we're cops. We know about a lot of stuff. So, don't bullshit us, pardner."

"Please, Detective," the lawyer protested. "May I remind you that my client is here of his own free will because he wants to help the police?"

"Sure, no problem."

"You may answer the Detective's question, Earl," the attorney prompted.

Lee cleared his throat. "Oh, yeah, the trip. We all went to Sequoia National Park. It was their honeymoon, I guess, since they hadn't had one. Anyway, they held hands, kissed, and seemed to have a fine time."

"Didn't you get sick on that trip?"

"Well... yeah, a little. Probably because of the altitude. I wasn't used to it. I spent a little time in a local emergency room."

Jenkins felt skeptical of Lee's claims. He knew the elevation in the park wasn't much higher than six-thousand feet, which he didn't believe would cause altitude sickness. But he let Lee continue.

"The thing is, Bill hired me to protect Connie Lynn. She seemed so paranoid. But he didn't want to take any chances of anything happening to her. But she never liked me much."

"Why did she dislike you?"

"Well, maybe it wasn't that she disliked me. But Bill told me she wanted him to fire me and to hire her brother as a bodyguard."

"If you were her bodyguard, hung around with them, and even went with them on their honeymoon, how come you weren't there protecting her the night she got shot to death?"

"A few days before she got murdered, to ease the tension, Bill asked me to take some time off. So I spent a few days in the San Francisco area. I wasn't in L.A. when it happened."

"Ease the tension. You mean because she disliked you and all?"

"That's right."

"Who do you think might have murdered her?"

"Well, here's the funny thing about it. Bill and I believe he was the actual target of a hit, but the person who did it shot her by accident."

Jenkins rolled his eyes, barely disguising his irritation.

"So, you and Lake think it was a real stupid hit man who couldn't tell the difference between a man and woman? Why would anyone want to kill Lake? What's the motive?"

"Connie Lynn had a motive. If Bill got killed, she would have benefited financially."

"How do you figure?" Jenkins said with disgust. "He made her sign a prenuptial agreement before they married. She wouldn't have inherited his estate. She would have just lost her meal ticket."

When Lee offered no response, Jenkins continued.

"Will you take a polygraph exam?"

"No, I don't trust those things."

"And the results aren't admissible in court because they are unreliable," the lawyer said to support his client.

"Okay, thanks for coming in," Jenkins said impatiently, pushing away from the table and standing up. "If we need anything more from you, we'll circle back."

"Okay," Lee said after glancing at his attorney.

Jenkins could feel the man's unease. He had obviously hoped coming in for the interview would have been the end of involvement for him.

·······

After Jenkins returned to the squad room, after escorting Lee and his attorney out, he slumped into his desk chair and looked at Ross.

"Well, partner, where do we stand?"

"Lake did it, man," Ross said. "She tricked him by getting pregnant, so he had to marry her. But he didn't want to spend the rest of his life with her, so she had to go."

"What about Lee? You think he could have pulled the trigger?"

"No way. He doesn't have it in him. I think he tried to do it when they went to Sequoia National Park. But he couldn't. The stress got to him and that's what made him puke."

Jenkins nodded. "I think you're right. I believe Lake popped her himself out of desperation when he couldn't find anyone willing to do it for him, no matter how much he offered to pay them."

Twenty-Seven

DREW AND LI FOUND Nash's office in a strip mall on Saticoy Street in Van Nuys. Li parked the car, and the detectives went inside. An attractive bleached-blonde smiled at them when they walked in. Li took the first shot.

Displaying her badge, she said, "LAPD. We need a few minutes of Mr. Nash's time. Is he in?"

"Do you have an appointment?" the receptionist asked, smiling sweetly.

"No, we don't," Li said, smiling back malevolently. "Of course, you're his receptionist. So, you already know that."

"Then, I'm sorry, ma'am," the woman said without missing a beat. "Mr. Nash is very busy. But if you would like to make an appointment..."

The gatekeeper, Drew assumed, stepping up beside Li and interrupting.

Turning to Li, he said, "Here, hold my beer." Then he eyed the receptionist. "Please pick up that phone right now and tell Mr. Nash LAPD Detectives Drew and Li are here to see him about a P.C. 538, and how violations result in the revocation of a private investigator's license."

The receptionist's eyes widened, and she grabbed the phone and dialed. After relaying the message, she hung up and smiled up at the detectives.

"Go right in, please."

Drew nodded and he and Li went through the door to the right of the receptionist's desk into a private office. A man, stocky with a shock of white hair, wearing a rumpled suit, sat behind the desk. He didn't bother to stand.

"What can I do for you, Detectives?" he asked.

"Mark Nash?" Drew asked.

"The one and only. Now what's this bull about a P.C. 538?"

"It's a funny thing," Drew said. "We got a report that you flashed an LAPD badge at a woman named Connie Lynn Manley at an L.A. hotel a couple of months ago, and represented yourself to her as an active LAPD detective. The funny part is this. That hotel keeps its security video recordings in the cloud, so they preserve them indefinitely."

"Bullshit," Nash said. "Do I look stupid to you? I used to do the same job you guys are doing. You think I didn't check for video cameras and make sure my back was to it?"

"What do you think, partner?" Li asked Drew. "It sounded to me like he just admitted to a P.C. 538."

"Bullshit, I admitted nothing. Besides, I think you're short a witness, so you have no complaint."

"Don't worry, Nash, we aren't here to jam you up over a misdemeanor," Drew said. "We're with Homicide Special. We want to talk to you about the Connie Lynn Manley murder."

"Don't know a thing about it, besides what I see on television and read in the paper."

"Oh, we think you know plenty," Drew said. "You worked for William Lake. You pulled that little sting on our victim and got her to fly back to Arkansas. Then you made sure the authorities were waiting at the airport to arrest her to keep her there. And we suspect you probably dug up most of the dirt on her that Lake's attorney is spinning to the media."

Nash held up his hands, palms up, in mock surrender. "I'd like to help you, Detective. But I'm sure you've heard of confidentiality privilege. I can't ethically even confirm or deny that I've ever worked for the individual you mentioned."

"Look, Nash. You're not an attorney, and you're not a priest. You have no confidentiality privilege claim to hide behind. Either you answer our questions, or we're going to talk about obstruction of justice. Or maybe, conspiracy after the fact to commit murder."

"Oh, that's how it's going to go, huh?"

"That's how it's going to go."

"What is it you want to know? I had no involvement in the murder you're investigating. I was a cop for twenty-five years, and would have nothing to do with something like that."

"But you didn't have a problem helping facilitate a kidnapping and then doing your best to help Lake dirty up a murder victim, did you?"

"I know nothing about any kidnapping. I had no involvement in any criminal activity."

"Fine. Just tell us what you did for Lake. You can leave out the part about impersonating a police officer."

"Just a routine background investigation on Ms. Manley. He had an idea she was doing sex work over the Internet and hired me to determine the extent of it. And what I found out shocked him more than a little. I learned that she and one of her ex-husbands, back in Arkansas, ran a shady Internet business. A con, we might say. She emailed amateur photos and videos that appealed to certain prurient interests of older, lonely men, promising them sex and taking them for cash without delivering the sex."

"Do you think any of the men she conned might have been angry enough to track her down and shoot her?"

Nash shook his head. "I don't think so. It was small stuff. A thousand here, a few hundred there. The marks caught on pretty fast when she never showed up to be their personal sex slave and stopped sending money. Then she just moved on to greener pastures. I only saw one example with any real money involved."

"What was it about?"

"She flew out here once, hooked up with a college student from China, and had sex with him two or three times. Then she had some friends dress up in suits and show up at the guy's front door. They told him they were FBI and threatened to arrest him for facilitating Internet prostitution. Or they told him he could pay a twenty-five thousand dollar fine and they would drop the charges. They scared the crap out of the poor guy."

"Did he pay them?"

"Sure did. And she would have got away with it, except she got greedy and went back to the guy for more money. He got suspicious and called the actual FBI and they descended upon her like a cloud of locusts. They gave her a choice. Give the guy his money back or spend some time in federal lock up. She coughed up the twenty-five grand, and the FBI dropped the charges. Someone might get angry enough to commit murder over that kind of money. But the kid got his money back. He was happy, she was happy, the feds were happy. And I checked. He's already finished school and gone back to China."

"So, nothing else big?"

"Well, she tried to pass a stolen six-hundred-thousand-dollar check once, but the bank stalled her until the Little Rock cops arrived. She never got the money, went to jail, and no one suffered a loss."

"Where did you get the information that you turned over to Lake?"

"Usual places. Criminal histories, court records, and she left her laptop unattended once, and I copied the hard drive. I'd never seen so much amateur porn on one computer."

"Why did Lake want the dirt on her?"

"She conned him. Manley swore up and down she was on the pill because he was super worried about her getting pregnant. So, a few months in after they hooked up, when she came to him and told him she was pregnant and he was the daddy, he knew she had got pregnant on purpose to trap him into marrying her. Or at least to collect child support. When he became convinced that the kid was his, he didn't want her anywhere near the kid and sure didn't want to spend the rest of his life with her."

"So why did he marry her? Did he ever say?"

"Yes, he thought it was the only way he could get sole custody. Lake had some issues in his background, too. Drugs, alcohol, assaults, etc. And he had been a little too open about it all. He couldn't be sure of getting custody unless they married and he got her declared an unfit mother."

"You ever meet his handyman-bodyguard? A guy named Earl Lee?"

Nash smiled. "Yes, I saw him at Lake's house a few times. He was always around, actually."

"You think he could have killed her?"

Nash grinned again and shook his head. "Doesn't have the stones for it. I don't see that ever happening."

"How about Lake? You think he had it in him to pull the trigger?"

"Good question. He has this whole tough-guy image he tries hard to project, although I think it's bullshit. Typical Hollywood actor mentality. The inability to distinguish between reality and fantasy. But you should know he really hated that woman. He did not want to marry her, and he didn't want her around leaching off him the rest of his life. I spent time on the murder table at Hollywood before the department moved all homicide investigations to the bureaus. As I'm sure you understand. I arrested several people for murder that I wouldn't have believed capable of killing someone. But I'm not talking about people like Earl Lee. I'd be shocked if I was wrong about him. Lake, he's a different story. I think maybe he's one of those individuals who, given the right circumstances, could do it. Would do it if he felt it was the only way to get something he considered very important. That kid became very important to him once he decided it was his. And he also wanted Manley out of his life permanently."

"He ever mention anything that made you think he was considering killing her or having someone else do it?"

"No, never. And if you're curious, he never asked me to do it. Of course, he knew I was a retired cop. And you better believe if he had offered me money to kill her, I would have turned him in to the cops in a heartbeat."

"Okay, Nash, we appreciate your cooperation. We'll let the P.C. 538 violation slide this time. But I wouldn't make a habit of doing that. Not when every person in this city over the age of six carries a camera-equipped phone on them."

Nash raised his hands in mock surrender again. "What can I say? You're right. That was a really dumb move. I mean, it would have been dumb if I'd done it, which I vigorously deny." Then he grinned.

Drew chuckled and shot Nash with his finger. "See you around, Nash."

"Sure. If I ever run into you in a bar, I'll buy you both a beer, Detectives."

Li and Drew left Nash's office and passed the smiling blonde on their way out the front door.

Twenty-Eight

JENKINS HAD PHONED DREW with the details of the Earl Lee interview while he and Li were driving back to the PAB. Back at the Open-Unsolved squad room, Drew shared with Jenkins and Ross the salient points from the interviews with Alvarado and Nash.

"Man, it all points right at Lake," Jenkins said. "But we still have nothing but a bunch of witness statements. We need something solid. We need to put that gun in Lake's hand."

"Or we need to find someone Lake told he did it," Drew said.

"That's never going to happen," Ross said glumly. "Jenkins is right. We need physical evidence. We need the lab to come through with something. These celebrity cases are insane. Think about all the physical evidence they had on O. J. and he still walked."

"That differed from our case," Li said. "The O.J. verdict wasn't about him. It was the jury getting payback for the Rodney King beating. That's why they acquitted him."

"Huh?" Jenkins said. "I always thought they had to acquit because that damn glove didn't fit."

Everyone chuckled. But it wasn't a laughing matter. While technically, the murders of Nicole Brown Simpson and Ron Goldman were still open. But no one in the LAPD had done any meaningful investigation of the cases since the day O. J. had walked out of the courtroom a free man, because everyone in the department, past and present, knew they had arrested the killer.

Jenkins and Ross went back to work on the documents they had printed from Manley's laptop. Li and Drew sat down at their desks to document their interviews.

"We need a warrant for Earl Lee's phone records," Drew said.

"I can get started on that if you want to handle documenting the interviews today, Howie," Li said. "What are we looking for?"

"The GPS data," Drew said. "He told Jenkins and Ross he was in the San Francisco area the day Manley died. We need to check that."

"Okay, on it."

Drew noticed a stack of tip line phone messages someone had left on his desk, and flipped through them. The problem with tip line calls was that detectives had to sort through so many red herrings. Calls from psychics, dog psychologists, dream interpreters, and ordinary people seeking attention. The plausible tips that eventually turned out useless were the worst because they consumed valuable time detectives couldn't afford to waste. But when the police were desperate for leads, they could leave no stone unturned.

"Oh, great," Drew said as he read one message.

"What?" Li asked.

"Here's a message from a psychic who talked to Manley after she was killed and wants to talk to the detective in charge."

Li laughed. "Maybe she senses where Lake got the gun from, too. You better get on that one, Howie."

Drew rolled his eyes, wadded the message, and tossed it in the trash can beneath his desk. "If they are such a good psychic, why didn't they ask for me by name?"

He continued scanning the messages.

"Hey, wait a minute," he said. "This one might be legit."

Li stopped typing on her keyboard and looked at her partner.

"What does it say?"

"This guy said he lives a few miles from Lake's house. He told the operator even though it hit close to home, he hadn't been following the case in the news. But after talking with a neighbor, he went to a cable network television website forum covering the case and saw the photo of a guy he knows and a handgun he thinks he's seen before."

"Whoa? You think he might give us a connection to the murder weapon?"

"Maybe," Drew said, hurriedly punching in the callback number. But his excitement turned to disappointment when the call went to voicemail. Drew left his name and office number and hung up.

"If he doesn't get back to me today, I'm going to do a reverse search on the number and get his address. We'll go out and try to catch him at home tomorrow."

"Sounds good, partner."

· · · • • · • • · · ·

At four-thirty, Drew told Li, Jenkins, and Ross they could check out for the day. After the three detectives left, Drew stayed behind, finishing up his reports and waiting in hopes the tipster he had called would call back. At five minutes past five, he was about to try the number again and leave another voicemail with his cell phone number if the man didn't answer. But before he picked up the receiver, the phone rang and Drew grabbed it and answered.

"Detective Drew."

"Yeah, Detective, I just got your message from earlier. This is Gilbert Robertson."

"Yes, Mr. Robertson. Thanks for getting back to me. You told the tip line operator you had something to tell us about the Connie Lynn Manley case?"

"That's right. I hadn't been following the case until recently. A neighbor, who has, since it concerns someone here in the neighborhood, told me about this television channel website that covers true crime and court cases. It sounded interesting, so I checked it out. And in the forum on the website, I saw something that blew me away."

"What was that?"

"I saw a photo of a guy I know. I've seen him at Lake's house a few times. Before, I only knew him by his nickname, Squeaky. But according to the online forum, his name is Roy Cooper. Anyway, besides his photo, I saw something else, a photo of the gun I understand was used to shoot that woman. Well, I think I've seen that gun before."

"You recognized it?"

"I think so."

"What type of gun are we talking about?" Drew asked, trying to keep his excitement in check.

"It was a Walther P38," Robertson said. "I'm sort of a gun enthusiast, so I know. Besides, my grandfather had one of those when I was a kid growing up. He was a vet and brought it back from Germany as a souvenir after the war. So the gun I saw in the photo was a Walther P38."

"And you think you've seen a Walther P38 recently?"

"I sure did. Maybe a month or six weeks ago."

"Where did you see it?"

"The guy I mentioned, Squeaky, had it tucked into his waistband."

"Where did you see this, Mr. Robertson?"

"Inside the garage at Lake's house. I was there at the time. And so was Squeaky, along with Lake and some guy who works for him. I think his name is Earl."

"You're acquainted with William Lake?"

"Well, we're not friends or anything. But, yeah, I know the guy. He is the closest thing we have to a celebrity living in our neighborhood. And I've seen reruns of that old private detective show he was in."

"Why were you at his house the day you saw Roy Cooper there with the Walther?"

"I'm a motorcycle mechanic. Lake owns a Harley, and he was having trouble with the carburetor on the bike. I guess someone in the neighborhood told him I fixed motorcycles, and so he dropped by one day and asked me to look at the Harley. So, it just so happened that I stopped by his house the day Squeaky was there. You think this connects with your case, Detective?"

"It might. Would you recognize the gun if you saw it again, Mr. Robertson?"

"Well, I couldn't be one-hundred percent sure it was the same gun you guys have. Squeaky let me hold it and look at it, but I wasn't looking for a serial number or anything. The one my grandfather had was in rough shape, but this one was in excellent condition. Especially for an antique. Someone took great care of it. All I can tell you for sure is it was a Walther P38."

"I'll tell you what, Mr. Robertson. Are you willing to come downtown in the morning for an interview? We need to document your statement."

"Yeah, I could do that, I guess. What time?"

"How about ten o'clock tomorrow morning?"

"Sure, I can do that."

"Okay, I'll see you in the morning, Mr. Robertson. And thanks again for calling."

"No problem, Detective."

Drew said goodbye and hung up. He leaned back in his chair with his hands behind his head and a smile on his lips, feeling giddy. It wasn't the physical evidence he had hoped for, but Robertson's statement could be another important piece of the puzzle. And it gave them a reason to yank Roy "Squeaky" Cooper back in for another interview, and this time they would have leverage to pry the truth out of the old stuntman.

Twenty-Nine

IT WAS AFTER SIX o'clock on Wednesday evening when Drew left the PAB after a long day that had begun with the flight back to L. A. from Little Rock. He felt bone tired, but he wanted to talk to someone. So, he had made one more call before leaving the squad room, this one to his first partner and mentor when Drew had joined the West Bureau homicide squad. When Drew had called his cell phone number, Rudy Ortega had answered on the third ring. Drew asked if they could meet, and Ortega said they could if Drew wanted to drive to the Formosa Café, his current location. Drew had agreed and made the twenty-five-minute drive to West Hollywood.

When he walked inside the legendary café, Drew found Ortega sitting at the bar.

"Hey, Youngblood," Ortega said, using his favored sobriquet for Drew from back when they had worked together. "You never call. You never write."

Drew grinned and sat down on the bar stool beside Ortega.

"You're looking good for an old murder cop," Drew said with a grin. "How is retirement treating you?"

"Can't complain," Ortega said, raising his empty glass to flag the bartender. "You still drink scotch?"

"Not today," Drew said. "Maybe a beer. I don't want to fall asleep driving home."

"Long day, huh?"

"Yeah, pretty long."

When the bartender arrived, Ortega said, "Another bourbon and a Dos Equis for my lightweight friend."

The bartender grinned, nodded, and shuffled away.

"I heard you made the big time," Ortega said. "Look at you. Working a celebrity case for Homicide Special."

"Surprise you?"

"You've got the skills, Youngblood. I trained you myself. But you were working cold cases at Open-Unsolved the last I heard."

"The Homicide Special assignment is only temporary. But the rumor is, the department is shutting down Open-Unsolved because of the budget cuts."

"Yeah, heard that too."

"That's what I wanted to talk to you about."

The bartender refilled Ortega's glass, set a bottle of beer in front of Drew, and then moved down the bar.

"About what, exactly?"

"Well, Rudy, you know more about the LAPD than anyone else. At least anyone else I trust. What can you tell me about Deputy Chief LaChasse and Captain Mann at RHD?"

"You still butting heads with LaChasse? I told you before that wasn't smart."

"I've stayed away from him. But he hasn't returned the favor. I've bumped into him twice since I got the lead on the Manley case."

"Okay, what do you want to know about them?"

"History. Connections."

Drew drank some beer.

"LaChasse and Mann graduated from the academy together. LaChasse's star rose faster, and he's used his influence to help Mann along. They're friends. LaChasse is the reason Mann got the job commanding RHD."

"That's what I was afraid of."

"Why is that?"

"I think LaChasse is behind me getting the temporary assignment to Homicide Special and the lead on this high-profile murder investigation."

"From what you've told me, I can't imagine LaChasse doing you any favors. Rumors I've head say he still wants you out of the LAPD."

"That he does," Drew said before drinking more beer. "He thinks I'll screw up the case, let it turn into another O.J. thing, and the city council will blame Chief Sandoval. Then he thinks he will get the chief's job. According to LaChasse, the chief's stock with the city council has already dropped, and I would be the final nail in his coffin."

"Well, Sandoval only beat out LaChasse for the chief's job by a hair. LaChasse still has friends on the city council. So, he could be right. If they made a leadership change, I could see LaChasse getting the job. But he has underestimated you, Youngblood, if he believes you don't have what it takes to solve a murder case. Even a celebrity case."

"Well, I guess he has because he confronted me today and told me how confident he was that I'll fuck it up and it will pave the way for him to the top job on the tenth floor when I do."

"Don't let him mess with your head, Youngblood. Just do your job and I know you'll close the case successfully and put that fool Lake in jail for murder."

"You think he did it too?"

"Of course he did it. In my experience, no criminal defense attorney tries as hard to convince the media his client is innocent as Oberlin has, unless he knows his client is guilty as sin."

"Everything is pointing right at him," Drew said. "But all we have is a circumstantial case at the moment. We don't have a shred of physical evidence."

"Just keep digging, Youngblood. Breaks don't fall out of the sky. You make them with good old-fashioned police work."

Drew nodded.

"So, you think LaChasse and Mann have cooked up a conspiracy and are out to get you?"

"I know LaChasse is. He made no bones about it when he confronted me. Maybe all Mann did was assign me the case because LaChasse asked him to do it. I haven't seen him but once since I got started and only talked to him once on the phone before that."

"What do you think of Moreno?"

"I suspected he was against me at first. But we had a talk, and he changed my mind. I think we're good now."

Ortega nodded. "I worked with Moreno a long time ago. He's a stand-up guy and a good cop. And he earned his job. He owes nothing to LaChasse, Mann, or anyone else, as far as I know."

"Good to know."

"The thing is, Youngblood, is you have that leverage with LaChasse. He knows the only to neutralize it is to discredit you. If he can do that, if you dropped the dime on him, he hopes you won't have the credibility to do him any real damage. It sounds like he needed to draw you out because he didn't see a way to get at you while you were in Open-Unsolved. That probably explains why he got you put in your current position. Still, I don't see how he can influence how you choose to run your investigation. I wouldn't waste time thinking about him. It's only a distraction."

"Yeah, you're probably right, Rudy. I haven't noticed him interfering overtly in any way. Maybe I'm only borrowing trouble worrying about it."

"There is something else you should know."

"What's that?" Drew asked.

"About the history between LaChasse and William Lake."

"What history?"

"LaChasse is one of those cops who has always wanted to be in books, be on television, be in films, wanted to make money. He and Lake go way back. Lake got him a few small speaking roles on the television series that made Lake famous. And he hired LaChasse as a law enforcement adviser for some films Lake produced or directed. I don't have to tell you LaChasse has a checkered past as a cop. And I wouldn't put it past him to compromise your investigation if Lake offered him enough money."

"Thanks a lot, Rudy. You tell me not to worry about him, then you drop that little gem on top of me like a cement truck."

Ortega chuckled. "It's one of those things, Youngblood. Worry about him, but don't worry about him."

Drew shook his head and finished his beer. He reached for his wallet. Ortega put a hand on his arm.

"I got it. You sure you don't want to have another one?"

"I'm sure," Drew said. "I started the day getting up early in Little Rock, Arkansas, to catch a morning flight back to L.A. to attend Oberlin's press conference. And I've done several interviews. I need some sleep."

"Okay, Youngblood. I'll keep my ear to the ground. If I hear anything through the grapevine, I'll circle back."

"Thanks, Rudy. I appreciate it."

The men shook hands and Drew walked out the door.

Thirty

DREW AND LI WERE first in on Thursday morning and met in the parking structure. When they got upstairs and had cups of the less than tasty department supplied coffee, Drew quickly updated his partner on his conversation with Gilbert Robertson. Then he told Amy Li about his conversation with Rudy Ortega.

"Howie, don't take LaChasse lightly," she said. "Maybe it's time to take the evidence you found during the Stepanchikov case to the chief and let him handle LaChasse. You have credibility now, and I'll back you up. I think Chief Sandoval already suspects LaChasse is bent. What I don't get is why he thought pushing LaChasse out of the PAB to the Valley Bureau would solve anything. He should have cleaned house and got rid of him."

"Chief Sandoval couldn't push him out of the LAPD, even if he knew," Drew said. "LaChasse has forty years with the department. He has connections that reach outside the department and into City Hall. He has allies on the city council. And he knows where a lot of the bodies are buried. If the chief made a move against him, it would likely blow back on him. And I owe Chief Sandoval. I don't want to put him in the position where he might have to cut his own throat, especially if he really has lost support with the city council, as LaChasse claimed."

"Then what's the use of having the leverage against LaChasse if you have no intention of using it, Howie?"

"Because LaChasse knows I have it and I'm sure he doesn't want it to come out. At least not until he can destroy my credibility, so no one would believe me. I'm not saying I don't believe it's possible he might try to sabotage the case. I've just got to be very careful and ready to react if he tries."

Li shook her head, looking wistful. "If the chief doesn't even have the power to do anything about him, I'm not confident you're going to be much more than a speed bump, Howie."

"We've just got to keep this case moving," Drew said. "We've got momentum and we need to stay in front of things. That way, I don't see how LaChasse can derail it."

"I guess we'll find out," Li said. "I'm just sick of all the politics in this department. Why won't people just let us do our jobs?"

"I don't like the politics either," Drew said. "But with any large organization, politics is always going to be involved."

"Okay, so what's the plan for today?" Li asked, shaking her head in frustration.

"Did you get the warrant affidavit for Earl Lee's phone records finished?"

"Yes, I finished it all before I left yesterday afternoon. All it needs is a judge's signature and I'll fax it to the cell phone service provider."

"Okay, then we'll interview Gilbert Robertson when he gets here at ten o'clock. Then you can take the warrant to the CCB and get a judge to sign off. As soon as Jenkins and Ross get here, I'm sending them to pick up Roy Cooper and to bring him back here for a second interview."

"Without waiting until after we talk to Robertson?"

"Yeah, I have a plan to make him tell the truth this time. I already got the basics from Robertson on the phone yesterday, so I'm confident the plan will work."

Jenkins and Ross walked into the squad room together.

"Just the guys I'm looking for," Drew said.

"What's up, Howie?" Jenkins asked.

"Go pick up Roy Cooper and bring him in for a second interview," Drew said.

"Try to get him to come in voluntarily, you mean?"

"Yeah, try that. But if he refuses, arrest him and bring him anyway."

"Arrest him for..."

"Murder. We're going to put the murder weapon on him if we have to."

"What? What's changed?" Jenkins asked.

Drew quickly explained his phone conversation with Gilbert Robertson to Jenkins and Ross.

"He's coming in this morning for a formal interview."

"I don't get it," Jenkins said. "You just said he told you he can't say for sure it was the murder weapon he saw."

"Yeah, but Roy Cooper doesn't know that, and we won't tell him," Drew said.

Jenkins grinned. "Tell me lies, tell me sweet little lies," he sang off-key.

It was the worst imitation of Fleetwood Mac's Christine McVie Drew had ever heard. The other three detectives had a good laugh at Jenkins' expense. But it didn't deter Jenkins. He kept singing the lyrics of Little Lies all the way out the door as he left with Ross.

·•••••••••

Gilbert Robertson arrived ten minutes early. Drew and Li ushered him into the interview room and got his story on video. He related the same story he had told Drew on the phone the previous evening. He was certain the gun he saw inside Roy Cooper's waistband at the home of William Lake was a well-maintained Walther P38, but even if the detectives showed him the murder weapon, he couldn't swear it was the same Walther P38. But that wasn't a problem for Drew. He felt confident that with a little embellishment, he'd spin Robertson's story just enough to put the burden on Roy Cooper to explain where he got the Walther P38 Robertson had seen him with and what he had done with it. Drew didn't believe Cooper had shot Manley. His theory was Cooper had given the handgun to William Lake and Lake had pulled the trigger on Manley.

·········

After they finished interviewing Robertson, Li left for the CCB to get the warrant signed. Previously, the police simply subpoenaed phone records, but a recent U.S. Supreme Court ruling required a search warrant when the police sought GPS data with phone records.

Twenty minutes after Li had left the squad room, Jenkins and Ross arrived with Roy "Squeaky" Cooper, who looked both angry and frightened. Since Cooper hadn't arrived in handcuffs, Drew assumed Jenkins had convinced him to come in voluntarily. Ross took Cooper back to the interview room.

"You and I will interview him," Drew said. "Ross can work on the documents you guys printed until we finish. Hopefully, we'll get something out of Cooper that will inform the rest of our day."

"I hope so," Jenkins said. "We've got about all there is to get out of the laptop. I'm just glad Moreno got us those plainclothes patrol officers to work on the boxes of documents that Oberlin dumped on us."

With Ross returning glumly to working on the documents, Jenkins and Drew went to the interview room. They found Cooper sipping the coffee with a grimace that Ross had got for him.

"This is the worst coffee I ever tasted," Cooper said to the detectives.

"How do you think we feel?" Jenkins asked without cracking a smile.

The detectives sat down across the table from Cooper.

"Roy, you're in a world of shit," Drew said. "You lied to Detectives Jenkins and Ross when they spoke to you the first time."

"I don't know what you mean," Cooper said, but with little vigor.

"You claimed you didn't know why William Lake wanted you to set up the meeting with Grayson Cohen. Now we've found out you also set up a meeting between Lake and Ronald Saunders. It's time to tell the truth, Roy. You're in a lot of trouble, and the truth is the only thing that will get you out of it."

"I didn't lie to the detectives I talked to," Cooper protested. "Like I told them, I didn't know why Bill wanted to meet with Gray. He never said. I only assumed it was some movie project. And they never asked me about Ron or I would have told them. I have nothing to hide."

"I think you do, Roy," Drew said. "I think you have a lot to hide and I think you're protecting William Lake."

"I've done nothing wrong. I swear I haven't."

Drew shook his head in feigned sadness. Then he opened a folder, took out a photo, and slapped it on the table in front of Cooper.

"Tell me about that gun, Roy."

Cooper glanced at the photo and then back at Drew, looking like his eyes might pop out of his head.

"I've never seen that gun," Cooper said, his voice breaking at the end.

"Oh, but you have, Roy. We have a witness who saw you with it. A witness who saw you with it inside the garage at William Lake's house in Studio City. He said you even let him hold it and look at it when he told you his grandfather used to own a similar Walther P38."

"Oh, that gun. I forgot all about it. I didn't have it long, because I sold it to a guy I know."

"To William Lake?"

"Bill? Hell no. I didn't sell it to him. Another guy I know."

"Let me explain something, Roy," Drew said, as if speaking to a dull child. "That gun in the photo is the gun someone used to shoot Connie Lynn Manley to death last Friday night. And remember the guy who saw you with the Walther P38 at Lake's house? He noticed a small anomaly when he handled your Walther P38. The guy was a gun enthusiast, and he noticed it right away. A minor defect most people wouldn't even notice. But he noticed. And guess what, Roy? When we showed him the murder gun, he pointed to that tiny imperfection and told us he knew for sure it was the same Walther P38 he saw you with that day."

Speechless, Cooper glanced nervously from Drew to Jenkins and back again.

"I want a lawyer. That's my right, isn't it? I don't have to answer your questions until I get a lawyer."

"Yes, you can have a lawyer," Drew said. "If that's how you want to play it. Right now, we're interviewing you as a witness. Once you have a lawyer, then we must treat you as a suspect. I'm not trying to discourage you if you want a lawyer. But I want to be honest with you."

Cooper remained quiet.

"And once your lawyer gets here, if that's what you want. We're going to put that gun on you, Roy. We're going to arrest you, put handcuffs on you, and take you straight to Men's Central and book you for first degree murder."

"I want a lawyer," Cooper shrieked, spittle flying from his mouth.

"Okay, Roy. No problem. Calm down. Detective Jenkins, please read Roy his rights and have him sign the document attesting you did so, and that he understands his rights."

Reading from a form, Jenkins said, "Mr. Cooper, you have the right to remain silent..."

After Jenkins finished reading Cooper the Miranda Warning, Cooper signed the form showing he understood his rights.

"You have someone in mind to call, Roy?" Drew asked. "Or do you want us to provide you with an attorney?"

"I know a guy."

"Fine," Drew said, sliding his cell phone across the table. "You get one call. Make it count."

"Don't I get any privacy?"

"Nope. If you want to call your lawyer, call him."

Cooper sighed in frustration, picked up the phone, and punched in a number.

"Yeah, this is Roy Cooper. Let me talk to Derrick. Just tell him it's Squeaky."

"Listen, this is an emergency. The cops are with me and I have to talk to Derrick right now... yeah, okay. Thanks."

After a momentary pause, Cooper spoke into the phone again. "Derrick, I need you to come down to the police department. What? Yeah, the Los Angeles police. Downtown. The big building on First Street."

Cooper cocked his head and listened for several moments.

"They are trying to frame me for a murder."

He listened some more.

"Derrick, I don't care what kind of lawyer you are. You went to law school, didn't you? You know about rights, don't you? Just come down here and see what's what. Then, if you think you can't help me, we'll figure something else out. Otherwise. they are going to haul me to county jail and I don't want to go to jail, Derrick."

Cooper listened impatiently for a few more moments.

"Okay, thanks, Derrick. I'm sure you will know more about it than I do. Please hurry. I'll be waiting. Goodbye."

Cooper passed the phone back to Drew.

"All good?" Jenkins asked.

"Yeah, he's a buddy of mine. His name is Skinner. Derrick Skinner. And he's on his way here right now. He said maybe twenty minutes, depending on traffic."

"This is L.A.," Jenkins said. "It always depends on the traffic. Get you anything while you wait, Roy? More coffee?"

"No coffee. I'll be lucky if I don't already have a hole in my gut after the cup that other guy brought me."

"I don't blame you, Roy. The coffee here is nasty. How about a bottle of water? Or a soda maybe?"

"Water is fine."

"You got it, Roy," Jenkins said, standing up.

Drew got up too. "Sit tight, Roy, until your pal Derrick gets here."

The detectives left the room, and Drew closed the door.

"Something tells me Derrick Skinner is no F. Lee Bailey," Drew said.

Jenkins chuckled. "I think you're right. If we're lucky, it will be another entertainment attorney. And hopefully one not as sharp as Lake had that night at North Hollywood."

Thirty-One

WHILE WAITING FOR COOPER's lawyer to arrive, Drew went to Lieutenant Moreno's office. He had already updated Moreno the previous day before Gilbert Robertson had called him back, so Drew hadn't mentioned Robertson. He figured he owed the lieutenant another update, given the rapidly changing circumstances. Moreno seemed pleased with the progress. After the early contentious private meeting with Moreno when they had cleared the air, the tension between the men had evaporated and Drew felt he had Moreno's full support.

Derrick Skinner arrived about ten minutes after Drew got back from Homicide Special, and almost forty minutes after Cooper had called him. Drew escorted the lawyer back to the interview room where Jenkins was waiting with Cooper. Drew brought in another chair for Skinner, and after everyone sat down, he explained the situation for the lawyer's benefit and showed him the photo of the Walther.

"We can prove Roy possessed the murder weapon," Drew said. "If he didn't shoot Connie Lynn Manley, it's time for him to convince us by telling us what he did with the handgun. Otherwise, we have no choice. We'll arrest him and charge him with murder."

Skinner, who reminded Drew of the George Costanza character from Seinfeld, seemed visibly uncomfortable after hearing Drew's summary of Cooper's predicament. He took out a handkerchief and mopped his brow.

"I'd like to confer with my client," Skinner said.

"Sure, counselor," Drew said, nodding to Jenkins. The detectives got up and left the room, and walked a short distance away from the closed door.

"What do you think?" Jenkins said.

"Skinner will ask for a deal, unless he bails and tells Cooper to get another lawyer."

"He looked pretty shaky," Jenkins said. "My money is on him bailing."

After about five minutes, Skinner opened the door and waved the detectives back in.

"My client will tell you what he knows, providing you first tender in writing a grant of unqualified immunity from prosecution."

Drew shook his head. "That won't fly with the district attorney's office, counselor. We already have him with the murder gun. Until he tells us what he knows, we don't know what else he may have done."

Skinner slumped, deflated. He looked at Cooper. "Squeaky, this isn't the type of law I practice. Don't you want me to find you a criminal defense attorney? This is serious."

"You know someone else who will accept monthly payments?" Cooper asked.

"No, Squeaky. They will want a retainer."

"Then, I'll stick with you, Derrick. I trust you to handle this."

"I'm an entertainment lawyer," Skinner said to detectives almost apologetically. "The closest I've ever got to practicing criminal law was defending my brother-in-law in a DUI case."

"How did that go?" Jenkins asked.

"Don't ask."

"I'll tell you what, counselor. We can't make any promises about immunity. I'll call and ask a prosecutor to join us. You can talk to him about terms attorney to attorney."

"Okay, Detective. Let's do that."

"Get you anything while you're waiting?" Jenkins asked Skinner.

"Got any coffee?" he asked.

"You don't want their coffee, Derrick," Cooper warned.

· · · • • • • • · ·

Drew called Scott Kelly, a filing deputy, and one of the deputy district attorneys on hand for the search of Lake's house on the Saturday morning after the murder. Kelly agreed to help and arrived at the squad room about fifteen minutes later. Drew briefed him on the situation and revealed the ruse he had used, hoping to get Roy Cooper to talk. Kelly grinned.

"Well, the U.S. Supreme Court has ruled consistently that law enforcement officers can use deception when interrogating suspects. Whether your ruse works depends on his attorney."

"He's not entitled to see the video of our interview with Gilbert Robertson unless we arrest and charge Cooper, right?" Drew asked.

"Right. But a good defense attorney would advise Cooper to say nothing for now, even if he must go to jail. Then the attorney could get the interview video in discovery and would find out you've got nothing."

"I'm banking his attorney isn't that sharp," Drew said, explaining that Skinner was an entertainment lawyer who seemed out of his depth.

"In that case, let's give it a shot," Kelly said. "I brought with me a standard qualified immunity agreement. If his lawyer agrees to our offer, I'll fill in the blanks and sign it."

Drew and Kelly walked to the interview room. Since four people already made the room crowded, Jenkins stepped outside, giving up his place to the deputy district attorney. Drew introduced Kelly to Skinner, and then he and Kelly sat down across from him and his client. Skinner told Kelly what his client wanted in exchange for answering the detective's questions.

"We can't and won't offer your client unqualified immunity," Kelly said. "As Detective Drew already explained, possession of the murder weapon, which we believe we can prove, puts your client in a tough spot. What I can do is tender an offer of qualified immunity."

"What are the qualifications?" Skinner asked.

"In exchange for his truthful statements, we will grant immunity for any criminal act besides murder or conspiracy to commit murder. Not yet knowing what your client may tell us, for all we know, he might implicate himself in the murder of Ms. Manley. If he shot the victim or took part materially in her murder, he's not walking out of here no matter what else he might tell us."

Skinner looked at Cooper. "I think that's the best deal we will get, Squeaky."

Cooper nodded. "I'm innocent. I feel okay with it."

"My client accepts your terms," Skinner said to Kelly, "as long as we get it in writing."

"Not a problem," Kelly said, opening his briefcase and pulling out a document. "This is a standard qualified immunity agreement. I'll fill in the exceptions we just discussed, sign it, and give it to your client."

Skinner nodded, and Kelly completed the form. He handed it to Skinner. Skinner scanned the document and then allowed Cooper to sign in. Kelly signed as the representative of his office.

"Okay, Roy," Drew said. "I want you to start at the beginning and tell us in your own words about when William Lake first contacted you about setting up the meeting between him and Grayson Cohen, and later Ronald Saunders. I'll stop you whenever I have questions."

Cooper swallowed hard and nodded. Then he began.

"Bill called me one day..."

Kelly interrupted. "When you say Bill, are you referring to William Lake?"

"Yeah," Cooper said.

"Okay, just wanted to make that clear for the record. Please continue Mr. Cooper."

"Anyway, I've known Bill for many years and have worked for him on movies and television shows. But I hadn't heard from him in maybe four or five years when he called around two months ago."

"Is that when he asked you to set up the meeting with Grayson Cohen?" Drew asked.

"No, that was later. When he called that first time, he asked me to meet him at Du-Par's in Studio City to discuss a job. He said he'd buy me lunch. He didn't explain the job, so I assumed naturally it was a movie deal. I'd done stunt work and also worked for Bill as a stunt coordinator in the past."

Drew nodded for the man to continue.

"Well, we met and after some small talk, Bill told me about his wife and what a bad person she was. He said she got pregnant with his child on purpose to trap him into marrying her. And she was costing him a lot of money. Then, he came right out with it and said he wanted her whacked."

"Whacked? What did you think he meant by that?"

"Right away, I figured he meant he wanted her dead. And if I had any doubts about it, as the thing continued, Bill sure removed them. That's what he meant."

"Okay, then what happened?" Drew asked.

"I went along with it, just to see if he was serious or joking around. Or maybe just angry and talking nonsense. I've heard people say things when angry about killing someone, but they didn't mean it."

"Did you think he was joking, or wasn't serious?"

"At first, I hoped it was only a joke or just anger at her talking, but soon I had to accept that Bill was serious."

"When did you first feel certain he was speaking seriously?"

"By the time that first meeting ended. We were walking out to our cars. Bill turned to me and asked me if I'd take the job. I asked him what job, and then he asked if I'd snuff his wife for him for ten thousand dollars."

"Just to clarify, did you understand he was talking about Connie Lynn Manley?" Kelly asked.

"Yes, he had used her name a few times when we were inside the restaurant. I knew she was his wife."

"He used the word snuff?" Drew asked, recalling Ronald Saunders had used the safe term when Jenkins and Ross had interviewed him.

"Yes, he never said kill her or shoot her. Bill only used words like snuff her or whack her. I could tell he was being cagey about it. Like protecting himself in case anything came back on him, he could claim I'd misunderstood and that he hadn't asked me to kill his wife."

"Okay, what did you say when he made the offer?" Drew asked.

"Well, I told him I honestly didn't know if I could do it," Cooper said. "Understand, I had no intention of doing it. But Bill scared me. We're friends and have been for a long time. But Bill can get violent and he has a temper. When he asks you to do something, it's more like he tells you to do what it is he wants. It doesn't sound like a request when he asks."

Drew nodded. "So, did that end the discussion at that meeting?"

"There's a little more. Bill asked me to think it over and he'd call me in a few days to talk more. And that's when I suggested the burner phones."

"What about the burner phones?" Drew asked.

"I told Bill it wasn't a good idea to discuss that sort of thing on our usual phones," Cooper said. "I mentioned if anything happened and the police got involved, they could get our phone records. He didn't seem to know much about burner phones. I had to explain they were cheap, disposable phones that the police couldn't trace. Understand, I only suggested it because while I didn't intend to accept his offer, I didn't want it blowing back on me if something happened to that woman. I didn't want the police to think I'd done it by finding phone records showing Bill and I had talked about it."

"Did Lake take your advice?"

"Yes, we both bought cheap, prepaid phones and exchanged numbers the next time we met."

"You met again after the meeting at Du-Par's?"

"We met several times after that. Sometimes at his house. Once, when his wife was out shopping, Bill took me to the guest house behind his house and told me she stayed there and then took me inside. He has a gym set up on the first floor, but upstairs there is an apartment with a bedroom, bath, kitchen, and living room. We went into her bedroom and Bill told me someone could come in while she was asleep in the middle of the night and pop her."

"Where else did you meet?" Drew asked.

"Lots of places. Sometimes Bill drove me to places where he said someone could snuff her, places where there would be no witnesses around. He once drove me to that restaurant where the murder happened. Another time, he drove me out to the desert and showed me a place where he said someone could bury her and no one would ever find the body."

"Do you still have the prepaid phone you bought to communicate with Lake?"

"Yeah, it's at my house. I'll turn it over to you if you want it, but I always deleted his calls after we talked."

"That's okay. We have people who can recover deleted calls. Do you have a problem giving us the key to your place and letting one of my detectives go get the phone right now?"

Cooper looked at his lawyer.

"I don't think we want the police searching his house," Skinner said.

"He can tell us where to find the phone," Drew said. "I give you my word. We won't search his house. My detective will only go straight to the phone, get it, and leave."

Cooper leaned in and whispered something to Skinner.

"My client is agreeable."

Cooper pulled out a key ring and took one key off it. He slid it across the table to Drew.

"Let's take a ten-minute break," Drew said. "Roy can use the restroom and get something to drink while I get this key to my detective. That way, they should be back with the key by the time we're finished."

Kelly offered to show Cooper and his attorney where the restroom and break room were. Then Drew went back to the squad room. Li had returned with the warrant for Earl Lee's phone records and was faxing it to his telephone service provider. Jenkins and Ross were still digging through their stack of documents. Drew called the team together. He handed the key to Li and gave her Cooper's address.

"Just go in, grab the phone, and come right back," Drew said. "He said the phone is on the top of the refrigerator in the kitchen."

Li nodded, gathered her things, and left with the key.

"I have something for you and Ross," Drew said to Jenkins. "Lake bought a prepaid cell phone, and I'd like to know where he got it. It's a long shot, but I want you to drive to his neighborhood in Studio City. Starting at his house, look for places that sell those cheap, prepaid phones. I'm betting he bought it close to home. Give it two hours, moving further out from the house as necessary. If you find nothing in two hours, come on back."

"That sure beats working on the documents," Ross said, grabbing his jacket off the chair.

"We'll let you know if we find anything," Jenkins said.

The detectives left the squad room and Drew walked back to the interview room. He still had a lot of ground to cover. For one, he wanted the details about the Walther.

Thirty-Two

BACK IN THE INTERVIEW room, Drew picked up where they had left off.

"Okay, so you met with Lake several times to discuss his plans for killing his wife. How did Grayson Cohen, and later Ronald Saunders, come into the picture?"

"The whole thing made me more and more uneasy the more we talked about it," Cooper said. "It reached the point finally when I had to turn Bill down, even though I worried he would get angry."

"So, you turned him down. Then what?"

"When he realized I wanted no part of it, he asked if I knew someone who might do it. I told him no. He asked if I'd do it for more money. I said no, but I told him I doubted anyone would do it for only ten thousand. They would probably want more because it was risky. He called me again a few days later, and asked me to call Gray and set up a meeting between them at Du-Par's. So, I got Gray's number from the union, called him, and set it up."

"And you knew why Lake wanted to talk to him?"

"Yeah, okay, I had a good idea by then. But I was scared. I didn't know what else to do. I already knew too much and felt that put me in a bad situation."

"We know Grayson Cohen also turned him down."

"Yeah, and that's when Bill called me and told me to set up a meeting with Ron."

"Let's move on to the gun," Drew said. "Where did you get it, and what did you do with it?"

"About twenty years ago, I got into an argument with another stuntman on a set. He had a rough reputation. And he threatened me. So, I bought the Walther from a guy I knew and carried it for protection for a while. I had had it ever since. One day, after I'd told Bill I didn't want the job. I think it was maybe a few days before he met with Ron. He called and asked me if I knew where he could get a pistol that couldn't be traced to him. I didn't, but I had the Walther and told him about it. Bill asked me to bring it by his house and if it looked okay, he said he would buy it from me."

"And you took it to him?"

"Yeah, I drove to his house. He and Earl, his handyman, were out in the garage with the door up, messing with an old Harley Bill owns. He was having trouble with it. I walked in and we shot the shit for a while. He saw I had the pistol inside my waistband at the front, but about the time he said something about it, this guy walked up. I can't remember his name. My memory isn't what it once was. But Bill mentioned the guy was a neighbor and worked on motorcycles. I guess Bill had asked him to look at the Harley, and he just happened to stop by while I was there. He saw the gun right off and mentioned it. He said his grandfather had owned a Walther and asked to look at mine. I didn't know what else to do, so I took it out and handed it to him. He said it was in much better shape than the one his grandfather had owned, looked at it for a few minutes, and handed it back."

"Then what happened?"

"I could see it made Bill furious. Furious the guy had even seen the gun, much less handled it and looked at it closely. So, he told the guy he'd already fixed the Harley, thanked him for stopping by, but said he didn't need him to look at the bike any longer. So, the neighbor left."

Cooper drank some water from the bottle in front of him, and then continued.

"Bill closed the garage door and then asked to look at the Walther. He worked the slide a few times and looked it over. Then asked if I was sure no one could trace it to me. I told him I was sure and had bought it twenty years before from a guy who had since died in a car accident. No one knew I had it. So, he reached in his pocket, took out a roll of bills and offered me two thousand for it. I'd only paid about three hundred for it and I'd looked it up on the Internet and saw that antique Walther pistols went for an average of around fourteen hundred. So, I sold it to him."

"Lake had the pistol since that day, as far as you know?"

"Actually, as soon as we made the deal and he paid me, he handed it to Earl and told him to hold on to it. The last time I saw that gun, it was tucked inside Earl's waistband."

The story was getting better and better, Drew thought.

"Did Bill ask you to set up meetings with anyone else after Ronald Saunders turned him down?"

"No, I think he gave up on the idea of finding someone after Ron turned him down. He still called me using the burner, but never asked me to meet him again or do anything else. I think he was only checking in from time to time to remind me to never talk to anyone about any of it."

"When was the last time he called you?" Drew asked.

"He called me a few days before the woman got shot, and then the last time he called was early the morning after it happened. That's the last time I heard from him."

"What did he say when he called the morning after Manley died?"

"Bill asked me if I was sure no one could trace the burner to him. I said, I was sure. Then he reminded me to never speak to anyone about what we had talked about. The way he said it made me feel like it had been a threat. That's why I was reluctant to talk openly to the other detectives."

Drew nodded. "Okay, you've satisfied me you didn't kill her. But you will have to tell this story again in court."

"I don't mind telling you, Detective, I'm scared of what Bill might do when he finds out I snitched on him. But I'm an old man and I have serious liver problems. I can't go to prison. For me, any sentence would be a life sentence."

"Well, you won't get charged with anything, Roy, as long as everything you've told us is the truth and you cooperate with the district attorney's office. Lake won't find out you've talked to us until after we arrest him. He will be in jail then, so I wouldn't worry about him."

Cooper nodded, looking relieved. Drew ended the interview. When they walked out into the hallway, Detective Li was there. She had the phone inside a plastic evidence bag and handed the key back to Drew. He returned it to Cooper. Then Li escorted Cooper and Skinner out. Drew and Kelly went to the squad room.

"You've got a solid case against Lake for soliciting murder," Kelly said. "Really good work. When you're ready to file the packet, bring it to me, and I'll accept it."

"Thanks, Scott, but we have more work to do. I want Lake for more than just soliciting. I want him for the murder. The gun is another piece of the puzzle. We can't put it in his hand the night of the murder, but we can put him close to it now. But we need more."

"I hope you get more, Howard, and believe you're getting close. But as I understand it, you've got mostly a circumstantial case. I've seen those go either way, even strong ones."

"We'll get there," Drew said. "Any idea who will get the case when it goes to trial?"

"Well, it isn't official. But the rumor around the office is Cheryl Wheeler will get it. She has twenty-five years of experience as a prosecutor and has forty-eight murder convictions out of the forty-nine she has prosecuted."

"Good enough," Drew said. "I know her and she is a solid prosecutor. Thanks for helping, Scott."

"Happy to do it, and it got me out of the office for a while. But I better get back over there."

The men shook hands, said goodbye, and Kelly left for the CCB.

Thirty-Three

JENKINS AND ROSS GOT lucky. When they arrived in Lake's Studio City neighborhood, the first place they checked, a convenience store only blocks from Lake's house, turned out to be the source of his burner phone. They waited until the clerk finished with a customer at the counter and then Jenkins badged him and asked him if he knew William Lake, and recalled selling him a prepaid phone.

"Oh, sure, I know Mr. Lake," the clerk said. "He comes in to buy smokes and other things all the time. He lives here in the neighborhood. And, yes, he bought a prepaid phone here. A month ago, I think. It may have been six weeks or a little longer, but I remember it."

"You must get a lot of customers here," Jenkins said. "But you seem to recall it clearly."

"Yes, I do. Mr. Lake came in for smokes. But we were out of his favorite brand. He always gets the shorts, and all I had were the 100s. He took them, but he became a little upset."

"How about the phone?" Jenkins asked.

The clerk turned and pointed to a rack behind the counter. "The boss only started carrying them a few months ago. We keep them back here so the kids don't steal them. Before we only carried phone cards. But a salesman talked the boss into the prepaid phones. The thing is, they haven't sold well. You can buy the same phone in the big box stores for much less. They get them at a better wholesale price. So, if we ever get rid of these, the boss isn't carrying them anymore."

"But William Lake bought one here?"

"That's right. While paying for the cigarettes, he noticed them on the rack. And he asked for one. I told him they came with two-hundred minutes and he bought one. Strange. A famous guy like him I'd think would have the top-of-the-line smart phone."

"Let's have a look at the phones," Jenkins said.

"Sure, Detective."

The clerk took one of the clam shell packages from the shelf and put it on the counter.

"No, we want to see all of them," Jenkins said.

"They're all the same."

"We still want to look at all the packages."

The clerk shrugged and put six more packages on the counter beside the first one. Jenkins and Ross blew the dust off the plastic packaging and examined each one.

"The numbers are sequential," Ross said to Jenkins.

"Yeah, that's what I was hoping. They are all from the same lot."

"You sell anymore phones since William Lake bought his?" Jenkins asked.

"I haven't, but I can't be sure whether someone on another shift might have."

Jenkins took out his phone and photographed the phone packages, front and back.

"Thank you," he said to the clerk after he finished. "We appreciate your help."

"You don't want to buy one, Detective?"

Jenkins grinned. "No thanks. I have a top-of-the-line smart phone. It's all I need."

·······

Back in the car, Jenkins took his phone out and called a guy he knew at Piper Tech. When the tech answered, Jenkins explained the circumstances and asked if there was a way to get the phone number for a prepaid cell phone. The tech told him there was if he had some information on the phone. Jenkins told him he had images showing all the information from the backs of the packaging for other phones from the same lot as the one he wanted the number for, but not the phone he wanted to know about. The tech gave him a cell number and asked him to send him the images and he'd see what he could do with them. After ending the call, Jenkins sent all the images he'd taken in the convenience store to the tech. Then Ross started the car, and they headed back downtown.

Before they arrived at the PAB, the Piper Tech guy called Jenkins back.

"What have you got for me?" Jenkins said. "Yeah? Cool. Hang on a second."

Jenkins pulled out his notebook and pen.

"Go ahead."

As the detective listened, he scribbled down three telephone numbers.

"Hey, thanks, pal. I appreciate it."

Jenkins ended the call and put his phone back inside his pocket.

"My guy at Piper Tech checked it out," he said to Ross. "All the telephone numbers are sequential too. This prepaid phone brand gets their numbers from Verizon. He said that the phones at the store came in a box of ten, so they've only sold three phones, and we know Lake bought one. He got the phone numbers for all ten phones from the manufacturer, checked them somehow, and verified someone has activated three of the numbers. So, one belongs to Lake's burner."

"How does that help us?"

"Now that we have the phone numbers, we can get search warrants for the phone records on all three numbers. Then we'll check the call records and find out which number called Roy Cooper's burner. That gives us Lake's burner phone number."

"Okay. Then that gives Cooper's story some credibility."

"Yeah, but the Piper Tech guy said we'll also get GPS data that might be helpful. Remember Lake said he forgot his phone the night of the murder and left it at home?"

"Yeah."

"Maybe he was carrying the burner."

"Excellent stuff."

·········

"We need another search warrant, Amy," Drew said. "This one for Earl Lee's residence. Cooper told us he sold the Walther to Lake, but Lee had it in his possession the last time he saw it."

"Okay, on it, Howie," Li said.

"We're getting very close to putting a conspiracy to commit murder charge on Lee. Hopefully, we'll find something at his house that pushes us over the line."

Li was typing the warrant and Drew was updating the murder book when Jenkins and Ross returned.

"We got it, Howie," Jenkins said.

"You found the place he bought the burner?"

"Yeah, we got lucky. The first place we checked was a convenience store just blocks from Lake's house. The clerk who sold it to him was working today and remembered it. And I already checked with a guy at Piper Tech and we have three phone numbers, one of which is Lake's burner."

"Good work. You guys exceeded my expectations."

"If you're good with it, we want to grab lunch. Then we'll knock out the search warrants on the phone numbers. Since you got Cooper's burner, we just have to review the phone records when we get them and look for Cooper's phone number to find which number belongs to Lake's burner."

"Sounds like a plan," Drew said. "Amy is typing up a search warrant for Earl Lee's residence."

Drew gave Jenkins and Ross the chief points from the Cooper interview.

"Now that we have him with the murder weapon, getting a search warrant shouldn't be a problem, and maybe we'll get something we can use to put a conspiracy charge on him. As soon as Amy finishes, we'll head to the CCB and get a judge's signature. Then we'll get lunch, meet you back here, and this afternoon we'll all go to Lee's residence and execute the warrant."

Thirty-Four

THEY ARRIVED WITH A search warrant in hand. Lee lived in a studio apartment above a garage on a side street in Burbank. All the buildings in the neighborhood were beige, with speckled concrete exteriors. Jenkins pounded on the door and announced.

"LAPD. Search warrant. Open up."

If it surprised Lee to see the detectives, he didn't show it when he opened the door. He greeted the detectives with the same heavy-lidded eyes and hangdog expression that Jenkins remembered from the first interview at the PAB.

Lee's apartment was like most bachelor pads the detectives had seen. Not much thought had been given to the interior decor except for the strategic placement of the large flat screen television that dominated the wall in front of the sofa.

After Jenkins patted Lee down and put him on the sofa with an order not to get up, he joined Drew and Li in the search of the apartment. Ross told Lee the warrant also covered his pickup truck. After picking up the keys from a table beside the front door, Ross went downstairs to the driveway to search the truck.

During the first few minutes of the search, the detectives found two thousand dollars, two shotguns, and two pistols. When Drew asked

Lee about it, he said he just cashed his paycheck. The guns he explained belonged to his father, a gun collector and gunsmith.

After two hours of combing through the small apartment, Drew was ready to call it, but then Ross came upstairs and pulled him aside.

"When I searched Earl's truck, I found this antique pistol." It was a Mauser nine millimeter. The weapon intrigued Drew. The gun used in the murder wasn't a Mauser, but was an antique. Ross handed Drew the ejected magazine and Drew examined the base of the top cartridge. It was a Federal factory loaded nine millimeter cartridge, the same ammunition SID had recovered with the Walther.

"And look what I found at the bottom of the cup holder." Ross unfolded a sheet of paper containing a handwritten list of items. Two shovels, 25-auto, get blank gun ready, old rugs, black duct tape, Drano, pool acid, lye.

"Holy shit," Drew said.

Ross agreed. "Quite a list, isn't it?"

"Looks like someone planned to get rid of a body," Drew said.

After the detectives finished the search, Drew handed Lee a copy of the warrant.

"Am I under arrest?"

"No. Not yet," Drew said. "But don't leave Los Angeles County. If you do, we'll get a warrant, find you, and put you in jail."

The detectives then left the apartment with the items they had collected.

·········

The next morning, one week after the murder of Connie Lynn Manley, the lawyer who had accompanied Lee to the first interview and still represented him, phoned Drew and tried to explain it all away. He said most of the items on the list had been intended for maintenance at Lake's house, where Lee still worked as a handyman. The pool acid and lye had been for cleaning the pool. And the 25-auto referenced a 25,000-mile oil change for Lee's truck that had been due. Drew didn't buy any of it. There was still a lot of legwork to do, but Drew believed he had evidence connecting Lee to Manley's murder.

Howard Drew knew all about the "48 Hour Rule" in homicide investigations. Experts commonly believed that the first 48 hours were the most critical part of any murder investigation. Some believed a homicide became fifty percent harder to solve after the first 48, and with each passing day thereafter, the likelihood of solving it diminished even further. Drew felt depressed over the slow progress of the case, but there was nothing he could do about it. They were still waiting on the results of the GSR tests from the LAPD lab that shared the same building as the county lab at Cal State L.A., and it would be several days before his team got their hands on the phone records they had sought with search warrants. That's why he focused now on Earl Lee. By arresting Lee on a conspiracy to commit murder charge, they might turn him and get something on Lake that could make the difference. Because of the close relationship between Lee and Lake, Drew felt sure Earl could tell them plenty about Manley's murder if they could pry it out of him. He made a mental note to call Scott Kelly to discuss arresting and charging Lee.

Drew was alone in the squad room. Li had left on a coffee run. Jenkins and Ross had gone to the firearms analysis unit to drop off the ammunition they had found with the Mauser during the search of Lee's apartment. Then they would go to Pasadena to interview Manley's brother, Dean. Dean Manley had called the previous afternoon to ask about progress on his sister's case. He had told Drew he was in L.A. from Mexico since the family expected the coroner's office to release his sister's body and that he wanted to be on hand to help his sister Regina with the arrangements for sending Connie Lynn back to Arkansas for burial.

Drew picked up the copy of the Times he'd bought to work with him. The above-the-fold story he read on the front page incensed him. Patrick Oberlin had given the reporter another interview, and the story was a hit-job on one of Drew's key witnesses, Grayson Cohen. Oberlin, after revealing to the reporter that Cohen had gone to the LAPD with an outrageous story about Lake soliciting him to kill his wife, gave the reporter background information about Cohen. Oberlin had told the reporter his private investigator had learned that Grayson had a long history of drug abuse, to include cocaine and methamphetamine. The reporter quoted Oberlin as saying that Cohen had once believed the police were tunneling beneath his house, that the federal government had bugged his house, and that his drug-fueled hallucinations had led to Cohen's confinement for seventeen days in the psych ward of a Glendale hospital. The story concluded with Oberlin's assertion that his client was innocent, that there was no evidence, direct or circumstantial, that William Lake had shot his wife, and with an attack on the LAPD. "They thought they had the killer on the first night, and they have never looked further."

Oberlin was already trying the case in the press by attacking the credibility of an LAPD key witness. And Drew expected this had been only the beginning. Even more troubling was media relations hadn't revealed Cohen's name or anything about his statements to the press. That meant only one thing. There was a leaker inside the department. Someone had leaked confidential police information to Oberlin, and he had fed it to the press. Drew trusted everyone on his team, and he now trusted Moreno. He didn't believe they had leaked anything. He still wasn't sure about Mann. One thing he knew was the leaker was likely high in the LAPD food chain. Now that the department files were computerized, anyone with sufficient credentials could access any file in the department's database. This leak had the name of one person all over it, that of Deputy Chief LaChasse.

Drew's phone rang. Still fuming over the newspaper article, he answered.

"Detective Drew," he growled.

"Oh, my, did someone wake up cranky this morning?" a female voice asked.

The voice sounded familiar, and then Drew realized who was on the phone. It was Nina Garraway, the pathologist.

"Oh, sorry," Drew said. "How are you, Doctor Garraway?"

"Well, I'm fine, Detective Drew," Garraway said with a chuckle. "Must we be so formal? Call me Nina, please."

"Okay, sure. What can I do for you... Nina?"

"You haven't called, so I thought I'd make the first move. I'm making spaghetti this evening, and it's always too much for one person. I wondered if I might entice you to come over for dinner this evening?"

Drew thought about it. He'd been so busy he had forgotten all about Garraway's invitation to call her that day at the autopsy. He couldn't think of a good reason to say no, and maybe it would be just the break he needed from thinking about the case every waking hour.

"Uh, sure. That would be great. Can I bring anything?"

"No, I've got it covered," Garraway said. "I've even got a nice bottle of Sangiovese I've been dying to share with someone."

"Okay, what time?"

"Seven o'clock?"

"That's fine," Drew said.

Garraway gave Drew her address.

"See you at seven then," she said.

"I'm looking forward to it," Drew said.

They said goodbye and hung up.

"Who was that?" Li said, putting a cup of coffee on Drew's desk before sitting down in her chair.

"Uh... Doctor Garraway."

"Ah, the cute blonde pathologist," Li said. "I've been meaning to ask if you had called her."

"No, I hadn't got around to it."

"Hm. The toxicology results came back?"

"No... well, I don't know. She didn't mention it."

"Then what did she want?"

"She invited me to dinner."

"Oh, my, that sounds exciting. And kudos to her for making the first move. She must have realized you never would."

Thirty-Five

AFTER STOPPING FOR LUNCH, Jenkins and Ross arrived to interview Manley's brother Dean in his room at a Best Western motel off a bustling stretch of Colorado Boulevard in east Pasadena. Dean Manley told the detectives he lived in Mexico with his boyfriend, and had recently arrived in Los Angeles after his sister Regina had called and told him the coroner's office planned to release the body of their sister, Connie Lynn.

"We wanted to arrange transportation for Connie Lynn back to Little Rock for burial," Dean said. "But he is fighting us over it. Lake insists on burying her here in Los Angeles."

"That's tough," Jenkins said. "I hope it works out for you."

Dean, who was thirty-seven, wore a shirt with an NYPD logo on it and answered the door barefoot. He was about five feet eight, chubby, and unshaven. He told the detectives he used to pave roads for a living, but now, after a work injury, he lived on disability.

"Connie Lynn had some problems," Dean admitted. "But she was a good person, and I loved her. She didn't deserve to die that way."

"No one does," Jenkins said sympathetically. "Was she having a problem with anyone?"

"Only him," Dean said with disdain.

"How long had the problem been going on?"

"Since day one. He's a snake, in my opinion. I warned Connie Lynn to get away from him before she got hurt. But she wouldn't listen."

After Dean related a story about the first time he met Lake, Jenkins asked, "With the Internet business, was there ever anyone your sister mentioned who was trying to get even, or had threatened her?"

"No one she had met online even knew she was out here," Dean said.

"Do you have any sense her ex-husband, Paul Hudson, had any motive to kill her?"

"He's pussy-whipped," Dean said bluntly, sounding disgusted. "And he's never even been out here. I'm not sure he could even find Los Angeles."

"No one ever stalked her? No one, to your knowledge, ever tried to hurt her or threaten her?"

"No."

"Did she ever tell anyone outside the family that she was coming out here to live?"

"No. He did it, Detectives. William Lake murdered my sister. If you're looking at anyone else, you're only wasting your time."

After Dean told the detectives about Connie Lynn telling him on the phone that Lake had told her he had a bullet with her name on it, Jenkins and Ross offered their condolences and thanked him for his time. They promised to call the family if there was a break in the investigation, and then they left the motel room for their car and drove back downtown.

· · · · ● · ● · · ·

After reading the morning paper himself, Lieutenant Moreno had summoned Drew to his office.

"Any idea who leaked to Oberlin?" Moreno asked. "Was it one of your detectives?"

"No way, Lieutenant. I'll vouch for everyone on my team. They are all good cops and solid investigators. We all want to put Lake in jail so bad we can taste it. Besides, what motive would any of them have?"

"Well, there is a leak somewhere. That's the only way Oberlin could have got Cohen's name and details about what he told us."

"I agree," Drew said. "It wasn't me, anyone on my team, and I know it wasn't you, Lieutenant. We may have got off to a rough start, but I've learned I can trust you and I know you want the same thing I do. I think it was someone higher up the chain."

"Are you accusing someone, Detective?"

"No, sir. I have no proof. But I have my suspicions."

"Suspicions about who?"

"Remember when I talked to you about Deputy Chief LaChasse that time? Well, he confronted me again since we talked about that. He as good as told me he wants this case to turn into another O. J. disaster."

Moreno leaned back in his chair and rubbed his face with both hands. Then he looked back at Drew.

"Care to explain why a member of the command staff would want to see a killer go free, Drew?"

"I know why the deputy chief wants it," Drew said without backing down. "He told me. He believes if we don't get a conviction in another high-profile case destined to become a media spectacle, the LAPD will get embarrassed again, and the city council will push Chief Sandoval out in favor of new leadership. And Deputy Chief LaChasse believes he is the odds-on favorite to get the chief's job."

"He told you that?" Moreno asked incredulously.

"Yes, sir, and I'm not exaggerating."

"Okay, Drew. Listen to me. This is way above your pay grade. Stay out of it and I'll try to get to the bottom of it. And I don't want you starting any rumors. Understand?"

"Don't worry, Lieutenant. I'm doing my best to stay out of the deputy chief's way. He confronted me both times. I didn't go looking for him."

· · · · • • • • · ·

After leaving Moreno's office, Drew and Li headed to UCLA Medical Center to follow up on a call to the tip line. A doctor had called in stating he had been at Spirito's the night of the murder and had observed William Lake briefly at the murder scene, behaving strangely. After they arrived and Li found parking, the detectives walked in to the ER to find the doctor.

After a nurse paged him, a doctor in green scrubs met the detectives at the desk and introduced himself as Andrew Strickland. He then escorted the detectives back to a vacant treatment room to talk.

"You mentioned when you called you were at Spirito's last Friday evening when the incident occurred there," Drew said. "What did you want to tell us?"

"Yes, I took a date to the restaurant that evening," Strickland said. "I didn't know at the time a man I saw outside the restaurant was William Lake. I guess I've never seen his movies or reruns of his television program. But I saw him banging on a door and shouting, 'She's bleeding. Help. Call 911.' Because I found his behavior peculiar, I hesitated to approach at first."

"Where were you at the time, Doctor Strickland?"

"My date and I had just finished dinner and were walking back to the car. I'd parked on the street across from the parking lot at the restaurant. And when I heard the commotion, we stood beside the car and watched for a while. I thought maybe someone badly hurt might need a doctor."

"What else did you see?"

"Another gentleman came out of the house where Mr. Lake had banged on the door and they ran over to a car parked across the street diagonally from the house. The man from the house opened the front passenger door and Mr. Lake stood there for a moment. Then I saw him vomiting. He turned away and started walking toward the restaurant. I intended to ask him if he needed medical attention when he got to where I was standing. But suddenly, he stopped and walked back towards the car."

"So, he never made it to the restaurant?"

"No, he turned around about halfway there. I think he spoke to the man leaning inside the car briefly, then he walked over and sat down on the curb. When the paramedics arrived, I thought it was probably safe to approach to see if they needed a doctor. So, I asked my date to wait in the car, and walked toward the car Mr. Lake was sitting beside. The other man sat down beside him on the curb and seemed to console him. I heard Mr. Lake asking him repeatedly. 'What's wrong with her?' Two things struck me as odd about his behavior, even before I knew what had happened."

"What was that?"

"First, he was sitting off at some distance away from the car. At least fifteen feet. Things were going on with her and he seemed distraught. But he didn't show any interest in what was happening with her. I just thought his words, 'What's wrong with her?' seemed unusual given the circumstances."

"In what way?"

"Here in the emergency room, it's usually very hard to keep families away. I've had family members try to force their way into treatment rooms here many times. So, that's what I found so odd about his behavior. He did not involve himself at all and showed no interest in what was going on with her throughout the entire time. I just felt something wasn't right, that it seemed strange. I thought that from the time he first called for help. From my experience as an emergency room physician, I hear people calling for help all the time. I know what that sounds like. And with Mr. Lake, it just didn't sound... genuine."

"You mean like he was only acting?"

"Exactly. It didn't sound like genuine cries for help at all."

"Did you ever make it down to the car?"

"No. A police car arrived right behind the paramedics. A crowd was gathering, people from the houses in the neighborhood. And before I got there, the police officer was already asking people to stay back. From what I could tell, the paramedics had things under control and quickly they put the woman on a gurney and inside the ambulance for transport."

Drew felt the doctor's story could prove important at trial. Strickland was the second witness to question Lake's behavior that night. And because seeing grief-stricken family members and spouses perhaps every day as an emergency room doctor, his opinion would impress a jury.

"I should have called sooner," Strickland said apologetically. "But this place keeps me so busy, I just kind of unplug when I have time off. I hadn't followed the story at all. But this morning, I read an article in the paper during breakfast about what happened that night. I hadn't even known the woman had died. Then, when I saw the photo of William Lake that accompanied the article, I realized the man I saw was Mr. Lake and the story was about the incident I witnessed last Friday evening. So, I felt I should call you."

"We appreciate it, Doctor," Drew said. "You're the second person who has told us they found Mr. Lake's behavior that night very odd."

Thirty-Six

Drew envied Nina Garraway her morning commute. She lived on Mercury Avenue in Montecito Heights, a family friendly community situated only about five miles from downtown Los Angeles with some of the best views available in the city. He suspected her commute to and from her office on North Mission Road never exceeded ten minutes, even during rush hour. The Ernest E. Debs Regional Park and nature preserve next to Montecito Heights offered miles of hiking and biking trails and picnic areas, making the neighborhood ideal for outdoor lovers.

Garraway's house was a multi-level affair on a hillside with a white stucco exterior and a red tile roof. The lower level was a garage with the living quarters at the top. Drew found parking on the street and climbed one long flight of dark gray painted steps that matched the color of the wooden trim on the exterior. Then he made a right turn at the landing and took another shorter flight of steps to the porch. He rang the bell and Nina greeted him at the door with a kiss on the cheek and then grabbed his arm and escorted him inside.

"Pour yourself a glass of wine and make yourself at home," Nina said, gesturing to an open bottle already open on the bar separating the kitchen from the living room. "I'm at a critical stage putting things together in the kitchen."

As Nina hurried back to the kitchen, Drew poured a glass of wine and sat down on a stool at the bar to watch. Jazz music played softly from a stereo and it surprised Drew he recognized the artist. It was Norah Jones. He was more a fan of country than jazz, but he'd heard Norah Jones before and enjoyed her music.

"How is your case going?" Nina asked.

"It's coming along," Drew said. "But we still have a way to go."

"I'm sorry," Nina said. "Work is probably the last thing you want to talk about, and I promise not to tell you about the body I dissected today. Well, at least not until after dinner." She finished with a laugh, and Drew realized he liked the sound of it.

"Yeah, I don't really want to talk shop," he said. "I love your house. How long have you lived here?"

"Oh, let's see. I bought this place after my divorce, so a little over five years."

"Kids?"

Nina laughed again. "No, we talked about it, but we never got there. Jack, my ex-husband, and I attended medical school together. Then we got married after graduation. But I guess the stress of both of us in residency was too much. We drifted apart and divorced about a year after we finished."

"Sorry to hear that."

"It's fine. We parted amicably and we've remained friends, believe it or not. He remarried and he and his wife have two kids."

Drew got up and walked over to a faux-fireplace and looked at the framed photographs arranged on the mantel.

"Looks like you've traveled a lot," he said. He recognized the Sydney Opera House in the background of one photo with Nina standing arm and arm with a guy. And in another Nina and two other attractive women were standing in front of the Sagrada Familia, the famous unfinished cathedral in Barcelona, Spain. There were photos of Nina taken on Waikiki Beach and another with the ancient Colosseum in Rome looming behind her.

"Yes, I love to travel, and I've done quite a bit. You?"

"Yes, I've traveled some. I see we've been to some of the same places."

"Have we?"

"Yes. Australia, Europe, Hawaii."

"That's Jack in the one taken in front of the Sydney Opera House."

"Good looking guy."

"That was taken before the divorce," Nina added hastily.

It looked to Drew she was making traditional spaghetti, given the smell of the tomatoes and spices.

"Smells good."

"Thank you. I hope you like it. It's a Spaghetti Bolognese recipe I picked up during a vacation in Italy."

"You enjoy cooking?"

"Love it. But sometimes I wish I had a bigger kitchen. This one is compact. It's a small house, just under eight-hundred square feet. But it's open and airy and more than enough room for me."

"It seems bigger than that," Drew said, looking around. "Two bedrooms?"

"Yes, and two baths. The laundry room is below the porch. You probably noticed the door coming up. And I have a nice sized garage."

As Nina continued working at the stove, stirring a pot of sauce with a wooden spoon. Drew walked up behind her and put his hands on her shoulders. She offered no resistance and her muscles felt relaxed.

"Smells even better when you get closer," he said.

Nina chuckled. "Does it?"

"Your glass is empty. Want me to pour you more wine?"

"Yes, please."

Drew retrieved the bottle from the counter and refilled her glass. Nina picked it up with her free hand, turned and clicked it off the side of his and took a sip.

"What are we toasting?" he asked.

"New acquaintances?"

Drew smiled. "To new acquaintances," he said, taking a sip of wine. "This is good."

"Yes, another discovery from my travels," she said. "I usually have Zinfandel with traditional spaghetti, but thought I'd try something new."

Nina removed the pot from the burner. Then she turned, put her arms around his neck and kissed him, this time on the lips.

"Almost ready," she said with a wide smile. Pulling away and turning back to the stove, she dumped a pot of cooked linguine into a strainer in the sink.

"Anything I can do?" Drew asked.

"There's a salad in the frig if you want to put it on the table. The dining room is back there behind the kitchen. I'll plate the spaghetti and take the bread out of the oven."

Drew opened the refrigerator and grabbed the salad bowl and a bottle of Italian salad dressing from the shelf beside it. He carried it through the door into the dining room and set it on the table. Nina breezed in and put a plate of spaghetti pasta topped with a rich, thick sauce on the table at the two place settings. Then she went back to the kitchen and returned moments later with a plate of sliced hot bread and a small bowl of grated fresh Parmesan cheese. Drew stepped past her and picked up the wine bottle and their glasses.

"Sit and let's eat," Nina said with a grin.

They enjoyed dinner. The food was delicious and the natural flow of conversation pleasantly surprised Drew. There was none of the awkwardness that often went with spending time with someone for the first time. Even the moments of silence felt comfortable. He enjoyed Nina Garraway's company and was already hoping they would spend more time together by the time they finished eating. He helped her clear the table and while she put away the leftovers, Drew rinsed the dishes, pots, and utensils and put them inside the dishwasher. After they had cleaned up, Nina opened another bottle of wine, Pinot Noir, a light-bodied red wine. And they retired to the living room sofa and talked for a while longer. Later on, Nina leaned over and kissed him deeply, and then took Drew's hand. She stood up, pulled him up from the couch, and led him into the bedroom.

After they made love, Nina lay on her back, head propped on a pillow. Beneath the sheet, Drew put his arm across her and pulled her tightly to him. She looked at him, smiling, with her eyes roaming back and forth as if searching his face.

"Well, I guess I should get going," Drew said.

Nina sat up, the sheet falling away from her breasts. She folded her arms across them.

"Oh, you're the love them and leave them type, huh?"

"What? No... I just thought... well... I didn't know..."

"If you were welcome to spend the night?"

"Yeah, that."

Nina grinned. "Well, you are. I spent a lot of effort getting you here and I'm not letting you off that easily, Detective."

Drew smiled back. "Okay, if you insist. You're the doctor."

Thirty-Seven

THEY HAD BUILT MOMENTUM with the case early on, but two weeks later, the investigation had stalled. The detectives were still waiting on the GSR test results from the lab and the records on the burner phones from Verizon. They had received the phone records on Lee's phone and the GPS data showed the phone was in L. A. on the evening of the Manley murder. He might claim he'd left the phone at home when he had gone to San Mateo, but Lee had made several calls with the phone. One had gone to a pizza restaurant the Thursday evening before Manley's death. Jenkins and Ross had followed it up and the delivery driver recalled delivering a pizza to Lee's apartment. He had delivered there before and knew Lee. He had told Jenkins and Ross he had delivered the pizza to Lee and remembered because Lee hadn't tipped him. That made it unlikely Lee had left the city at all since he'd told the police he'd been in the San Francisco area several days before someone killed Manley, and hadn't returned until the following Sunday.

Connie Lynn Manley's lifelong pursuit of fame ended at a Hollywood cemetery on a warm, clear Los Angeles morning. The service lasted only fifteen minutes. The funeral took place exactly three weeks after Manley's murder. Her family had wanted to bury her in Arkansas, but William Lake fought them. He said he wanted his daughter to have the chance to visit her mother's grave while growing up. As Manley's husband, the law came down on Lake's side of the contentious issue. Connie Lynn's family refused to attend the funeral. Her sister Regina told the press that she wouldn't stand at her sister's gravesite beside the man who had murdered her.

As Drew and Li stood and watched from a respectful distance, Lake was the first to arrive. He stepped out of the dark limousine provided by the funeral home carrying his and Connie's baby daughter. He wore a navy suit and striped tie and sported freshly dyed black hair, collar length and styled high in the front. The wind blew it back as he strode across the plush green lawn to the gravesite. He glanced at the detectives and scowled as if to say, "I'm not going down." Drew recalled seeing those words scrawled on a bathroom mirror when they had searched Lake's house.

About a dozen people joined Lake under a green canopy. His adult children, a few of his friends, his lawyer, and the priest. Like Drew and Li, none of them had known Connie when she was alive. Everyone stood quietly. Eerily, there was almost no sound. Just the soft clicks made by news photographers snapping photographs with their digital cameras as the pallbearers carried her polished rosewood casket with brass fittings and a large spray of white roses on top of it to Connie Lynn Manley's last resting place.

A Catholic priest began the service. He spoke a few general words about Connie and quoted the standard scripture verses so often heard at funerals about the inevitability of death and the promises of an afterlife. When the priest finished, Lake handed Holly to his adult daughter, Miranda. He placed a hand on Connie's casket. Then he spoke.

"It's because of Connie that Holly was born. It was her will, her conviction. Not mine. It was her dedication that brought Holly into this world. And for that, I thank God. And I thank Connie."

When he finished, Lake sat down on a white folding chair, and the priest recited The Lord's Prayer and that ended the service. The mourners headed back to their cars. Lake remained at the gravesite alone. He watched as the cemetery workers lowered the casket into the ground, gently depositing Connie in her final resting place.

It wasn't an unpleasant view, the detectives thought. The Hollywood hills in the distance, and just below the cemetery, the Warner Brothers' lot. They couldn't help thinking that Connie Lynn would have approved, spending eternity in the company of many Hollywood greats. Betty Davis, Lucille Ball, Buster Keaton, and Liberace all rested nearby.

When Lake returned to the car and the limousine drove away, Drew and Li walked to the gravesite and stared at the headstone. Below an inscription, they read: "Connie Lynn Manley Lake."

"I guess she finally got what she wanted," Li said.

"Yeah, but maybe she never expected dying was part of the deal," Drew said.

"I don't know about that," Li said. "Everyone she knew and had talked with about Lake all warned her she would get hurt if she stayed with him. I think maybe she wanted fame so much that she was willing to die for it if necessary."

"Well, if that's true, it's all very sad."

"Her entire life was very sad, Howie."

"Maybe, but Lake treated her like a zero. And nobody is a zero. I can't wait for the day when we arrest and book him for murder. Watching him today, playing the role of the loving, grieving husband, made me sick. He didn't shed a single tear. His demeanor looked more like relief than grief."

"You can't make this personal, Howie."

"I already have. I take the murder of every victim personally. Everybody counts, and every victim deserves justice. And I intend for Connie Lynn Manley to get justice. Whatever it takes."

The detectives turned and walked across the lawn to their city ride.

After leaving the cemetery, Drew and Li drove to the Los Angeles County Criminal Courts Building. The county had renamed it the Clara Shortridge Foltz Criminal Justice Center, but every cop at the LAPD still called it the CCB. They took the elevator, after the obligatory ten-minute wait the elevators in the building were infamous for, up to the district attorney's office. After checking in, Scott Kelly came out and escorted them back to his office, where the detectives found Cheryl Wheeler waiting. She stood and shook hands with the detectives.

"Cheryl wanted to sit in," Kelly explained. "She will prosecute the case."

"I know you're here to talk to Scott about arresting and charging Earl Lee," Wheeler said. "But I wanted to discuss William Lake while you were here. To see where we are."

The rumor Kelly had shared with Drew had been true. Cheryl Wheeler had the job of prosecuting Lee and Lake. As long as they could make the case. Drew handed the charging packet to Kelly, the filing deputy. While he reviewed the documents, Wheeler and the detectives discussed William Lake.

"Tell me why you think Lake did it?" Wheeler said.

"He wanted the kid for his daughter," Drew said. "She's in her thirties, wants kids, and can't conceive. And maybe he truly believed the victim was an unfit mother and the kid would be better off without her influence. The bottom line was Lake thinks he's streetwise, and he was angry because a two-bit Arkansas grifter conned him. She tricked him into marrying her with the pregnancy, but no way he intended to spend the rest of his life with her. He wanted her gone. Permanently."

"Take me through your theory of the event."

"Simple," Drew said. "He leaves her in the car after telling her he left his gun in the restaurant. He brought the Walther with him and had it on him the entire time, or else had stashed it nearby earlier. Either way, instead of going back to the restaurant as he claimed, he walked up to the car on the passenger side after leaving the electric windows down and taking the keys. Then he popped her through the window, coated the Walther with motor oil to eliminate fingerprints, and then tossed it into the construction dumpster."

"You don't believe Earl Lee shot her?"

"No, based on the story that the victim told her sister Regina about the trip to Sequoia National Park. I think Lake asked Lee to kill her then, but he couldn't pull the trigger and even got physically ill. He claimed it was altitude sickness, which doesn't stack. People don't get altitude sickness at only six-thousand feet. It was nerves. He couldn't do it, and according to the victim's story, Lake told him not to worry. He'd get someone else to do it."

"Then maybe Lake finally found an actual hit man to do it. He hired them and they shot Manley and dumped the gun in the dumpster."

"That's kind of too Hollywood," Drew said.

"This is Hollywood," Wheeler retorted.

Everyone laughed.

Then Drew shook his head and turned serious. "A pro wouldn't have dumped the gun in the dumpster."

"Why not?"

"I've worked on a lot of murders and studied many more. I've never seen or heard of a contract killer dumping a gun at the scene. Besides, a pro would have used their own gun, not an antique pistol provided by Lake. And we can put the gun near him at his house, albeit through Earl Lee, even if we can't put it in his hand the night of the murder. And he bought it."

"That's another issue," Wheeler said. "Patrick Oberlin has been destroying the credibility of our three key witnesses in the press for weeks. He's painted them all as longtime abusers of illegal narcotics, hard drugs, who have all suffered from drug-induced mental problems. While I believe I can rehabilitate Roy Cooper and Ronald Saunders at trial, I'm less sure about Grayson Cohen. I'm uncertain a jury will find him credible once Oberlin takes him apart on the stand. And he was the first to come forward and led you to the other two men."

Drew shrugged. "We have three guys who all tell the same story. And Roy Cooper ties it all together. When we get the records from those burner phones, his testimony will be even stronger. And with Cohen, it all depends on how he does on the stand. He might survive Oberlin's cross. Yeah, he's shaky, but I'm not ready to write him off as a total loss."

"Let's review your evidence to date," Wheeler said.

Drew, with Li's help, spent thirty minutes presenting everything in their file.

"And we're only waiting on the GSR test results and the burner phone records," Drew said. "We expect those to drop any day now."

"I went directly to the TAU," Wheeler said. "I called them this morning. The test on Lake's hands was positive for particles of gunshot residue. It was a small amount, but if he washed his hands like the North Hollywood detectives told you, we would expect that. And the lab found trace amounts of gunshot residue on the shirt Lake wore that night. Anyway, a lab supervisor told me you'll get the written report on Monday."

"That's good then, right?" Li asked.

"It helps," Wheeler said. "But Keith Oberlin is a smart criminal defense attorney. He'll ask to have his own lab test fire the murder weapon. Then he will bring in his own firearm expert witness who will tell the jury the LAPD lab should have found far more gunshot residue than they did. Then he'll spin the many other ways small amounts of gunshot residue could have got on his client's hands and shirt and try to explain it all away."

Drew nodded. He'd seen other smart criminal defense attorneys do that before.

"Are you expecting to find a silver bullet soon you haven't mentioned?" Wheeler asked.

"No. Beyond the burner phone records, we have nothing else on the horizon as far as I can see. I wish we had more physical evidence, but we don't and I don't expect to get any. That's why I want to arrest Earl Lee and put him in jail. Hopefully, we can turn him and get him to snitch on Lake to save himself. And we have a mountain of circumstantial evidence."

Wheeler nodded. "Getting Earl Lee to turn isn't a sure thing, but I'm willing to make a deal with him if he can give us something that hurts Lake. And there is a lot of circumstantial evidence. I don't think even Keith Oberlin can explain it all away."

"So, where do you think we are, counselor?" Drew asked.

"I have high confidence we will get a solicitation conviction," Wheeler said. "He tried to hire three different men to kill his wife. Four if you count Earl Lee, although we can't prove that one unless Lee talks. But I'm less confident of getting a conviction on the murder charge."

Drew felt deflated. He trusted Wheeler's judgement, but if it were his decision, he would at least try.

"That said, with the right jury, it isn't impossible," Wheeler said.

Drew brightened.

"We have two options. Wait and hope you turn up something we don't know about now, or that Lake gets stupid and brags to someone he did it and they come forward. Or we arrest and charge him, go forward, and do the best we can with what we have to work with."

Drew nodded expectantly.

"I'll recommend going forward to the district attorney, but he'll make the call. If he agrees to go forward, then we'll arrest William Lake on Monday and charge him."

Drew smiled.

"And as far as Earl Lee, you've got solid probable cause," Kelly said. "You have a witness that puts the murder weapon on him. That's probable cause on its own. I'll file the conspiracy charge today and get a warrant for his arrest. I'll have it by the end of the day. When do you want to do it?"

"Tomorrow morning," Drew said without hesitation. "That gives us the weekend to work on him and see if he will make a deal and give us something useful. Then, if the district attorney accepts Ms. Wheeler's recommendation, we'll be ready to arrest Lake on Monday."

Wheeler looked at Drew. "We'll probably be spending the better part of the next year together, Detective. So, we might as well get on a first name basis. You can call me Cheryl."

"Howard," Drew said with a grin, reaching out and shaking hands with Wheeler again.

"Or Howie," Li said. "Drew likes his friends to call him Howie."

Everyone laughed.

The two-hour meeting ended. Wheeler left to confer with her boss. Kelly walked Drew and Li out and they left for the PAB to close out their day. Both hoped they could finish with Earl Lee on Saturday and maybe take their first Sunday off and relax for the first time in almost a month.

Thirty-Eight

BACK AT THE OPEN-UNSOLVED squad room, Drew shared the news from the meeting with the prosecutors to Jenkins and Ross.

"We should have the warrant ready to go by the end of the day," he concluded. "We'll arrest Earl Lee tomorrow morning and bring him here for questioning before we book him into Men's Central."

Jenkins and Ross nodded, happy that they would finally make an arrest in the case. They hoped the district attorney would accept the recommendation of Cheryl Wheeler so they could arrest Lake on Monday, after the weekend.

"We were watching the television news while you were gone," Jenkins told Drew. "It's amusing how inaccurate the news reports are. I saw one reporter who said the LAPD is replacing the entire Lake investigation team."

Ross said, "I saw another one last night who said some crimes never get solved and this will be one of them."

Drew nodded.

"After we arrest Earl Lee and, hopefully, Lake, we need to sift through the stacks of emails sent to Manley again to ensure we haven't missed a threat," he said. "I predict right now that Oberlin's strategy will be a third-party culpability defense. He will try to make us all look like incompetent assholes who never gave a serious look at anyone but Lake. He will borrow a page from the O. J. playbook and try to convince the jury we engaged in a vendetta against his client. We need to show we looked seriously at other suspects."

"Is there anyone else we need to interview right now?" Jenkins asked.

"One person. On the way back from the CCB, it occurred to me we should find that woman who posed as the nanny the day Lake sent that private investigator to Manley's hotel and duped her into returning to Arkansas without the baby. We need a sense of her role in that drama."

"Depending on what she tells us, that could produce a kidnapping charge," Li said. "That's another motive right there. Lake wanted to keep her from making a kidnapping complaint."

"Ross and I could handle it on Monday, depending on how things shake out with Lake," Jenkins offered.

Drew nodded his agreement. "We've almost reached the finish line. I'm going over to Homicide Special to update Moreno. If he has no objections, I'm planning for us to take care of business with Earl Lee tomorrow and then take Sunday off for a change. And we can all check out at the usual time this afternoon."

"I'd sure appreciate getting Sunday off," Jenkins said. "My golf game has really suffered since we started this case. I haven't played a round in nearly a month."

The team meeting concluded, Jenkins and Ross went back to work on the emails, and Li updated the murder book while Drew went to brief the lieutenant.

·········

"Hard to believe we can see light at the end of the tunnel on this," Moreno said, after Drew brought him up to date on the meeting with the deputy district attorneys. "I only hope we have all our ducks in a row."

"I think we have everything there is for us to get," Drew said. "Other than interviewing the fake nanny and sifting through the emails sent to Manley one last time, I can't think of anything we've missed."

Moreno nodded. "Yes, I agree. I guess it's time to turn it over to the prosecutors."

"I'd like to give the team Sunday off if that's okay with you, Lieutenant."

"As long as you feel you've done all you can do with Earl Lee after you arrest him tomorrow, I have no problem with it."

"They will appreciate it. Jenkins says his golf game is suffering."

Moreno laughed, then he said, "We need to discuss what comes next, assuming the district attorney green lights arresting Lake on Monday."

"Okay," Drew said.

"As you know, the department is shutting down Open-Unsolved at the end of the month when Ed Howard retires. Actually, they are cutting it back, not shutting it down entirely. The chief will leave one detective in charge, since some things will require a sworn police officer. That person will supervise volunteers that the chief plans to recruit to work on cold cases. Retired detectives and other civilians with research skills applicable to the job. Because you and Li have the best closure rate in Open-Unsolved, he wants one of you to take charge of the scaled down unit."

Drew nodded. "What happens to the rest of the detectives in the unit?"

"Most will go to the bureaus or a community police station. But Captain Mann asked me for recommendations to fill three vacancies in Homicide Special. I'm impressed with the work ethic of your team.

So, I'm going to recommend Jenkins, Ross, and either you or Li for the three vacancies, depending on which one of you takes the lead in Open-Unsolved."

Drew felt uneasy. He'd prefer to stay on at Homicide Special permanently. But he and Li had grown close working as partners and he didn't want the circumstances to provoke a rift in their relationship.

"I can choose who stays in Open-Unsolved and who comes to Homicide Special," Moreno said. "But I'd rather let you and Li work it out to avoid any hard feelings. If you can't agree, then I'll decide."

"I appreciate that," Drew said. "I'll talk it over with Amy. We've had a good working relationship and I think we can come to an agreement."

"Okay, Drew. Let me know when you do. The transfers will become effective the first of next month. You will all have to be available for the trial when it comes around, so having three of the four team members in Homicide Special will facilitate that. Of course, the three filling the vacancies here will go into the rotation, so you'll be working on other cases."

"Understood. If there's nothing else, I'll head back and talk things over with Amy Li after Jenkins and Ross leave for the day."

"Fine. I want you to talk with Detective Li, but don't mention any of this to Jenkins and Ross. I'll tell them after I've given my recommendations to the captain and we've made the final decisions."

·· • • • •• • • ··

When he returned to Open-Unsolved, Drew pulled Li aside and told her they had something to discuss in private. Then, after telling Jenkins and Ross the team was meeting at the unit at 6:00 A.M. the following morning to prep for the arrest of Earl Lee, he let them check out for the day a little early. After they left, Drew suggested to Li that they go downstairs and talk over coffee. They took the elevator down and then walked to a nearby coffee shop to put some distance between them and the PAB. Then, after they had their drinks, they sat down at a table and Drew related the details of his conversation with Lieutenant Moreno.

"This sucks, Howie," Li said. "Moreno is putting us against each other. We both want to stay at Homicide Special permanently. I'd like us to remain partners and we'd do great work there. Why can't they put Jenkins or Ross in the new Open-Unsolved position?"

"Moreno said the chief wants either you or me in the position," Drew said. "It seems non-negotiable."

"You've been a natural as the lead in this investigation," Li said finally. "If only one of us can go to Homicide Special, then I think you deserve the third vacancy. I'll stay in Open-Unsolved."

"You're every bit as good a detective as I am, Amy. Better in a lot of areas. You deserve a shot at Homicide Special as much as I do. And, the more I've thought about it, the more I think heading the scaled-down version of Open-Unsolved wouldn't be a bad gig. I've enjoyed working cold cases. And I'd answer directly to Mann, so I could pretty much set my agenda and choose the cases I wanted to work."

Li shook her head. "I know how much you've wanted to move up to Homicide Special. And if I feel dissatisfied with the new Open-Unsolved position, I could always put in for a transfer to a bureau squad. That would be harder for you to do, Howie, and we both know that. As long as Deputy Chief LaChasse is around, you've got a big target on your back."

"I'll tell you what, Amy. Let's both think about it over the weekend. Then we'll talk again on Monday and decide. I'd rather we work it out together than leave it to Moreno to make the call. I consider you not only a partner, but a friend, and I don't want that to change."

Li nodded. "Same here, partner. We'll discuss it again on Monday. I want to talk to Mandy about it, anyway. Now that we're married, I think she deserves to have input into the decision."

"Good enough," Drew said. "We'll revisit it on Monday, hopefully after we've arrested Lake and put him in jail."

Drew's cell phone rang. He pulled it out and looked at the screen. It read, "Unknown Caller," but his gut told him to answer the call. And when he did, he couldn't believe who the caller was.

Thirty-Nine

THE "UNKNOWN CALLER" ON the screen had put Drew on high alert once he heard the caller's voice.

"I almost didn't answer, Chief," Drew said to LaChasse. "I usually let 'Unknown Caller' calls go straight to voicemail."

"This is a confidential matter, Detective," LaChasse said. "Obviously, I don't have to explain myself to you and, beyond the previous statement, I won't."

"Okay, Chief," Drew said. "What can I do for you?"

"Are you available, Detective?"

"It's the end of watch, so I'm not working on anything," Drew said. "Available for what?"

"William Lake wants to talk with you, Detective."

"Then why did you call me, instead of Lake?"

"You have no reason to know this, Detective, but William Lake and I know each other well and he trusts me. He must talk to you because you're the lead investigator. But he doesn't trust you. He believes he is a victim of an all-out vendetta, chiefly orchestrated by you. He asked me to make this call, and I agreed."

"What does he want to talk about?"

"That I do not know, Detective. He didn't tell me. I didn't ask. While I don't believe he murdered his wife, maybe he wants to confess.

Or perhaps he has information he believes you can use to identify the actual killer."

"Okay, when and where does he want to meet and talk?" Drew asked. "I admit this intrigues me. And by happenstance, I'm here with my partner. We'll be happy to come to Lake wherever he wants."

"No, he will only meet and talk with you, Detective. No one else. Those are his terms and he's adamant. He is not even inviting his attorney to attend."

Drew sensed someone planned to spring a trap, and he wasn't falling for it.

"Chief, we both know I can't agree to do that. Regardless of what you believe, Lake is a murder suspect and policy states I cannot meet with a murder suspect without my partner."

"Well, Detective, it gratifies me you have learned something from your past misadventures. But I misspoke. Mr. Lake also wants me to be present during his conversation with you. He wants a witness. As I said, he doesn't trust you. He knows all about your checkered history with the department and fears you might fabricate an excuse to harm him. Since I'll be there as a witness, you will also technically have backup, so it will all be within policy."

Drew's mind raced. He knew there was some angle here, and that LaChasse expected him to trip over it. But he couldn't imagine what it was. When he said nothing immediately, LaChasse prompted him.

"Well, Detective? Are you willing to meet with Mr. Lake and hear his side of the story before you and the district attorney's office do something rash that they and the LAPD will long regret?"

That settled it. LaChasse and probably Lake already knew the district attorney was considering green-lighting Lake's arrest. How had they found out so quickly? It hadn't yet been an hour since he had told Moreno about the discussion with Wheeler and Kelly. But he knew

Moreno had probably updated Captain Mann. Maybe Mann was the source of the leaks. Still, the idea of finding out what Lake wanted to tell him intrigued him.

"Okay, Chief. I'll meet with him, and will come alone since you will be there. But if his attorney won't be present, I'll have to advise him of his rights and get him to sign a waiver before I'll talk with him."

"I'm certain Mr. Lake will agree to that, Detective. I'll explain it to him when we arrive."

"Fine. When and where?"

"At Mr. Lake's residence at eight o'clock this evening. Does that give you enough time?"

"Yes, no problem. I'll be there."

"I can't stress this enough, Detective. Come alone and I want none of the tricks you're infamous for. We're going to respect Mr. Lake's terms. I've given him my word, and I won't allow you to embarrass me. Understand?"

"I understand, Chief. We're on the same team. I'm comfortable meeting with him as long as you will be there."

"Very well. I'll meet you there at eight, Detective."

LaChasse abruptly hung up without waiting for a reply.

"Who was that, Howie? And what the hell is going on?"

"Looks like we're working late, partner," Drew said with a grin. "That was LaChasse. He just set up a meeting between us and Lake. Lake wants to talk."

"Us? You and me?"

"No, LaChasse made it clear I must come alone. He said those are Lake's terms, and he has given him his word that we'll respect his terms. LaChasse will be there as a witness."

"Are you insane, Howie? This is some kind of trap. You aren't seriously considering going, are you?"

"I am going," Drew said. "How could I turn down the opportunity to hear what Lake wants to say? But, no. I'm not going there alone. I'm sure it's a trap, but I can't imagine what the angle is. We'll go together, but I'll drop you off a block from the house. Then you can ninja around to the back of Lake's house and stage there while I meet with him and LaChasse. And I'm going to call Jenkins. I want him and Ross there also, staged a couple of blocks away in case things go sideways."

"Don't you think you should notify Lieutenant Moreno and get his approval?" Li asked.

"Yes, I have to notify him, but I'm going to hold off on that until we get to Studio City. That will give us time to allow things to develop before he shows up if he intends to come out."

"I guess that will work. There's no way I would let you go in there alone."

"They set the meeting for eight o'clock," Drew said. "So, we have plenty of time to make a plan. Here's how we will play it..."

Forty

LI DROVE THE UNMARKED car while Drew called Jenkins and then Ross. He told the detectives to meet him and Li at the convenience store a few blocks from Lake's residence where Lake had bought the burner phone. After disconnecting with Ross, he turned to Li.

"Can you record a telephone conversation with your phone?" he asked.

"Yes, it's easy if you have an Android phone, as I do," Li said. "You just activate the recording app, place a phone call, and then save the recording when you're finished. Why?"

"I want to record the meeting with Lake, and for you to hear what's going on inside the house. So, before I drop you off, activate the app and call my phone. I'll leave the call active and keep the phone in my pocket. I'm not sure how good the quality will be, but we'll get the meeting recorded and you can hear what's happening."

"A wire would have been better, but that will probably work as long as they don't ask to see your phone," Li said. "It's a quiet neighborhood. But I hope no emergency vehicle running code three comes through the area while you're inside. If that happens, you're screwed."

"I'll accept the risk."

Li pulled into the parking lot at the convenience store, shifted into park, and killed the headlights. She and Drew discussed various scenarios until Jenkins and Ross arrived about fifteen minutes later at 7:40 P.M. Ross had driven to Jenkins' house and they had come together in Jenkins' car. Jenkins drove up beside the unmarked car on the passenger side and Ross lowered his window. Drew explained the situation, giving them details he hadn't taken time to share when he had called and told them to meet him at the store.

"What do you think he wants to talk about?" Jenkins asked. "This is bizarre."

"Yeah, it's strange all right," Drew agreed. "Especially with LaChasse as part of the equation."

"You better loop Moreno in, Howie," Li said. "He may nix the entire idea."

"I'm still going through with it, no matter what Moreno says," Drew said. "As long as you guys will take the weight from backing me up."

"Hey, man, we're in," Jenkins said. "I won't be able to sleep if I don't find out what this is about."

"Yeah, Howie, I guess we'll all go down together if that's how it turns out," Li said. "You aren't going in there alone."

"Okay," Drew said. "Wait one."

He dialed Moreno's cell number. When the lieutenant answered, and Drew had explained his situation, Moreno wasn't entirely happy with the circumstances Howard had outlined. But like everyone else, he was curious about what LaChasse and William Lake were up to. So, reluctantly, he approved the plan.

"Where are Jenkins and Ross going to stage?" Moreno asked.

Drew gave him the cross streets where the detectives would wait two blocks from Lake's house.

"And Detective Li will have eyes on you from the back of the house?"

"That's the plan," Drew said. "If possible, I'll insist we stay in a part of the house where she can see us from a window." Then Drew explained their makeshift audio arrangement.

"Okay, I'm on the way. I'll link up with Jenkins and Ross and we'll wait for you or Li to call when you need us at the house. Listen, Drew. Be careful. You don't know what you're walking into."

"Don't worry, Lieutenant. I plan to be very careful."

···•••••···

At 7:55 P.M., after they had set up the phones and Li had got out of the car, he pulled to the curb in front of Lake's residence and parked. He found it strange that LaChasse's car wasn't there. He wondered if the deputy chief was just running late, or if things had already gone off script. But the porch light was on and he saw lights on inside the house. So, with his phone inside the breast pocket of his jacket with Li's call active, Drew got out of the car and walked to the front door. He rang the bell. When no one responded after several moments, Drew knocked on the wooden door. A moment later, William Lake, wearing a white T-shirt over denim shorts, opened the door. Lake had on yellow rubber gloves, the type used for household cleaning, and was holding a plunger.

"I'm sorry, Detective," Lake said. "I have a clogged kitchen sink drain. Earl isn't answering his phone. He usually takes care of things like that. So I'm trying to unstop the drain myself. Come on in."

"Where is Deputy Chief LaChasse?" Drew asked before stepping inside. "He told me he would be here."

"Yes, Greg called a few minutes ago and is running late. But he is on the way. You can wait in your car until he arrives if you're frightened to come in alone."

Lake's smirk as he suggested Drew feared entering the house alone seemed like a challenge. He couldn't let that pass.

"No, I'm fine with coming in. But since your attorney isn't joining us, we can't talk about anything related to the case until LaChasse gets here."

"Agreed," Lake said, stepping aside to allow Drew to enter.

"If you don't mind, I'm going to work on the drain until Greg gets here," Lake said. "You know anything about plumbing repairs?"

"No, afraid not."

"That's fine. Have a seat and make yourself comfortable, Detective Drew."

"I'm fine with standing," Drew said, taking several steps toward the kitchen for the benefit of the recording.

"Suit yourself," Lake said, as walked to the sink and went to work with the plunger.

Drew heard the water sloshing in the sink and watched as it occasionally splashed out onto the floor. He wondered what Li was making of the noise. Soon a good size pool of water formed on the floor beside the sink cabinet.

"Damn, I better wipe that up," Lake said after he appeared to slip and almost fall on the wet floor. "You wouldn't think this would be that hard."

Lake set the plunger on the counter, opened a drawer, and reached for a kitchen cloth. But then, he rapidly spun toward Drew and in his hand, he held a semi-automatic pistol, not a cloth.

"What are you planning to do with the gun, Lake?" Drew asked, mostly for Li's benefit, and hoping the audio was good. "Shoot me? That won't solve your problems. Shooting a cop will only make your situation worse. It won't stop the investigation, either."

·············

Li had been peering through a window with her phone in one hand and her Glock service pistol in the other when she saw Lake spin towards Drew with a gun in his hand. A knot had immediately formed in her stomach, and her heart pounded. She thought about calling Moreno and the other detectives, but if she did that, she would have to disconnect the call to Drew's phone and couldn't restore it. She decided she would wait a few moments longer to see how things played out. But she was ready to shoot Lake from the window if it came to that. She felt grateful the audio was remarkably good.

Forty-One

DREW TOOK A DEEP breath. He thought the best tactic was to keep Lake talking. Since he knew how arrogant the man was, he expected that wouldn't be hard. A man like Lake would probably want to brag to show his cleverness.

"I think you're wrong, Drew," Lake said. "Not only do I believe it will solve my problems, it will also take care of the investigation."

"How do you figure?"

"First things first, Detective. You can try to pull your gun, and I will happily shoot you. Or you can take it out slowly and place it there on the bar. Then I'll answer some questions I'm sure you must have. We have plenty of time and I feel you deserve that much. Which will it be?"

Drew had heard from several of Lake's associates that the man knew guns and spent time at the gun range. So, he entertained no illusions he could draw his weapon before Lake shot him.

"Okay, Lake. I'll take it out and put it on the counter, just like you said."

"Go ahead. But no sudden movements, Detective."

Gingerly, Drew pulled his Glock from the holster on his belt and carefully put it on the bar.

"Very good," Lake said. "Now step back away from it."

Drew retreated three steps.

With his pistol still trained on Drew's chest, Lake stepped forward and picked up the Glock in his gloved hand. He backed up, reached back, and put the Glock inside the open drawer. Then he closed it.

"Now, you can step back up to the bar, Detective," Lake said.

"Why did you do it, Lake? Why did you shoot your wife?"

"You wouldn't understand, Detective. Cops only think in black in white. She conned me and I didn't appreciate it. And I didn't want her tainting my daughter. She had to go. Miranda, my adult daughter, will raise Holly to become a good, upstanding person. So, you might say I did it for Holly. But I don't want to talk about Connie."

"What do you want to talk about? You must have had some reason to bring me here."

"Indeed. I'm sure you are curious about that. And I don't mind telling you. The night I shot Connie, I called Greg LaChasse. After declaring I hadn't shot her, I told him I feared the LAPD would frame me for her murder. After all. Isn't it the husband or lover cops like you always go after first? I asked Greg for his help, as the only Los Angeles cop I trusted. We've known each other for a long time. And I told Greg I'd make it worth his while."

"And he agreed?"

"Of course. Greg has always enjoyed earning extra money, and told me not to worry. Greg said he would make sure the detective assigned to the case wasn't a seasoned investigator and he would do what he could to turn Connie's death into another O. J. failure. He told me to leave it to him. He'd take care of it. But it seems Greg chose unwisely. I think he underestimated you, Detective. He let his hatred for you blind him. And now it seems you've built a case strong enough to worry my lawyer. That's what he told me today when he learned the police planned to arrest me on Monday and charge me with Connie's murder."

"Mind telling me how your lawyer found out about that?"

"It's not important, Detective. Let me continue, please. I called Greg on my burner after talking with my attorney. Ironically, the same phone he used to call you this afternoon. I asked him to come over and when he arrived, I told him I felt I hadn't got what I'd paid him for. And I presented a plan to Greg, a way for him to redeem himself. I also reminded him there were several things I would tell his colleagues at the LAPD that would cast him in an unfavorable light if he refused to go along with the plan. Reluctantly, he agreed."

"So, he called and led me into this trap?"

"Yes, but don't be too hard on Greg, Detective. I shared a plan with him, but it was only a ruse. We're working from a script now he knew nothing about then. Yes, he knew I planned to kill you, but not the how and why. The plan, as Greg understood it, was he would get you to come here. Then I'd shoot you and stage a break in. The story I'd tell was you went off the rails out of frustration, as I understand you've done before. You broke in. Threatened me with a gun and said you would kill me if I didn't confess to shooting Connie. So I had to shoot you in self-defense. Then, fearing your colleagues would kill me if I just called 911 and told them I'd shot you, I had to call Greg, the trusted deputy chief. Then Greg would respond and back up my version of events when the police arrived."

"Good thing you scrapped that one," Drew said. "It wouldn't have worked."

"Oh, I think it might have. But it left a loose end. Greg. I know Greg can be greedy and it would have left me too exposed. Greg might have blackmailed me and come back to me repeatedly for more money."

"So why aren't you worried about that now, since he is still involved in whatever your new script is?"

"That's the beauty of the script, Drew. I even think you might admire the complexity of it."

"I might. I'd love to hear it, and you said we have plenty of time."

Lake smiled. Drew could tell he couldn't wait to reveal his genius.

"It starts with this gun I'm holding, Drew. This is Greg's gun. I disarmed him and tied him up right after he called you earlier from my burner phone."

"Where is LaChasse, anyway?"

"He's out back in the garden shed, waiting to perform his role," Lake said. "Want to hear the story from the new script?"

"I'm dying to hear it."

"Well, you will soon, of course," Lake chuckled. "You called and threatened me. You told me you were on your way and I would confess to killing Connie, or else. Frightened, I called Greg, a man I know well and trust. When he arrived, I told him what you said on the phone. He tried to assure me you wouldn't show up. You had only tried to rattle me. But while we talked, someone pounded on the front door. Greg assured me he would protect me and told me to let you in, so I did. You were furious. Even Greg couldn't deter you. He tried to calm you, but you kept shouting, demanding that I confess. When I refused, you pointed your pistol at me. Greg tried to reason with you, but to no avail. Then you told us both what you intended, and you pulled this."

Lake withdrew a small nickel-plated revolver from his left pocket. "No one can trace this pistol," he said. "Someone removed the serial number. Earl got this for me from his father, a collector and gunsmith, and Earl assured me no one ever registered this gun, even when it bore a serial number. But in our script, you brought this here and told me it's what cops used to call a 'throw down' gun. Is that still a thing?"

"We don't plant weapons on suspects," Drew said. "That's only Hollywood."

"Maybe it isn't done often," Lake said. "But I have had cops who worked with me on movie projects tell me it has happened. They even laughed about it. But I digress. Enraged, you told me and Greg if I didn't confess, you would kill me and put this gun beside my body before the other police arrived. Isn't that what you call a brass verdict? When the police kill someone that they believe is guilty but can't prove it? You would claim I invited you here and then pulled this little gun on you. So you had to shoot me in self-defense."

"I'm confused," Drew said. "I thought I was getting shot, not you."

"You are, Detective. You haven't heard the entire script yet."

"Excuse me. Please continue."

Lake put the small revolver back into his pocket and resumed his two-handed grip on the semi-automatic.

"Obviously, Greg, a fine, ethical police officer, couldn't stand by and watch you murder me. And since you were beyond reasoning with, he drew his weapon. This weapon I'm holding now. You argued, and while I couldn't be certain who fired first, you both fired and shot each other. So, I will not kill you, Detective. Greg will. At least that's the story I'll tell when I call 911 and the other police arrive."

"Then you will shoot him with my Glock, right?"

"Very good, Detective. I told you I believed Greg had underestimated you. Once I finish with you, I'll go out to the shed and shoot Greg with your gun. I'll put the revolver on the floor beside you, along with your pistol. Then I'll bring him inside, put his pistol beside him, and stage the scene to match my story. I've had these gloves on since you arrived. I have touched none of these weapons without the gloves, so the fingerprints will all match perfectly. Then, I'll make sure your prints are on the throw down too."

"It might work," Drew said. "If you do a good job staging the crime scene. But that's more difficult than you might think. For example, the blood can throw things off when it isn't where the SID people expect to find it, or in the right amounts or patterns."

"I'm confident it will work, Detective. You can't discourage me, so don't waste your time. I've given this much thought. And imagine the mental anguish I'll suffer after watching two police officers kill each other. The very people who take an oath to protect the innocent. My lawyer will tell the press all about it, the PTSD, the need for years of therapy to help me get past it. Once that runs in the press for months, do you really think anyone will care about Connie? I'll be the victim in the spotlight. I'll receive outpourings of sympathy over the LAPD vendetta and the attack on me by a rogue detective. Do you really believe they will find a jury who will convict me if they persist in prosecuting me over Connie's death? I think not. Actually, I think the new district attorney will dismiss the case you've built against me."

Drew's heart pounded. He knew that Lake, who had already killed once, would shoot him. It all depended on Amy Li. He had seen no sign of her, looking past Lake's shoulders and he had no way of knowing if she was hearing everything. But he trusted Amy. She had proven herself more than once and he couldn't think of anyone whose hands he'd rather have his life in right now.

It seemed Lake was tiring of the talk. Drew knew part of it was Lake had wanted him to see how smart he was. But he also knew Lake had been talking to work himself up to pulling the trigger and Drew believed the man was nearly there.

"Well, I guess you will graduate from killing Connie to becoming a serial killer, Lake," Drew said.

Lake laughed eerily. "You know something, Detective? I never thought of that way. But I suppose you're right. Still, the killing ends tonight for me. I can't expect to keep getting away with it, can I?"

"I guess not."

"Please know this isn't personal, Detective Drew. I know you only did your job and I can respect that. But in about four months, I'll be sixty-eight years old. I can't risk getting convicted, even on the solicitation charges. Any sentence, for me, would be a life sentence. I can't go to prison."

Drew recalled hearing that from someone else recently, but right now he couldn't for the life of him remember who had said it.

"Don't turn around, but move backward until I tell you to stop," Lake said. "I think more toward the center of the living room is best for our script. And I'm ready to raise the curtain on the first act."

Drew stepped backward slowly, careful not to trip, not taking his eyes off Lake and the gun.

"That's fine. Stop."

Drew stopped.

"I'll shoot Greg in a few moments," Lake said calmly. "Maybe that gives you some small comfort, since I know you two don't like each other very much. But for now, it's your turn, asshole."

Forty-Two

Li had watched the drama unfold nervously through the patio door. And she had heard every word. Her first inclination had been to stop Lake immediately. Yet, as he had talked to Drew, his explanation of his plot had fascinated her, and he had made several incriminating statements. Statements that incriminated him in the murder of his wife, and statements that incriminated Deputy Chief LaChasse for conspiring to murder an LAPD detective. So, reluctantly, she had waited, unwilling to cut Lake off too soon. She knew Drew expected her to get as much as possible on the recording before she acted. But she had not intended to wait too long and allow Lake to shoot her partner.

The moment Lake had uttered the last sentence, Li's blood ran cold, fearing she had waited a beat too long. She slammed her clenched fist against the glass patio door and shouted, "LAPD! Drop the weapon!" Later, she would admit to Drew, she hadn't expected Lake to hear her shouted announcement and verbal command. But she had wanted to get it on the recording to satisfy department policies and procedures.

Fortunately, the glass hadn't shattered when she struck it, but the sound was loud. Drew later described it as like the sound when a bird flies full speed into a freshly cleaned glass window, mistaking it for an opening. Li had already put her phone on the ground and was ready, holding her Glock in a strong two-handed grip.

It was even more fortunate that Lake hadn't reflexively pulled the trigger and shot Drew when he heard Li's fist smash against the door glass. No one would ever know what Lake had thought when he heard the unexpected loud noise behind him. Maybe he'd thought LaChasse had somehow escaped from the garden shed. Regardless of what he had thought, he committed an error that proved fatal. Just as he had uttered the last word before intending to shoot Drew, he heard the loud thump behind him, and had spun toward the patio door and fired what investigators later determined had been four chest high shots, blowing all the glass out of the frame. He had stopped firing for an instant, maybe to see if he had neutralized whatever he'd imagined the threat had been, and that was the fatal mistake. Li, on her knees beside the patio door, leaned around the door frame with her arms fully extended and returned fire with her Glock. Three quick shots, all of which struck Lake squarely in the chest. He pitched forward onto the floor face down, and the semi-automatic pistol he had held, which had already fallen from his hands, clattered across the floor.

Li sprang to her feet, jumped through the empty door frame into the room, and kicked the weapon further away from Lake's body. Drew was already on top of Lake's prone form, handcuffing the man's wrists behind his back.

After he had handcuffed him, Drew turned Lake over onto his back and pressed his fingers to the carotid artery. When he found no pulse, he looked at Lake's chest and saw three red circles on Lake's white shirt where Li's bullets had struck him. So, Drew got to his feet and looked at Li.

"My phone is out..." she began.

Drew put a finger to his lips, and then stepped over and whispered into her ear. "Get your phone and stop the recording."

Li nodded woodenly. She walked back through the empty patio door frame, retrieved her phone, and hit the save button on the app to stop the recording. Then she walked back inside.

"It's off now," she said. "I'll call it in and get EMS started."

"No hurry on that," Drew said with a wry grin. "You blew out his heart, which is a good thing, because I wouldn't have given the asshole CPR, anyway. Good shooting, partner."

"Then you want me to call Moreno?"

"Not yet. Show me how to work the app on your phone. I want to listen to the recording."

"You want to listen to the entire thing? Just push that button there."

"No, I only want to hear like the last thirty seconds."

"Okay, then push that button and then that one to stop it. Then push play. Do that until you get to the part you want to hear."

Drew's first attempt was close enough. He and Li listened as he waited for the part he wanted to hear.

Lake's recorded voice said, "I'll shoot Greg in a few moments. Maybe that gives you some small comfort, since I know you two don't like each other very much. But for now, it's your turn, asshole."

Drew pushed stop and smiled brightly at Li. "Perfect. It sounded exactly the same as when he said it. It's very clear."

Drew kept pushing buttons, playing back the recording and reversing it until he had the recording cued to the precise spot he wanted. Then he handed Li his cell phone.

"Here, call Moreno now and tell them to come to the house. His number is on my contact list."

While Amy called the lieutenant, Drew went to the front door and opened it. Then he waited for Moreno and the other two detectives to arrive. He didn't wait long. Both cars zoomed up to the front of the house and stopped with squealing tires. Moreno, Jenkins, and Ross all rushed inside. They looked down at Lake.

"You shot him?" a surprised Moreno asked.

"I told you it wasn't fireworks, Lieutenant," Jenkins said. "I know gunshots when I hear them."

"Not much blood," Ross observed. "Nice work, you guys. Zapped his heart."

"I shot him," Li said to Moreno. "No choice. He was about to shoot Drew."

"What?"

"Let me walk you through it, Lieutenant," Drew said. "But I'll make it fast because we have another matter to attend to."

Quickly, Drew summarized what had happened, from the time he entered the house until Li shot Lake. He didn't go into detail, because time was of the essence. But he gave Moreno a snapshot of the events.

"So, where is the deputy chief?" Moreno asked. "Did you have to shoot him, too?"

Drew shook his head. "He's fine. For now. I'm going to tell you what I'm about to do, Lieutenant. And if you don't want to be a part of it, I'll understand and won't think any less of you. Then Drew explained his plan."

Moreno nodded. "I have no problem with it. He conspired to lure you here to get murdered. Go for it and let's see what happens."

"Okay. You, Jenkins, and Ross can stand quietly outside the open shed door. Li will go in with me."

Everyone nodded. Drew took his phone from Li, opened the recording app, and showed Li how to record. Then he handed her his phone, keeping her phone.

"You understand what we're doing?"

"Yes, I wait until after you play the recording on my phone. As soon as it finishes, I hit the record button on your phone."

"You got it. Let's go."

The detectives filed out to the shed. Drew looked at Moreno, Jenkins, and Ross and put a finger to his lips to remind them to keep quiet. Then he opened the shed door. A single low-wattage bulb dimly lit the interior and everyone saw LaChasse sitting on a blue plastic tarp with his back against a wall. There was an identical plastic tarp on the wall behind him. Drew assumed the tarps were there to make for easy cleanup after Lake had shot the deputy chief. Drew led the way and Li followed, careful to not make a sound.

LaChasse had a blindfold positioned over his eyes and a rag stuffed into his mouth as a gag. Drew snatched the rag from his mouth. After gasping for a breath, LaChasse spoke in a shrill tone.

"Who's there? Is that you Bill? What happened in there? Is he dead?"

When he didn't get an answer, LaChasse spoke again, even more shrilly.

"Bill... talk to me. Talk to me. We can fix this. Just let me go."

Lake had wrapped duct tape around the deputy chief's ankles and knees to immobilize his legs. He had also bound the man's wrists behind his back, maybe with more duct tape, but Drew couldn't tell for sure since LaChasse had his back to the wall. Drew took out his Glock, which he had recovered from the kitchen drawer. Then he held out Li's phone and punched the play button on the recording app.

Just as the recording of Lake's voice began, Drew jammed the muzzle of the Glock against the forehead of LaChasse.

"Now, it's your turn, asshole," said Lake's recorded voice.

Drew thought it had sounded so lifelike inside the cramped garden shed.

"No!" LaChasse screamed. "Wait! Don't do it, Bill. Listen, you don't have to do this. Drew deserved what he got, but not me. I'm on your side. I'll tell no one. Never. And I helped you, didn't I? Drew wouldn't have come if I hadn't called him for you. Bill, I'll give you the twenty thousand back you already gave me."

Drew took the pistol away from his forehead, and the deputy chief whimpered and sobbed, while blubbering his thanks to his recently deceased pal, William Lake. Drew turned to Li and smiled. She smiled back. Then Drew reached out and pulled the blindfold off. LaChasse stared at him in confusion.

"Here you are, Chief," Drew said sarcastically. "I've been looking all over for you. Hey, what's that? Did you wet yourself, Chief?"

His face reddened as the gravity of his situation dawned on LaChasse, along with the bitter memory of his unwise pleadings before the blindfold had come off.

"Turn me loose, Detective, right now," LaChasse blustered, struggling to regain his dignity. Then he glanced at the doorway and saw Moreno's stony face and Jenkins and Ross who were struggling to stop laughing, but unsuccessfully.

"Lieutenant, cut me loose immediately. This man held a gun to my head and forced me to say those things. Release me now or I'll have the badges of the lot of you."

"Chief," Moreno said, seething. "With all due respect, shut your mouth. You're under arrest, asshole."

Moreno turned to Drew. We need to secure the scene and I'll call it in.

"I was thinking, Lieutenant," Drew said. "Earl Lee is unaccounted for. I would have expected him to be here. Lake might have warned him we're planning to arrest him, and maybe even told him what he planned to do here. If we don't get over to his place right now, he may be in the wind. If he isn't already."

Moreno thought about it for a moment. "You're right, Drew. Okay, Ross?"

"Yes, Lieutenant?"

"You stay here and secure this scene and watch LaChasse. Don't release him and let him set there in his piss. When patrol gets here, they can handcuff him and transport him to Men's Central. Tell them to book him on conspiracy to commit murder, after the fact, for now, so he doesn't get bail. On the Manley murder. And tell the patrol officers who transport to tell them at the jail there will be more charges to follow. Lots more charges."

"Got it, Lieutenant."

"Li, you're with me. You're on the bench for now until the OIS team gets through with you. Call a rep if you want one. I'll get them started when I call this in and get patrol and EMS rolling."

"Yes, sir."

Moreno turned to Drew. "You will need to make a statement to OIS, but it can wait. You and Jenkins go to Lee's apartment and see if he is there. If he is, hook him and book him. The arrest warrant is active now. I checked while we were waiting down the block."

"On it, Lieutenant," Drew said.

Drew exchanged phones with Li, put his hand on her shoulder, gave her a few encouraging words, and thanked her for saving his life. Then he and Jenkins sprinted away.

Forty-Three

Seventeen minutes after leaving Studio City, Drew and Jenkins arrived at Earl Lee's apartment in Burbank. They saw the man's truck parked in the driveway and that the apartment was dark.

"Maybe we got lucky, and he's already bedded down for the night," Jenkins said.

"Unless he took a taxi or ride share to LAX and is already in the wind."

"There is that," Jenkins said as the detectives got out of Drew's city ride.

They followed the cement path to the stairway and climbed the steps to the front door of the second-floor apartment.

Jenkins pounded on the door. They got no response, and no lights came on inside the apartment. Drew tried the doorknob, finding the door locked.

"Want to kick it or you want me to do it?" Jenkins asked.

"Hang on a second," Drew said, reaching for his wallet. He removed a compact lock pick set from the wallet. "Give me some light."

Jenkins produced a Pelican flashlight, and using his hand to shade the lens, illuminated only the lock of the doorknob. Drew went to work with a pick and tension wrench. Less than three minutes later, he had unlocked the door. Trying the knob again, he found Lee hadn't locked the deadbolt and felt more confident the man was asleep inside.

"Must be drunk or a heavy sleeper, since my knock didn't wake him," Jenkins said.

Drew eased the door open, and they stepped inside cautiously. Jenkins played the beam of the flashlight around the room.

"Uh-oh," he said.

"Let me find the light switch," Drew said.

After finding the switch beside the front door, Drew flipped on the lights, which caught Earl Lee in the bright glare. As their eyes adjusted from the darkness to the light, the detectives looked at him. Shirtless, wearing denim jeans, and shoeless, Lee hung suspended from an exposed beam in the high ceiling with a knotted rope around his neck. An overturned two-step stool lay on the hardwood floor beneath Lee's bare feet.

"Suicide," Jenkins said. "His hands aren't bound. He must have got the word from Lake we were coming to get him tomorrow, figured the jig was up, and checked out on his own terms."

It looked like a suicide at first blush, but something felt off to Drew. Walking over to the step stool, he snapped on a pair of latex gloves and then set it upright and slid it over beneath Lee's feet. Then he squatted on his haunches and stared for several moments. Turning his head to look at Jenkins, he spoke.

"I've seen a lot of suicides by hanging, but never saw one where a victim jumped two feet into the air to do it."

"Hey, you're right," Jenkins said, walking over to the body. "It's a homicide staged to look like suicide."

Drew stood and examined Lee's wrists.

"No ligature marks on his wrists. I see no signs of trauma. The killer probably drugged him, then hoisted him up there with the rope and tied it off. Then they staged the step stool. Only they must not have checked to make sure the hanging position matched Earl's height and the height of the stool."

"Lake, you think?"

"Be my guess," Drew said. "He showed me an untraceable revolver after he got the drop on me. Lake told me he had got it from Earl. With what he had in mind for me and LaChasse, I think he must have wanted to tie up a loose end. He didn't want to risk Earl Lee ever running his mouth about what he had known."

"Well, that's that," Jenkins said. "There's no one left for us to arrest, but I guess we closed the case."

"Then why so glum?" Drew asked.

"I was just thinking of all that time Ross and I wasted going through those damn emails."

Drew chuckled, took out his phone, and called the lieutenant.

·· • •·• • ••··

It was a warm, clear Los Angeles Sunday morning. Much like the past Friday morning. Drew parked his car on the access road and strode across the plush, green cemetery lawn to the gravesite. The white roses were already wilting, but the maintenance workers hadn't yet removed them. Drew stared quietly at the headstone for several moments. Then he laid the bouquet of spring flowers he had brought with him atop the marble stone.

"You lived a hard life," Drew said. "But I'm not here to judge. I only wanted to tell you that you weren't a zero. While it didn't turn out perfectly, I wanted you to know you at least got some justice. Even if it was a brass verdict. And to say that everybody counts."

Drew turned away from Connie Lynn Manley's grave and headed back across the lawn to his car. Moreno had given a full report on the events of Friday night to Captain Mann early on Saturday morning. Moreno told Drew that Mann had said nothing congratulatory, but neither had he chastised Drew for knowingly walking into the trap at the Lake residence, which had culminated with the shooting of William Lake. About Greg LaChasse, Moreno reported the captain had said nothing. Li was on routine administrative leave until the chief and the board ruled on her OIS. But Drew knew Amy had nothing to worry about. The shooting had been well within policy.

Amy had called him on Saturday evening with the news. "I only shared the briefest details about the shooting with her after she saw the news reports," Li had said. "But she freaked out." Li's partner, Mandy, a public school teacher, loved Amy. But she didn't love her partner's profession. Li told Drew that Mandy had cried and begged her not to take the Homicide Special vacancy. She believed Li was at least marginally safer from harm by taking the new officer-in-charge position in the streamlined Open-Unsolved unit. Amy ended the call by telling Drew to take the Homicide Special vacancy, and there were no hard feelings.

From the cemetery, Drew drove downtown to the Los Angeles County Men's Central jail. LAPD officers often referred to the facility as Bauchet because it was on Bauchet Street. While the Connie Lynn Manley murder and William Lake had dominated the Los Angeles media like nothing since the O. J. trial, it seemed all but forgotten now. Instead, the above-the-fold stories in the *Times* and on the television news were all about a disgraced LAPD deputy chief now confined at Men's Central.

After parking and walking into the main entrance, Drew produced his badge and told the deputy he wanted to see Greg LaChasse.

"No, he told the deputy. I don't want you to bring him down to an interview room. Can you have someone escort me to his cell in the high-power module? I only need about five minutes."

A deputy escorted Drew to the module and along the row of cells and then pointed out the one Drew wanted. Howard peered through the wired twelve-inch square window in the steel door. LaChasse was on "keep away" status and alone in the cell. As a former cop, he wouldn't have lasted ten minutes in gen pop before other inmates would have found out about him and beaten him to death. He didn't notice Drew staring at him for a long while, as he lay on the bottom bunk on his back, his hands laced behind his head, his eyes focused on the bottom of the bunk above him. Drew moved his mouth closer to the screen.

"Enjoying the accommodations, LaChasse?"

LaChasse looked over at the door, moving only his eyes.

"What was that?"

"Never mind. I already know the answer."

"What the fuck do you want, Drew? Here to gloat?"

"I just dropped by to see you locked in a cage where you belong."

"It's not over between us, Drew. I'll beat the bullshit charges. You'll see."

"I don't think so, LaChasse. The public who sits on the juries these days has no sympathy for cops. Especially corrupt cops. You might spend the rest of your life in a cage, depending on whether the sentences run consecutively or concurrently."

"Don't bet on it."

"I couldn't care less about how much time they lock you up for, LaChasse. You're done as a cop. That's what matters to me. You don't have the juice anymore, so I'll never give you a second thought. If you get out of jail and ever come near me again, I'll put you right back inside."

"Leave me alone, Drew."

"I will. I'm going right now. And believe me. It will feel great walking out of this place. Something you won't be doing anytime soon."

"Fuck you, Drew."

"No, fuck you, LaChasse. And thanks for the cheap entertainment."

Forty-Four

Early on Sunday evening, Drew stood beside Nina Garraway, leaning on the oak railing of the back deck of her hillside home, looking at the city of Los Angeles below and thinking about the question she had asked. "Do you think L.A. is a deadly place to live? I mean, compared to other comparable large cities?"

"Do you mean in general, or do you mean homicides in particular? Lots of people die on the freeways and from drug overdoses."

"Yes, I know. I guess I meant the murder rate here."

"Well, homicides here have already reached a fifteen year high in the first half of this year. Homicides increased twelve percent in 2021 over the previous year. And murders were up twenty percent in 2020, even with the pandemic lockdowns. So yeah, we live in L.A. deadly."

"My perspective is only from seeing what the violence has done to the bodies I autopsy," Garraway said. "But you live with the violence, Howie. You see it up close. How do you deal with it?"

Drew shrugged. "You get used to it, I guess."

"Do you really, or do you carry it around with you like a heavy weight on your shoulders?"

"I don't know. I just try not to bring it here with me to your home, Nina."

"What will happen to that little girl?"

"Ironically, Miranda Lake will get legal custody of Holly. So Lake got what he wanted. None of Manley's relatives wanted the responsibility. They all sold their stories to the tabloids and I guess they wanted to spend all their time enjoying the money, not raising Connie's daughter."

"Are you happy with how it all turned out? That the man died instead of going to prison?"

"I'm not unhappy. Lake deserved the death penalty and California hasn't executed a convicted murderer since 2006. It's only he didn't suffer enough for what he did."

"Is that your view, Howie? Criminals should suffer?"

"I believe predators who murder innocent victims should pay for their sins. So yeah. I suppose I think they should suffer. And I think Lake would have suffered more by spending the rest of his years in prison than he did getting the brass verdict."

"I suppose. It's important to you, almost a sacred duty, to make sure you get justice for your victims, isn't it?"

"Yes."

"You're a good man, Howie."

Drew chuckled. "You haven't known me that long. You sure about that?"

Nina smiled a little. "Yes, I'm sure. At least I hope you're a good man, and you seem to be. And you're an excellent police officer."

Drew looked at Nina and smiled back. She wore blue jeans and a red shirt, which went well with her blonde hair.

"I think you're a good woman, Nina. And having seen you in action, I know you're an excellent pathologist. Maybe we should get to know each other better and see if we still feel the same."

"I'm hoping we will. Get to know each other better, I mean. And I don't expect my opinion about you will change. I think I'm falling in love with you."

Drew nodded, but he wasn't looking at her. He couldn't bring himself to speak. He didn't know what to say.

"You already know, I've been through it all before with a man I loved. And it all fell apart. You know how it ended. There was a great deal of pain for both of us. And I never thought I could risk that again. But maybe you're changing my mind, Howie."

"All I know is I care for you, Nina. I want to see where things might go with us. I know love is never easy. It's hard and maybe the work I do makes it even harder. But that might make it all the better. Who knows?"

Nina turned and reached for him. Howard took her in his arms, kissed her on top of the head, and they held each other for a long while.

"Hey, do you want to go away next weekend?" he asked. "Get away from the city? I'm taking some time off before I report to Homicide Special on the first of the month."

"That sounds nice, and you know I'm off every weekend. Do you have a place in mind?"

"How about Catalina?"

"Sure, I love Catalina."

"That's good, because I already have the hotel room reserved."

She looked up at him and smiled slyly.

"Oh, you're pretty sure of yourself, aren't you? You knew all the time I'd say yes."

Drew smiled down at her.

"I didn't know, Nina," he said. "I hoped."

About Author

Larry Darter is the author of twenty-two previous novels, including the #1 Amazon bestseller *Come What May*. His books, which include the Howard Drew series, Malone series, and Rick Bishop series, have sold thousands of copies worldwide. Darter is a retired police officer and his law enforcement experience brings unique authenticity to his novels. Visit https://www.larrydarter.com to learn more.

Books by Larry Darter

Howard Drew

Omerta
The Pendulum
Darker Angels
LA Deadly

Malone

Come What May
Fair Is Foul and Foul Is Fair
Cold Comfort
Foregone Conclusion
Live Long Day
Foul Play
Black Deeds
Perchance to Dream
What's Done is Done

Rick Bishop

The Girl on the Beach
Dead End
Trouble in Paradise
Follow the Money
China Doll

T. J. O'Sullivan

Mare's Nest
Honolulu Blues
The Chinese Tiger Ying
Frisky Business